Praise for Nico Rosso and

Countdown to Zero Hour

"High stakes and sexual tension will keep readers
eagerly turning the pages."
—*Publishers Weekly*, starred review

"Rosso's talent for incorporating romance in the midst
of a gang war and military mission earns *Countdown
to Zero Hour* a spot on every bookshelf. It's an
enticing, scorching-hot read!"
—*RT Book Reviews*, Top Pick, 4.5 Stars

"THIS is how romantic suspense should be done!"
—*The Romance Reviews*, Top Pick

**Also available from Nico Rosso
and Carina Press**

The Last Night

Demon Rock Series

Heavy Metal Heart
Slam Dance with the Devil
Ménage with the Muse

And coming soon in the Black Ops: Automatik series

One Minute to Midnight
Seconds to Sunrise

COUNTDOWN TO ZERO HOUR

NICO ROSSO

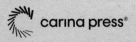
carina press®

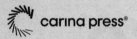

Recycling programs
for this product may
not exist in your area.

ISBN-13: 978-0-373-00407-2

Countdown to Zero Hour

Copyright © 2015 by Zachary N. DiPego

www.CarinaPress.com

Printed in U.S.A.

Dear Reader,

Welcome to book one of my new romantic suspense series, Black Ops: Automatik. You might be wondering, How do I find these former Special Forces soldiers who operate in the shadows as they fight for people in need? But you don't find them. They'll find you.

That's what happens to our heroine, chef Hayley Baskov, when she's caught up in a world way beyond her depth and is forced to trust a man she barely knows. Art Diaz has secrets that make him the perfect man to protect her.

I put both Hayley and Art in a pressure cooker in order to see what they're made of. They're tough on their own, but they'll need each other to get through this fight. It was a pleasure to find the details of Art's past that feed his present determination. Hayley's strength was an inspiration to me. And her cooking always made me hungry while I was writing.

Thanks so much for picking up this book. I hope you enjoy getting swept into the danger and romance with Art and Hayley.

Nico

For Ami. We're still cooking.

COUNTDOWN TO ZERO HOUR

ONE

HAYLEY BASKOV ALWAYS knew opening a restaurant was a risky proposition, but she'd never expected just how dangerous serving food could be. If all her plans had worked out, there would've been four walls around her, an industrial kitchen with a staff and a front door to pace the flow of customers. Instead, she manned a steam cart outside a shady Russian nightclub in a sketchy corner of San Diego, California.

Plans hadn't worked out.

But she wasn't ready to quit.

So far, business was going as well as possible. The night was cool enough to reveal the breath of the people standing in a long line on the side of the building, waiting for the doorman to mercifully let them in. Techno music bass thumped inside the Sea Weed and thundered louder each time the door opened. But the doorman only let a few of the partyers in at a time, leaving everyone else out in the chilly air in their thin designer jeans or short skirts.

Which turned the people into the perfect customers for Hayley's warm pelmeni. The pork dumplings simmered in broth, sending waves of unctuous steam out to the partyers waiting impatiently. When Hayley had first pushed the heavy cart up the hill from the closest parking spot she'd found, she'd cursed her ex,

Burton, every step of the way. But now that customers were breaking away from their line to drop five bucks for three pelmeni in a small paper boat, she had little time to think of how she'd wound up on this particular stretch of sidewalk.

Dudes in long shoes ambled up, chose whether they wanted a side of sour cream or vinegar then returned to the line with their food, thin napkin and plastic fork. Hayley watched the domino effect. The people in line around the customers would crane their necks to see what they were eating, then stare at her cart, then check their wallets, then skip over to her.

Girls balanced expertly on platform heels and maintained the shortest skirts Hayley had ever seen. They even managed to keep their glossy lipstick perfect while eating. Their shoes clicked back to the line. Hayley knew they'd make it inside long before most of the guys.

How would Hayley do in the club? She was wearing jeans and a chef's coat. Not the best fit for this venue. But that was how it had been for a long time. While the other kids had been clubbing and tearing it up, she'd been working. Catering gigs had carried her through high school. After that was culinary school and any kitchen jobs she'd been able to land. After-hours parties for Hayley and her friends had consisted of sitting around an alley behind a restaurant and killing off whatever wine bottles the customers had left unfinished.

It would feel good to get polished up like these girls sometime and do a little strutting. Especially if she could stomp past Burton on her way into the club. That justice would be way better than if he saw her sweating over her steam cart and hustling dumplings near midnight. But there'd be no revenge without money, and no money without selling food by any means necessary.

"Five dollars. Cash only," she explained again and again. "Family recipe. All homemade." After a taste of the dumplings, no one could doubt the truth.

Once her aunt had seen how serious Hayley had been about cooking, the older woman had given her the recipe and worked with her in the kitchen until she'd perfected it.

"No, I don't have a restaurant." Hayley tapped the butt of her metal spoon on the top of the steam cart. "You're looking at it."

She should've had a place by now. The lease was paid on a decent space with good visibility, but there wasn't enough money left over to pump any life into it.

Fucking Burton.

Man, she'd love to stomp on his chest in a pair of those high heels.

"No, this is the line." A guy in a trucker hat and sunglasses had grown impatient and pushy, and Hayley pointed him toward where people were patiently lined up. "Seriously, she was before you." Hayley took care of the woman, then served for the man. "See, no one has to wait for long."

The guy paid and took his food, grumbling, "Been waiting to get in the club for two hours."

Second thoughts banked any excitement she'd developed about a night out at a club. If that dude and his entitled attitude populated the dance floor, she'd want no part of it. But the effervescent thrill of flirting with a decent guy would be nice. She stirred the broth in her cart and tried not to count how many weeks or months it had been since she'd felt the heat of a nearby body instead of the stove.

"You're killing it tonight."

She glanced up from her food to see the man who spoke. His voice rasped, like he didn't use it much. From the look of him, he didn't need it. His fit body said volumes. Even in a T-shirt and a nylon bomber jacket with a trim knit collar, his muscles showed. But he wasn't a bodybuilder or a gym rat. He had the physique of an athlete. Or a fighter. She suppressed a swivel in her hips, as if her body was testing to see how they could bob and weave together.

He stood casually at the side of her cart. The man must've cut in front of everyone. She would've noticed a strong profile like his if he'd been waiting. "The line's over there."

"I know." He nodded and scanned over the people, giving her another opportunity to trace his defined jaw, angular nose and shaved head as he was outlined by an exterior light on the side of the club building. He brought his gaze back to hers. The guy was supremely confident, but there was also a playful glint in his dark blue eyes. "I'm Art. You can call me Art."

"Hayley. But you can call me Chef Baskov."

An easy smile made him look downright dangerous. Bedroom dangerous. This time the swivel in her hips was too strong to stop. But she was partially behind the steam cart, so he might not have witnessed her tight, needy grind.

What was his angle? Flirting with someone while the person was trapped working seemed a bit below his game. He looked too wise for that. Art appeared around her age, old enough to have a past.

Not that she minded a flirt with him, as long as he didn't screw up the flow of people to her cart. Business came first.

He took a deep breath of the steam coming from the cart, closing his eyes for a moment, then locking his gaze on her again. "I'd like two orders."

She informed without chiding him, "I showed you where the line was, Art." She pointed with her slotted spoon. More than a few of the waiting people started to get restless and glared at him.

When Art returned their looks, they quieted and steadied themselves into an orderly queue. Whoever he was, he wasn't with the other party people. He had a different purpose at the club. She'd known a few shady dudes, the kinds of guys who'd get you exclusive ingredients like Wagyu beef and heritage pork for "special" prices. Art's purpose, though, was direct. To what end? It wasn't difficult to recognize he was a man with a hard edge. But there was no threat in him when he brought his attention back to her. She felt his latent energy, though. This man could get dark.

"I'm not like them. I'm working." He glanced at the club.

"Had a feeling. You're not wearing dancing shoes."

His work boots were more rugged than stylish. Was he security? But not just a bouncer. He didn't have the requisite black T-shirt, and carried himself with a different swagger.

He stared at his boots as well for a moment. "I've stood in a lot of lines. And faced front lines, you know?"

A new resonant depth shone in his eyes. "Don't like them."

"We have to be fair, though." She was careful with the rapport they'd already built. "Let me take care of all these customers, then we'll put your order together. Special."

"You're right." He relaxed some, and the people in line took a long breath with him. "But I can't wait there."

"As long as you give me room to work."

"I'd never get in your way, Chef." He took a step back.

She kind of missed having him closer. It was just a little flirting, a little spice, but she was willing to see where it might go. She'd always been interested in different flavor combinations, and getting stirred up with dark and edgy Art would definitely be something new.

"But, man, smelling that takes me back home." He didn't look like the other Russians in town, but breathed in the aroma with real appreciation. "Don't think I can stay too far away. Tell me you make *draniki*."

The potato pancakes were a particular favorite of hers, simple and satisfying. "You bring the beer, and I'll fry them up."

"I've had a lot of raw deals in my life." A deep edge cut into the glint of his eye. "But if you're serious, Chef, I'll come through on this one."

Art was put together, head to toe. Taller than her by at least half a foot. His hands were broad, and she caught glimpses of scars across the knuckles. But for someone so capable, he looked like he was searching for something.

His quiet need triggered hers, reminding her how alone she'd felt. Every struggle, even pushing the cart up the hill at the beginning of the night, had been Hayley's. Her friends and family had been close, but a partner to shoulder the burden and encourage her on this difficult path had been absent for quite a while.

Whether or not Art was that kind of guy was way too early to tell. Yet he was clearly hungry for sensations other than food. Feeding him might satisfy her immediate wants, too. And he was built to satisfy. Tan. Strong. And that clever spark that let her know he'd pay close attention between the sheets. Her pulse bumped a bit faster.

There were quite a few people to get through in the line. She served them while thoughts of a steamy fling with Art distracted her. His body kept drawing her attention. He moved with awareness, constantly scanning the area. Legs balanced, but never static. At times he'd curl his long fingers around the lapels of his open jacket, and the cords of his neck flexed.

How could this guy go hungry? She saw the way the other women waiting to get into the Sea Weed peered at him. He wouldn't have to go home alone and would be shaking all the furniture in a bedroom by the time Hayley would be cleaning out her cart in her friend's backyard.

"My turn." He stepped close again.

She wasn't able to puzzle out his intent for a moment and just stared at him. Her heart raced harder to catch up to the new thrill.

"The line's gone. Two orders, please. Both with sour cream." He was talking about the food, while she thought he might be indicating other needs for her to fulfill.

An urgent heat rose into her cheeks and along the top of her chest. Switching gears out of her mental bordello, she focused on the dumplings, hoping the steam would justify her blush.

"You didn't eat dinner?" she asked. Victory swirled in the broth. She was on her way to selling out of pelmeni.

"Some new tapas place. Too fancy for me."

She knew of only one new Spanish restaurant. It was expensive and exclusive, and the chef ran the kitchen like a submarine captain with his finger on the trigger of nuclear annihilation. Art's mystery deepened. How the hell had he gotten in there?

"One of these is for me," he continued, taking a paper boat of dumplings. "The other is for my boss." Tipping his head, he indicated the front door of the club. Standing at the edge of the light, near the burly doorman, was a refined man with silver hair and a perfectly tailored suit. The man was so confident he had to be a crook.

And Art worked for him. Making him a...?

"Also—" Art pulled out his wallet and slipped a bill out. "He owns this place."

All the heat of the steam cart couldn't keep a cold chill from surrounding her. The traditional risks of opening a restaurant were blown away by the inherent threat of authority held by the man at the door. She'd parked herself outside a club owned by the Russian mob and was poaching his customers.

Art maintained his small smile and somehow didn't

menace her with the new imbalance in the power dynamic. The money he held was a hundred-dollar bill.

"I can't break that and still make change for anyone else."

He blinked, like he didn't understand anything she'd said. "Tip."

"I appreciate it, but…"

Slow and deliberate, he placed the bill on the cart. "I understand about running a small business."

"Does your boss?" She tried not to stare at the eerily tranquil man by the door.

"We'll see." He gave her a sympathetic look.

So even when he was on the clock, he could be human. But she knew not to let a sense of relief make her too comfortable. "It's a free sidewalk."

The edge returned to his eyes. "Nothing's free. You know that."

"I do." She'd paid for a lot through her life with money and sweat and had gotten very little back.

He took the second tray of food and tipped his head toward his boss. "I'll put in a good word with Rolan, but I think your pelmeni will do most of the talking."

His smile was only slightly reassuring. He was working for the guy who could make life very difficult for her. This stretch of sidewalk had paid well. It was a small start, but a start. She didn't know if she'd be able to muster any energy to overcome yet another setback.

Art walked the food over to his boss, leaving her alone on an island. The people waiting for the club watched her, but didn't approach for food. Wary, they glanced at the boss, and she busied herself organizing the cart so she didn't watch him eat the food. It would've been interesting to see Art eat, though. He appeared to take the world in with all his senses. Where would her food take him?

He wasn't the one she needed to win over, but she wanted to see him taste.

Damn it, they were still eating when she finished distracting herself with a jar of relish and peeked up toward the club's door. The boss nodded his head with approval. Art chewed slowly, savoring.

She fought the urge to duck back behind the cart. She was a chef, had earned the title, and would watch as people ate every bit of her food. Showing any weakness now would send the wrong message to the man Art called Rolan. Not that she was going to be too ballsy with the Russian.

His lean body radiated supreme confidence from within his lustrous suit as he strode toward her. Art remained close at his side, always picking apart the environment with keen awareness.

Rolan smiled, ticking his finger at her, and praised with a heavy Russian accent, "Very good."

Art nodded agreement. "Best I've ever had."

She soaked in his honesty. "Don't tell your mother that."

"She'd agree." Again, Art curled his hands around the lapels of his jacket and balanced on his legs.

Rolan planned something quickly in Russian. Art replied to him, and their conversation ran for a moment.

"…good…nights…home cooking…"

She picked out words and phrases here and there, wishing her family had taught her more growing up. They'd spoken mostly English at home. She'd only heard the steely opera of her ancestors' native tongue when her father and aunt would talk without wanting anyone to know what they were saying.

But her aunt had taught her to cook the family recipes, and those damn pelmeni had gotten Hayley into this situation. No, that wasn't right. She tried to blame Burton for her position behind the steam cart but knew that wouldn't fly either. A ton of circumstances had blended together to put her on that sidewalk. Ultimately, it had been her choice. And look where it got her.

New dimensions to Art unfolded in front of her. His mastery of Russian deepened his mystery. He wasn't just common muscle. She bet that anything she threw at him, he'd handle: leap from rooftop to rooftop, land a space shuttle, make a feast out of her body.

A tingling awareness swept low in her belly, hungry for something other than food. She threw the thoughts of sex into a quick ice bath, setting their lurid color but keeping the heat from overcooking her.

"Rolan loves your food." Art licked his lips. "And so do I." The growl in his voice let her know just how much her cooking shook him. "He says that you're doing a good job, keeping his customers from getting too restless while they're waiting to get in."

"Thank you." She made a curt bow to Rolan. *"Spacibo."*

Her accent for her kitchen-table Russian was good enough to let people know her last name wasn't just an ornament. Rolan appeared pleased and rattled off a string of sentences she couldn't follow.

Art translated, "You're a fighter." He added an aside, "I saw it from the way you handled the line. And me."

Rolan cleared his throat, and Art resumed translating. "You can stay. But..."

Here was where the boss would name the price for letting her stay. Or he would lean on her for intimate compensation. She'd been subject to that kind of pressure before as a woman in a commercial kitchen. The answer was always an unwavering "no." Was Art the enforcer for that kind of leverage? He didn't seem like it, but nothing was certain outside the club.

He continued, "You have to include a salad next time. Something with tomatoes and cucumbers with fresh dill and sour cream. And beets."

She knew better than to breathe too much relief. "That I can do."

"And forty percent." Art's face was all business.

The hope of an easy deal crashed, taking her mood with it. Damn it, forty was a big chunk. And would make it harder for her to climb out of the hole. But how much leverage did she have? She pushed past the frustration and countered, "Ten."

"Thirty-five."

"Ten."

He chuckled. "Forty."

She stood up to him. "Your boss trusts you to negotiate for him?"

"I'm trustworthy." He casually crossed his arms over his chest. "Thirty."

"Fifteen."

Art shook his head, scanning the area before coming back to her. "It'll cost twenty percent of your nightly to stay and sell here. No less. Otherwise you'll have to find another club to hang out in front of, and I can almost bet their ownership is a lot less accommodating. And I'm damn sure their hired help isn't as friendly." He gave her a secret wink. "You're cash only, no receipts. Cook the food, not the books. We'll go with a general twenty percent. Feel me?"

"Not literally." The monetary terms would work, but anything else was a deal breaker. Her quick and raunchy sexual fantasies with Art were very separate from these negotiations.

He backed up. "Not what I meant, Chef. I was raised by my mother and sisters. I've heard the stories. We're talking business right now."

"Twenty percent it is."

Rolan patted Art on the back, satisfied, then extended his hand to Hayley. Under the best circumstances, running a restaurant meant making deals the county tax board would never hear about. This arrangement put her running headfirst into very shady territory. But she had to. There was a career to salvage and a lot of generosity she had to pay back to her mother.

Hayley shook Rolan's hand.

Art immediately broke the handshake with his hard forearm. He stepped between them, and she felt just how powerful his body was when he pushed past her. A shocked gasp cut off in her throat. Was he having second thoughts about Hayley making a deal with Rolan?

The boss exclaimed in Russian, but Art didn't turn around or answer. His focus was on two men hurrying away from the club line and toward Hayley and Rolan. They were coming on fast, but she saw the hard lines of their faces, their cold dead eyes. And the wicked combat knives in their hands.

Her muscles locked, not knowing what to do.

Art rushed the men, placing himself between them and Hayley and Rolan.

She'd seen fights before and had even been in a few. They'd been clumsy and drunken, or fueled with blinding anger that limited the combatants to shouting and grappling.

Art, though, moved with precise brutality. He engaged the closest attacker, who wore a leather blazer. Art used his forearm to knock a knife strike to one side. Before the second man dressed all in denim got too close with his blade, Art kicked him quickly in the shin.

That man stumbled, and Leather Blazer swung back with his knife. Art leaned away, balanced. He kept his hands high and ready. The man continued to push forward, slicing the air. Screams erupted from the line of people outside the club, and bodies scattered.

Art's focus didn't waver. When Leather Blazer overextended a strike, he countered with a quick jab to the man's throat. Sputtering, the man lunged with a wild stab. Art jumped to the side and caught the man's arm up under his. With a quick turn and a wicked elbow, Art broke Leather Blazer's arm. She winced, gritting her teeth at the sickening sound. The knife fell from a limp hand and clattered to the ground.

The man howled. Art kneed him in the chest, then kicked him to the pavement. The denim attacker had gathered himself and sprang at Art. Instead of facing the man, Art dove to the side in a tight roll. When he stood, he had Leather Blazer's knife.

To this part in the fight, Art had looked like a professional and trained combatant. A warrior. With the knife in his hand, he was feral. His face remained calm, his body coiled. He was a predator who understood life and death.

He and Denim Man circled each other, knives out, Art always shifting to keep himself blocking the path to where Rolan and Hayley stood by the steam cart. All she had was a slotted spoon to defend herself, and she hoped she wouldn't have to use it against the determined attacker with the huge blade.

Art made no indication that he would let Denim Man through. He was cautious with the man's knife but pressed his own attacks.

Tension bolted all her joints in place. She couldn't breathe while the conflict played out, just a few feet from her.

Leather Blazer groaned on the ground, holding his arm tight to his chest. The line outside the club was gone, only a handful of people remaining on the far limit of the outside lights. Men streamed from the front door, hurrying toward the conflict.

Denim Man saw the oncoming bouncers and bodyguards and doubled his attack. He swung and sliced quickly with his blade, showing murderous skill. Art remained nimble and stable, avoiding the razor edge. If she could've drawn a breath she would've shouted some caution to Art.

Just when he looked to be on his heels, Art launched his own assault. The knife struck out like a snake in his hand. The first jab missed, but he swiped the edge to the side and cut through the man's shirt and into his forearm. Denim Man winced, clenching his teeth. Art didn't let up. His knife flashed out, again and again. The man's arm was cut in long stripes.

Her heart thundered harder at the sight of blood in the violence. The blades were much more brutal than anything she worked with in the kitchen.

Denim Man tried to counter, but Art blocked him with a quick punch to the shoulder that knocked him back. Art stabbed out again and sliced across the back of the man's hand, forcing him to drop his knife.

She winced and drew her arms tighter to her body, knowing the pain must've been intense.

The man's terrified eyes stared wide at Art's blade. Art made him flinch with a fake stab. Denim Man never saw Art's other fist coming in. The blow landed square on his jaw. The attacker was unconscious before he hit the ground.

Art immediately picked up that man's knife and patted him down for any other weapons. He found only a cell phone and tossed it to the side with the man's wallet. He did the same for Leather Blazer, who was in too much pain to put up a struggle.

The other men from the club descended on the scene. Half surrounded the two downed attackers, while others whisked Rolan back into the building. For a moment, the only sounds were the low groaning of Leather Blazer and the quick, hard thumping of Hayley's pulse in her ears.

Art emerged from the group of men and went to her, his face focused. "You okay?"

"Yeah," she replied. Was this the same man she'd been flirting with? He'd changed so fast, the fighter just beneath the surface. He seemed human again, but all that violence couldn't go away that quickly. "You?"

Still holding both knives, he checked over his hands. "Couple of nicks, nothing bad." One of the knives had the other man's blood on it. Art's amazingly calm gaze moved on to her face again. "Get out of here before the cops show up."

She glanced down the hill to where her SUV was, trying to figure out how to switch gears between life-and-death struggles and the nuts-and-bolts details of hitching up her steam cart.

Art grounded her with his calm and even tone. "You're not part of this business. You just sell pelmeni, right?"

She nodded.

He continued. "I'll stay with your cart. Get your car."

Usually taking orders prickled her, but having a clear directive helped sort out all the chaos. She jogged away from the side of the club, realizing she still held the slotted spoon like a weapon. She had clenched her fist so tight her fingers creaked when she opened them to get her keys out.

She laid too much gas on, and the tires screeched up the hill toward the club. The group of men surrounding the downed attackers paid little attention when she double-parked. Art didn't hold the knives anymore, and pushed the cart over to her trailer hitch. Hayley helped him hook it up, but lost most of her dexterity to jumping nerves.

Selling her family recipe pelmeni outside a Russian nightclub had seemed like a perfect way of digging her way out of debt and turmoil. But in one night, she'd shaken hands with a mob boss and witnessed an attempted killing. The man who'd taken on and neutralized the attackers appeared way too calm. The same physicality that had flared vivid sexual fantasies had erupted into quick, devastating violence.

Art placed his warm palm over her trembling hand. "Chef. You've got this."

Part of her believed him. He'd stood between her and the attacker's blades, even if he was protecting Rolan, too. She was amazed that he could make her feel at all safe amid the violence.

"Thank you," she breathed.

He was dangerous. The depth in his eyes resonated through Hayley, making her think she understood a piece of him. But, *no*, she told herself. He was too different, too far away from anything she'd known.

"You're welcome." He walked her to her car door and opened it for her. Once she was inside, he tapped reassuringly on the roof. "I've got to keep you cooking. Besides, you had my back. If they'd gotten through me, you'd have taken them out with the spoon."

It rested on her passenger seat.

He smiled, slightly crooked, slightly honest. "See you next weekend."

Fear and a hidden thrill tumbled through her. She'd found a good place to start her life back up but had to make a deal with a bad guy to do it and had entered into a world of knife attacks and violent men. Art was one of them. And he seemed like something else. She'd see him again. She'd be back in the danger. Would he protect her? Or tempt her deeper into the shadows?

TWO

ART SHOWERED IN the dark and left the lights out as he toweled off. Soap had stung the hairline cuts on his knuckles and the backs of his hands. He'd had worse growing up with his sister's cats. He'd had worse fighting in the hills of Afghanistan.

Long ago, he'd memorized the layout of his simple apartment and now moved silently through the darkness without bumping into anything. Leftover warmth from the shower dragged at his tired muscles. After pulling on a pair of boxers, he used an app on his phone to deactivate the motion sensing area light in the living room. The glow of the floodlight would've warned him if anyone had come through, even if he couldn't hear the footsteps. A .38 special in a zip-top bag in the shower was always close at hand.

His feet creaked the floorboards as he walked to the kitchen and poured himself a tall shot of aged tequila. There was another revolver within reach, taped to the underside of the counter. The cooking knives were kept sharp, even though he didn't cook much.

He'd never make a grilled cheese sandwich or improvise a burrito from leftovers again if he could eat whatever was coming out of Chef Hayley's kitchen every day. The pelmeni continued to warm him. Perfect dough. Rich meat. He remembered it almost as vividly as he did turning to see Hayley after the fight, standing with the metal spoon in her hand, ready to defend herself. She earned a whole other level of respect when he'd taken in how she'd tried to control her fear and stand her ground.

The tequila burned a slow path down his throat. He hissed a breath through his teeth, erasing any thoughts of what would've happened if the sharpened daggers of the two hit men had gotten to her.

"Fuck that," he said out loud, then downed the other half of the glass and refilled it. There was no chance he'd have let them touch her. The only way they'd have gotten close was if Art was dead. Which was more dedication than he'd give his supposed boss, Rolan.

Art had just met her that night, but if he had to pick between them, he'd save her. As far as Rolan and the rest of his mob organization, the Orel Group, was concerned, Art's job was to protect the boss at all costs. But they didn't know he had another job. He'd taken it to protect innocent people like Hayley.

And, man, if he'd just been a normal guy chilling outside a club and eating an order of dumplings, he would've been happy to spend a few minutes in her company. Chef Hayley was as sharp as razor wire. Quick wits and agile without being mean. Easy to look at, too. A few inches shorter than him, with a cropped blond bob and blue eyes that collected the light. And the body? He sipped the tequila. The chef's coat wasn't formfitting, but he saw she was strong and curvy. Would she go for a guy like him? It didn't matter. She didn't know what kind of man he was. To her, he was a goon, working for the mob, and he couldn't tell her anything different.

He hadn't been a normal guy for a long time. Things were too complicated for anything other than a casual hookup that was quickly dismissed. Hayley wouldn't play that. Nothing was casual about her. Just eating her simple food was like a weekend in bed.

Luckily it hadn't come down to making the choice between her and Rolan. The two assassins were skilled, but rough around the edges and too confident. They weren't coordinated as a team. He'd picked them apart and only had small cuts like he'd been repairing the screens in the crawl spaces under his mom's house.

He took another drink, sorting the night's events and letting the tequila mingle with his slow, tired blood. Another mob had made a play on Rolan. The territory was in flux. It would ramp up the boss's plans to pull in the other Orel Group heads for the big meeting. There was strength in numbers, and Rolan needed their help to squash out the competition in the southwestern region.

Art would be there, undercover, running point for the operation to bust that meeting. He had a rendezvous with his strike team the next day and would relate the escalation to them. A lot of moving pieces needed to be in place before they could take Rolan and the Orel Group down. But Art and the other operators worked like the components of a machine gun. Maybe that was why the shady black ops soldiers who'd first formed the team had named it Automatik.

Sipping his tequila, he walked back through the dark living room. The sun would be up soon. How much sleep would he get before the day burned him awake? Living a double life took all his energy.

He sat on the bed, surrounded by the solid silence

of his blackout curtains. Tonight's threat had been neutralized. A broken bone and non-life-threatening knife wounds were easy to explain to the cops. The men had been taken away and would be released on bail as soon as their crime family came through. Art's cover hadn't been blown. A new civilian had arrived in the mix, and she hadn't been hurt in the attack.

From the way Hayley had held the spoon, she could've given anyone hell. He was sure she had at some point. Anyone willing to stand out alone and sell food in foreign territory had to have a huge set of radishes. And a reason. Her ferocity in the negotiations had proved that. She was fighting not to lose.

She didn't know it, but he was fighting for her, too. He'd seen that she knew what she was doing when she'd shaken Rolan's hand, but there was no way she understood how spiked and twisted the web was. Would he be able to end all this before she got hurt? He'd joined Automatik to keep people safe. The undercover job with Rolan and the Orel Group had a personal meaning, too.

Revenge.

He was in deep and wanted to be in deeper, twisting the knife.

HAYLEY PEERED AT normal life from a distance. Four days had passed since the incident at the Sea Weed. She'd gone over the events again and again and couldn't find anything she'd done wrong. Still, she felt like a criminal. And something as ordinary as a farmer's market was distorted and alien for her now.

It was the same set of stalls in the same parking lot in the same old part of town, near brick business buildings, but anything familiar appeared too distant to touch. She walked through the rows, examined the fresh food and interacted with the farmers and sellers, yet it all rang false. Or tenuous, like she was about to slip up any second and reveal a terrible secret. The sky would go dark, and the people would turn on her like she was a monster in the village.

But she couldn't figure out what the secret was. She'd witnessed a real knife fight, with a violence she'd never seen. Art had been brutal and precise. Men had been broken and hurt. She'd run before the cops had arrived, and there'd been no contact since. There had been one mention on a local website about trouble outside a club, and three or four of the people who'd been standing outside had mentioned the fight on social media, but there weren't a lot of details. Everyone seemed to know it wasn't their business, and to say anything about it would draw them into the danger.

She was in it. That was her secret. Since that night, she'd worn her denim jacket like armor, even though the days were warm. She was fully aware of a perilous criminal world and she was planning on going back to turn a profit, instead of running as far away as possible. Which made her a crook, too. Like Art, who was always at the center of her thoughts. Coiled, a knife in both hands, smiling.

"The daikons are fresh." Carol, the Chinese woman who ran one of the better food stalls, picked up one of the glowing white radishes and shaved off a slice with a pocket knife. "Sharp, but a little sweet."

Hayley took it, and the quick burn of the daikon's spice brought her a few miles closer to the rest of the world.

But could she look Carol in the eye without the other woman knowing she'd waded into deep criminal water?

She selected a couple of daikons and handed them to Carol to be weighed. "You have dill?"

"With the herbs." Carol pointed to the piles of green bundles. "Planning something?"

"Experimenting." Hayley picked through the dill stalks, finding the freshest and firmest. This was how it was supposed to be. Collecting what was in season, finding a way to use it and presenting it to the diners in her restaurant. "The daikon will go great in a simple cucumber salad. Sour cream, dill, lemon juice."

But she didn't have a restaurant. Just a steam cart and a handshake with a mob boss.

"Sounds excellent." The woman bagged the radishes and the dill Hayley gave her. "Still waiting for you to open your own place."

Hayley took a long breath. "It's going to be a while longer." The first night of sales from the cart had been decent. How many more of those would it take to pay her mom back? And how long after that until she got into the black?

Carol looked on with sympathy. News of Hayley and Burton's breakup had made the rounds through the restaurant and food service community months ago.

Then Carol's face lit up. "Just a whim, try bitter melon in the salad." The woman comped Hayley one in the bag. "Whenever you're ready, I'll be there opening night."

Opening night. She'd worked so hard for that moment, to see her mother and family there, sitting at a table, sharing her food and clinking generous glasses of wine over low candles. What had been so close now tasted impossible.

And the main reason was probably sauntering through the same farmer's market searching for just the right ingredient. Hayley fought the welling of hot tears.

"Thanks, Carol." She took the offered bag of produce from the woman. "Don't need a restaurant. As soon as I have a decent dining table, I'll have you over for dinner."

The woman's eyes glinted, mischievous. "I'll bring the wild card ingredients." Then she glared over Hayley's shoulder. "He's here. Just up the aisle to your left."

The muscles between her shoulder blades knotted. But she wasn't about to run and hide from Burton. He was a son of a bitch with cold feet and a cold heart. She had kept cooking.

She turned, a small sneer on her lips. Burton saw her and stared back, about three stalls away. The harsh sun beat down. Everything glowed in a haze except Burton. His shaggy blond hair was deliberately tousled around his clean-cut and handsome face. Lanky and muscular, he was at least a head taller than most of the people around him. He held a couple of bags of produce and wore his usual shorts and a T-shirt. His customary easygoing surfer-guy chill seemed frozen.

They'd run into each other a few times since the breakup but hadn't spoken more than a cupful of words. This felt different. Charged. Did he see that she was part criminal now? She tried to deny how much she embraced that darkness, when confronted with someone she wanted to intimidate. It was too intoxicating.

"Trouble?" A man's voice at her shoulder startled

Hayley. She twisted to face Art, whose focus remained down the aisle at Burton. That ready violence lurked dangerously close to the surface.

It was a shock to see him there, so out of context, in her world. "No trouble," she reassured him. But she had to wonder what he was doing there.

Art loosened his shoulders and relaxed. "Looked like a standoff."

She glared at Burton again. "That battle's over."

Her ex glanced from her to Art and back again. Slowly, Burton stepped up the aisle until he disappeared beyond a stall selling roasted nuts.

Was this how it would work from now on—she'd think felonious thoughts, and Art would show up out of nowhere, bringing his menace? Her head spun a bit from the criminal cocktail. So much potential. If they were outside the rules, they could do anything together.

She pulled her wallet from her purse and peeled out a few bills. "Tell me this is a coincidence and you're out here looking for the perfect basil for your pesto recipe." The money went over to Carol, who made change and deliberately eyed Art quizzically.

He was out of place at the farmer's market. Rough around the edges, wearing his light jacket in the warm day. Dark sunglasses obscured his expression, making his intent more mysterious. Her skin prickled, aware of how close he was. And how close she was to touching all that potential motion and energy.

Hayley managed to answer Carol with a quick shrug. Whatever information she did have about Art wasn't something she'd give willingly without implicating herself. Carol waggled her eyebrows before Hayley and Art moved away from the stall.

Yeah, Art was sexy. She was sure Carol and everyone else at the market saw it. Even Burton must've recognized Art's potency. But none of them knew about his job the way she did. And they hadn't seen his efficient violence the way she had.

He walked beside her while she continued on her rounds. Daytime Art was much looser than she'd seen him by the club. His shoulders swung slightly and his lower body turned like he had his own theme song, thumping with a heavy beat. It would be easy to match that rhythm. Her body wanted to, rocking her own hips.

She tried to examine his expression, but the sunglasses were too dark.

"Do I have any secrets anymore?" she asked. "Did you use your…contacts to find me?"

He stopped walking and took off his sunglasses so she could see his serious eyes. "I don't want your secrets. You don't want mine. I found you all by myself. Where better to find a great chef than near great food, right?"

"You're a smart guy, Art." And sensual. And rough. And brutal.

He held up a warning finger. "You can't know that about me. I said you didn't want any of my secrets." A wry smile twinkled his eyes.

"I won't tell a soul."

"*Bueno.*" His accent was authentic.

"But how are people not supposed to catch on that you have a brain when you speak Russian and Spanish?"

His fist was held low. "They usually only hear this."

She went silent. But she saw hints of sadness and distance in his eyes. Part of her wanted to cover that territory and find out more about the man behind the scarred knuckles.

He put his sunglasses back on, started walking again then paused for her to catch up. It didn't feel like she had a choice. They were in the same world together now. She walked at his side. He chewed on thoughts.

Eventually he spared a few words. "My father was *hecho en Mexico*. Mother from Mother Russia. She's the one who raised me."

"Makes perfect sense." She directed them to a stall where she found ripe tomatoes and bought them. While the transaction went down, Art waited, his hands holding the lapels of his jacket again. It made him lean back a bit and peer down toward the world while the sides of his neck flexed. There was something casual about the posture, yet he was still ready to spring into action.

Part of her wished he was merely there to market with her. It would've been so much simpler. Flirting, talking about food. She'd cook him a meal with everything they found. He'd be fun to watch eat. Despite the tough exterior, he sensed the world. She'd seen it when he'd tried her pelmeni. So she'd experiment on him with new recipes. After dinner and the last of the wine, that strong body of his would experiment on her...

Sweat rose on the back of her neck when she imagined his mouth there. Her breath fell short as if his arms were around her and she pressed herself back into his chest. The need came on too strong. She shook off the thoughts. It didn't matter how much physical potential there was between them. He worked for the mob boss she was paying a cut to. There was nothing innocent about strolling through the rows of food.

Pausing at the intersection of aisles, she turned to him. "You're not here for the produce."

He shook his head, mouth a serious, thin line. "I'm here for business." His whole posture changed, transforming into that wary predator. He glanced at the people around them. "There's got to be someplace more private we can talk."

She led them away from the farmer's market, toward a small food court on the other side of one of the office buildings. It would be quiet, but public. She wasn't ready to get behind closed doors with Art when he was acting this sketchy.

Once they'd cleared past most of the people, she asked, "Is this about the guys with the knives?"

"No. That'll never touch you."

Her mind spun, trying to think about what other business there was. The only deal she had with Rolan was for her steam cart. Maybe this was his way of renegotiating.

"They were really going after your boss?"

"Yeah." He rubbed absently at his knuckles.

"But no guns?"

He tilted his head toward her. "You ask a lot of questions for someone who only wants to sell dumplings."

"I can't sell dumplings if bullets are flying."

"You got that right, Chef." He chuckled. "For a hit in a public place like that, they use knives instead of guns to keep collateral damage down. Innocent bystanders get shot, and the cops get interested. Knives are quiet."

"Mine are just for cooking."

His temper darkened again. He hardly moved his jaw to utter, "Let's keep it that way."

They reached the contained food court and skirted to the far side of a wide stone fountain. It was the farthest spot from any of the other people at the small metal tables. They settled at their own table, joined only by the burbling of the fountain and the occasional bird flitting past.

Nerves ground into her. What was his business? It was something serious. And so dire that it appeared like he didn't even want to be here discussing it.

Art took a long breath and removed his sunglasses to stare at her. She was about to find out the cost of making a deal with Rolan.

The wry glimmer deadened in his eyes. This wasn't the man who'd stood by her at the cart, smelling the food and letting it transport him to whatever past he had. At the table with her now was what she expected from a mob enforcer. A hard, unfeeling mask. But she knew what was beneath that mask. Did that make her dangerous to him?

Her palms sweat and her chest tightened. Her mind traced back to when they'd entered the food court. Where were the exits? Could she get to them before he caught her? She wasn't sure if there was any possibility of running from what was coming. Art's role in everything remained a mystery.

"My boss, Rolan," he finally informed her, "wants you to cook for a weeklong retreat he's throwing for friends."

A sigh of relief caught in her throat. That kind of gig should be a piece of cake, and she'd kill for the opportunity. But if Art was making this big of a deal, something must be wrong.

She tried to keep her mind from flying to the worst possibilities: she would be on the menu, or other women who didn't want to be there, or it would be one of those mob meetings that turned into a bloodbath as they cleaned house.

"How many people?" she queried automatically, as if this was just business.

"Eighteen. Some will need fancier food than the others."

"One week?"

"Seven days."

"Food allergies? Special needs?" Normal questions she'd ask anyone.

"I'll try to find out."

The ordinary details didn't take the edge off. Art remained stony.

"I've done that kind of thing in Temecula for a group of people who'd been friends since college. Four days. They'd golfed and done wine tastings."

"No one's going to be golfing at this party," he said flatly.

"When?" she asked.

"You leave Saturday morning."

"That's in two days." Way too fast. No one booked a cook with that short notice. The offer started to slide away from the real world she understood.

His mouth remained stern. "I know."

"That's hardly any time to prep." She leaped into menu possibilities for that many people. "Breakfast, lunch and dinner?"

"It'll be a walking breakfast, but they'll need full lunches and dinner."

What was the catch that had Art so stony? "You know I can't do it for free."

"Of course." He nodded. "Twenty thousand. Ten before, ten once you're back home. Cash. No taxes."

She leaned back in her chair like she was hit in the face with a glass of ice water. The amount would almost clear the books with her mom. The temptation drew her in, but there were so many questions.

"That's more than this kind of job merits," she said.

"You negotiating yourself down?"

The pile of money wasn't enough to bend her yet. "What are you really paying for?"

"A very quiet chef." His gaze remained unfeeling. "Who cooks great and doesn't ask questions and focuses on the kitchen and keeps any details to herself once she gets back home."

"Where is it?" she pressed.

"The desert."

"Which desert?"

He shook his head. "I can't say."

This was getting downright crazy. "Then how am I supposed to find it?"

"You don't." He placed his finger on the surface of the table. "I pick you up." Dragging his finger, he drew a jagged line. "I drive you to the house. You cook. I drive you home." He moved his finger back to the first point.

"You make it sound so simple," she murmured. The invisible map highlighted just how far away she'd be, in territory she didn't understand, with Art as her only way back.

"It should be." Was there the smallest hint of doubt in his voice?

The money was incredible. She'd never dreamed of getting a gig this lucrative. It would take months of impossible best nights ever with the steam cart to make that kind of cash. Instead of pulling her into the job, the money was part of the reason she was pushed away. They were paying too much. Somehow, she would end up paying.

"It's short notice," she hedged. "I might have to say no, but I can give you some chefs who would take it."

Art remained motionless. "Like you have better plans? You'd just be slinging dumplings outside the Sea Weed."

Seething frustration bloomed in her. Art had been so easy to talk to. Mysterious and dangerous, yes, but also perceptive and genuinely listening. This steely version of him was like a robot programmed for intimidation. She missed the way they'd communicated. "You don't know everything I do."

"I don't need to." God, he sat there like a typical confident bully. "The deal's good. You should take it."

She hated being cornered. All the bullshit with Burton had pushed her into a dead end, and she'd done what she could to fight her way back. But things had just turned darker. Fuck the money. She'd find a way to get it somewhere else, somewhere cleaner where it wasn't being used to leverage her. "What if I say no?"

"You can't," he said, like stating a law of the universe.

"Then why ask?" Her legs twitched to stand and run.

"Because I'm polite."

"Barely."

That cracked a small, sad smile from him. Art kept his eyes on the table. "People don't say no to Rolan. The ones who do aren't people anymore."

Acid churned her stomach. The violence and blood she'd seen in Art's fight in front of the club were magnified a thousand times.

He continued, "Tell your friends and family you got a sweet job for those college yuppies again. Golfing in the desert for a week. No details. And your cell phone won't get reception out there."

Moving slow and deliberate, he reached into a front pocket of his jacket. She tensed and tried to remember all the vulnerable places to attack on a man. Art didn't seem to have any weaknesses. He finally pulled out a simple pen and a pad of paper. "Write down your address."

She left the pen on the table. Art waited, motionless. Was there any way out? The police? She was sure Art and Rolan could do a lot of damage to her and those around her before the cops even showed up.

"I'm just there to cook, right?"

Art nodded, dead serious. "I'll make sure of it." The edge in his voice sounded like a promise.

The choice had been taken from her.

She picked up the pen and put her temporary address at her friends' guest house on the pad. The handshake with Rolan was a shady deal. Putting ink on paper was like signing her soul to the devil. And Art was the head demon. Sometimes he was close, with a wry glint in his eye just for her. Other times he was hard like a desert snake looking for its next meal.

He stood, taking the pad and pen. "I'll pick you up Saturday morning."

"Time?" She tried to create a schedule leading up to that moment, but there was no order in jagged fear, sharp dollar bills and Art's steel will that all trapped her.

"Just before sunrise." His sunglasses blocked his eyes, then he was gone, easily gliding through an exit and disappearing in the glow of the day.

She knew he'd be back for her.

THREE

FOR YEARS HE'D been alone just before the dawn. If his life had turned out differently, those dark, quiet moments could've been shared with a woman. Crisp sheets surrounding a warm body. She'd sleep with her head on his shoulder, and he'd be awake listening to her slow, even breaths. It might have even been Hayley.

But he woke without a word or another soul close to his. These solitary moments were his to recover from the night before and prepare for what the day would bring. This morning he drove across San Diego, toward Hayley. The address she'd given him was a guest house in a decent area of town, far from his apartment in a working-class neighborhood. He had a few minutes of silence.

Streetlights slipped past. In another hour, they wouldn't be needed anymore. Hardly anyone else was on the road. These small hours reminded him of basic training, when the instructors would shock the recruits awake, then drill them with PT or long runs under heavy packs. That work had paid off in the mountains of Afghanistan. There hadn't been a time of day when he wasn't ready for a surprise attack or stealthy recon mission.

Normal people didn't go out at these hours. It was the time for predators. That was what Hayley thought of him. He was the muscle who'd forced her into the gig. He'd given her no choice and had none himself.

He was trapped. The whole day before he'd found her at the farmer's market, he'd tried to figure a way to get her out of this. But every option would've threatened his position with Rolan, and subsequently the operation for Automatik.

Sitting across from Hayley, he'd wanted to burn the city down to give her a cover for escape. But he couldn't tell her. He had to play his part: bad guy.

After the time frame for the big meeting had been moved up, he'd met with the other Automatik operators to accelerate their own mission parameters. Planning had raced ahead, barely keeping up. Jackson and Harper, the two former Navy SEALs who were his closest contacts, were tasked with trailing his SUV now.

It was reassuring to know they had his back. But once he was out in the desert, they'd have to keep low and far away. The meeting house was his environment to control, waiting until all five regional heads of the Orel Group were in the target zone.

He'd never done any undercover work, though he'd been in plenty of deadly situations. Time always felt short on the forward bases in Afghanistan. His unit had spent months on their own without regular support from command. Being undercover in the mob was almost the same. Cut off, but never quitting on the mission. And trying to stay out of the line of fire.

After being shot at in country, working at a home improvement store in Southern California had been a bit surreal and detached from the view of life and death he'd developed in the combat zone. He'd kept to himself in San Diego while waiting for a call from Automatik. He was still living on the outside. Most of his socializing had been jogging with two former SEAL team members on the beach. Then one day, Jackson and Harper had told him they were with Automatik and some mission specifics were coming up for him. The Russian mob in San Diego was prime for infiltration.

When Rolan had approached him at the Sea Weed after a quick and dirty back alley brawl Art had won, it had been a smooth transition into the cover job of protecting a boss. He'd built trust with Rolan and leaked bits of intel to Jackson and Harper for over a year. Nothing had spiked their interest until he'd told them about the five-head meeting in the desert. Two weeks into the trip's initial planning, he'd gotten the call from a voice he'd never heard before.

"You're the trigger."

He'd been briefed on what that meant. The bullet was in the chamber. Just a matter of time until shots were fired.

It would happen in the desert. He'd run point on the operation and would create the plan from the inside, then lead the charge. And he'd have to trust the strike team was ready when he made the call. And now, goddamn, because he couldn't do anything to keep Hayley out of this deadly world, he'd do everything to keep her from the cross fire.

Dawn was half an hour away, and she was already on the sidewalk outside the address, a duffel bag, a large cooler and several bags of groceries piled near her feet. A streetlight up the block revealed only the shadows of her face, but he saw the tension in her posture. That dread echoed in him. If he just drove past her, left her behind as he went into the desert, she'd be safe. But he wouldn't be. Rolan and the Orel Group would kick him out, or kill him. Then he wouldn't be at the meeting house to run the operation to take them down. Once their power was solidified, they'd be much harder to pick apart. And too many more innocent people would be hurt.

No one else should go through what his family had endured.

He brought the black SUV to a stop in front of Hayley. A knit cap was pulled low on her head, just to her dark, tired and wary eyes. He popped the hatch for the back and got out, leaving the engine running. There wasn't an ounce of trust in her and he deserved it.

From the trunk he pulled a small leather knockoff purse and handed it to her. She unzipped it cautiously, like it hid a snake. Her eyes went wide on bundles of cash, ten thousand dollars. She quickly closed the purse, fists clutching the strap.

"Drop it inside," he said. "I'll wait with your stuff."

The still air shimmered after she hurried away, stalking the darkness around the side of the house. After a moment and the sound of a door opening, then closing, she returned without the purse.

He tipped his head to the building behind her. "Nice house." There were no lights on, but someone could be watching from one of the dark windows.

"Friends." She was smart not to give any names and involve them.

He reached for her duffel, but she already had her hand around the handle. He picked up the heavy cooler, and they walked together to the back of the SUV. She carefully placed the bag in the cargo area, and he followed it with the cooler, then returned for the grocery bags.

Even closing the hatch as quiet as possible sounded like a felony in the silent neighborhood.

She winced.

He shrugged. "Get any sleep?"

"Not much." Her raw voice told as much.

"Me neither." Again, his mind tumbled to impossible scenarios, like he was picking her up for a weekend getaway at a state park, or a mountain cabin far from anyone else. They could hike, fake bird sounds, eat and have sex without any worries. An ache coiled around him, yearning to move, as he tried to extinguish the thoughts of him and Hayley under a pile of blankets while snow fell outside dark windows.

Before she walked to the front of the SUV, he put his hand out. She just stared at it, forcing him to explain, "I need your phone."

The muscles in her jaw jumped, and she hissed a whisper, "I told everyone a good story. A group of friends for a desert getaway. ATVs and barbecue and everything. And I said I'd get no reception. Do you know what it's like lying to your mother?"

"Yes." His mom didn't know he worked for Rolan. She thought he was a personal trainer and hardware guy at the home improvement store and a consultant for military officer recruits. "Nobody trusts anyone anymore." He kept his hand out.

She eyed him and slowly pulled her phone from a coat pocket. Communication was a lifeline. He understood that. His links to Automatik had redundancies. If all of those failed, he'd resort to smoke signals if he had to in order to bring in the heavy guns.

Her fingers were tight on the phone as she placed it in his hand. Then she released it and recoiled.

He confessed, "I don't like it either."

As he walked to the front of the SUV, he shut the phone down. After he climbed into the driver's seat, she tapped on the passenger door for him to unlock it. It would've been so much better riding with her next to him, but he had to maintain his safety concerns as Rolan's hired man. He thumbed her toward one of the back doors. The divide between them grew so much larger after she got in the backseat and closed that door.

She brought the morning chill with her into the car.

He locked her phone in the signal-blocking safe box in the passenger foot well, then put the car in gear.

"Comfortable?" He turned to check on her. The SUV had been modified, with only one row of seats and tons of leg room. The doors were also reinforced, and there was a rig for a glass divider behind the front seats. She was tiny in the black interior

"Not really." She tucked herself into one corner and snapped her seat belt on.

He watched her try to peer out the side window as they pulled into the street, but the tint was too dark. She switched her gaze to the front window for a moment, but quickly looked away when her eyes found his.

A selfish wish to get her to see him without all that mistrust made him want to tell her the truth about him and Automatik. Their relations might be repaired, slightly, but it wouldn't make the operation any easier.

And it wouldn't make her any safer. Giving her a secret that big to keep would only screw down increased pressure. Any leaks would jeopardize both of their lives.

She continued to stare past him at the dark streets of San Diego.

Talking to her had felt easy. Now it was a crawl through mud under barbed wire. "Sorry to abuse your taste buds, Chef, but can you handle a fast-food breakfast?"

"I'm not above a little drive-through."

He'd already mapped a place near a highway entrance. "About ten minutes."

"Works for me."

"The cooler and bags have all the ingredients you need?"

"Specialized things and some staples. It won't last the week, so I'll need to market once I get there to stretch it all out."

"I'll see what can be arranged." The building of the house had been arranged by one of the other Orel Group bosses. All Art had were the coordinates and directions. There was a small town nearby, so supplies could be had there. He was already itching to get to the house and start mapping the floor plan, then send it to his Automatik teammates.

"Otherwise it might be a lot of butter sandwiches," she said tersely.

"I'm sure you'd make even that great." He glanced at her through the rearview mirror.

She crossed her arms and didn't smile.

He tried to keep his voice casual. "So who was that dude at the farmer's market? I was a little too on task to ask, but it looked like there were a few miles of rough landscape between you two."

She snorted a laugh. "My ex. Burton. We were going to open a restaurant together, but he bailed. On everything."

Which explained why she was selling pelmeni and making deals with Rolan instead of marshaling the troops of her own kitchen. "Son of a bitch."

"Worse."

"Dick, *cabron,* douche bag, *payaso,* motherfucker."

She grudgingly smiled. "Better."

"However things went down, I'm taking your side." The complications of a serious relationship had eluded him. He'd never thought about moving in with someone, let alone starting a business together. Fighting wars had always kept him too busy. But he'd seen his sisters go through the peaks and valleys. "Who the fuck would keep you from having your own place?" Here Art was, driving her toward a situation she might not come out of alive. "You say the word, and I can make his life real uncomfortable."

She uncrossed her arms and held her palms toward him. "No need. Seriously. He's got it bad enough without me."

"I'll bet. He'll never find as good a chef as you."

Her head tilted, not buying. "You've only had my pelmeni."

"You've only seen me take down two hit men."

She peered at him through the rearview mirror with somber eyes.

He filled the quiet. "Your food says a lot. Just that

taste made Rolan want to have you cooking for some very important people."

The silence thickened.

Nothing he said would be right. The truth, another lie, just lit fuses leading to inevitable detonation. Turning around, returning her home, would put them both in the crosshairs. Taking all the fuel in the SUV to get as far away as possible would just be the first day of the rest of their lives on the run.

He broke the quiet. "When you're done dazzling them with your cooking for the week, you'll get back in this car, safe and sound, and I'll drive you home."

No answer. He was sure she took it to be just hollow reassurance coming from him. Whether she knew it or not, his words were also a vow he was determined to fulfill.

THE CAR WINDOWS had been too black for a last glance at Kendra's house. Hayley had assumed that as soon as the sun came up, she'd be able to see the passing scenery, but the morning was well under way and the only natural light came into the SUV through the front windshield. Art was transformed into a shadowy mass, which was how she imagined him anyway.

They'd had a brief conversation about their favorite hole-in-the-wall food joints in the city while they ate a fast-food breakfast, but silence had once again fallen. The neighborhoods outside were taken over by light industrial parks and sprawling storage facilities. If she'd had her phone, she could've texted Kendra and asked her if she knew anything about this area. Hayley was cut off. She'd pulled away from her friend's house knowing she'd never be able to return to any sense of normalcy. If she returned at all.

Kendra and her partner, Julieta, had been excited for Hayley's gig. They'd been super generous all along, letting her stay in their guest house for minimal rent while she put the pieces of her life back together. Both of them ran a successful bar in the Gaslamp Quarter, so they understood the difficulties of the food service industry. They didn't even blink when she'd suggested doing her steam cart in order to make ends meet. If they'd known the truth of Hayley's current predicament, the tough girls would've spent all night and a bottle of bourbon trying to come up with a solution to keep her from going.

She'd thought plenty on it, though, and couldn't come up with anything that wouldn't lift her from the frying pan and toss her directly in the fire. It was for the best that she hadn't brought her friends into it. If they'd gone asking for help outside their circle, it could've put everyone at risk.

"Any news on the dietary restrictions?" she asked. "Allergies?" It was a fucked-up situation, but she had a job to do.

"I asked around but no one came back with a problem. I'll find out more when we get there."

"Anything you won't eat?" From the way he talked about food, it seemed Art was up for all possibilities. The kind of guy who could be inspirational to cook for.

He clicked his tongue, thinking. "Eyeballs."

"There's a story." She'd have guessed broccoli or curry.

"Making peace with someone," he explained, voice

distant in memory. "They honored us with goat eye-balls."

If she could just see his face, she'd know how those experiences affected him. The same guy who'd lived that was now basically her captor. He'd offered her a deal with no out. It must've come down from Rolan, but she wouldn't let Art off the hook for "just taking orders."

"I'm going to bet," she said, "that where we're headed, you won't rate high enough for eyeballs anyway."

"You got that right," he confirmed with a slow nod. "Just grilled cheese for me."

"We'll see." The conversation could've slid forward. Volleys of question and answer had arced easily between them. He'd obviously had a lot of diverse experiences and wanted to hear from her, as well. But he didn't press, and she kept any curiosity to herself.

She was a chef, cooking food for pay. They could be friendly, but she drew the line on any further connection. What was the point of getting to know this man if he had her cornered? She dug her protective moat deeper. Art was business, same as Rolan and anyone else she met wherever they were headed.

But cutting herself off left her hungry. There were hidden tastes of Art to discover.

No, she convinced herself. *No. He's dangerous. Everything is dangerous. Cook. Survive. Get home.*

The SUV accelerated up an on-ramp to a wide high-way. She tried to see the signs, but they went by too quickly.

Art turned to look at her, dark resignation on his face. "Sorry about this, Chef."

After he faced forward again, a sheet of glass rose up from behind the front seats. It was as black as the windows around her.

Sunlight was sliced thinner and thinner by the glass until any natural glow was gone. Inside the SUV, rows of inset lights turned on, illuminating the spacious interior but revealing no details of the outside. Even Art in the driver's seat was invisible.

Her phone was long gone. Now her isolation was complete. They'd already strayed too far from familiar territory for her to try to puzzle out what turns on the highway might mean. It was impossible to determine what direction they headed.

All she knew was that as a last resort, her cooking knives were in their roll in her duffel bag.

SHE'D LOST TRACK of time, and her attention shifted between trying not to be bored or carsick or angry or terrified. The ingredients in the cooler and grocery bags were listed again and again in her mind, and Hayley created as many combinations between them as possible. Brief conversations with Art had squawked, mechanical, through an intercom in the wall. He'd given her meaningless time updates or instructions on how to use the TV/DVD player between the seats.

Her only options to watch were pirated copies of a porno and two bad action movies from the '90s. Time passed while a shirtless dude ran through industrial hallways on the TV and kicked other men in their heads. At one point the sound of gunfire overwhelmed, as if all the barrels were pointed at her. She punched the pause button and leaned into the intercom, hoping for a sliver of contact and a crumb of humanity.

"Is this you in the movie?" she asked Art.

He laughed through the speaker. "Is that the one where the guy has a nano-computer behind his ear and it's got the antidote to the virus, but the bad guys want to infect the world?"

"I bet you've seen it a hundred times."

"Rolan digs it for some reason." There was a break in the intercom, then, "But no, that's not me. I don't wax my chest, and he pays no attention to the twenty-one-foot rule."

"Educate me," she said.

"If you have a gun in a holster, and there's a bad guy with a knife in his hand, and he's within twenty-one feet, he'll get you before you get him." His voice came out robotic through the speaker, like getting instructions from a machine, telling her to leave her compassion behind.

"Good to know." She turned the TV off, not wanting to see the sensational violence.

"Trade me." The warmth increased in his voice. "Give me a handful of knowledge back."

"When you're cooking beans from scratch," she instructed, "don't salt them until they're just tender. If you do it too early, the skins will toughen."

"Got it. I've never made beans from scratch. Always just opened a can."

"Fresh beans are a good thing." Though she doubted she'd be able to capture the pure joy of cooking wherever she was headed.

Art's voice informed her, "Another couple of hours."

"Bathroom?"

A pause, then the intercom crackled. "Twenty minutes, okay?"

"Thanks."

After a span of time that might've been the twenty minutes or two hours, the SUV came to a stop. Art opened the side door, and bright yellow sunlight erased her vision. She got out and stood for a moment, letting her eyes adjust. Blinking the world into shapes, she expected to see landscape, hills or trees or mountains. Instead, the only thing in front of her was a drab cinder block building with a single door marked for a women's bathroom. The SUV was parked at an angle to block the rest of the view. It could've been part of a gas station or a rest stop.

She hadn't realized how strong the air-conditioning in the car had been until she was out in the desert heat. It felt like all the moisture from her body was sucked away into the thirsty atmosphere. She tossed her jacket and knit cap back into the black abyss of the SUV and headed past Art into the restroom.

She took care of her needs in the somewhat grungy bathroom, splashed water on her tired face and came back out to see Art leaning on the car. It had been a long time since she'd been on a road trip with a boyfriend, maybe Yosemite when she was in her early twenties, but this didn't carry the same positive excitement. Art was casual, but always ready. For a while, before the deal, she might've thought of him as a friend. And there had been other potentials to explore. Now, he was…? Driver. Captor. Muscle. Protector?

She returned to the car, bringing her next to him as

he waited by the door. He didn't back off. She paused. The nearer she stood to him, the more her skin prickled with awareness.

He held most of the power. She clutched at what little she had, saying, "This is closer than twenty-one feet."

The desert-bright sun made him squint, and he slowly scanned over the space between them. "You armed?"

They both knew she didn't have a weapon. But she rallied as much danger as possible. "I might be." She might be able to take that one step closer to him. To feel how hard he would be against her. To feel how his active body could feed hers.

"Doesn't matter." He shook his head with a darkness that persisted even in the day. "I've got no defense if you're coming at me."

The moment drew out, tension between them buzzing hotter than the desert breeze. Attraction drew her toward him, but she didn't move. Since first meeting Art, the possibility of the two of them crashing together had seemed almost inevitable. But this job had derailed the momentum. She was left yearning for what might've been. And bitter that something that had shone so new and appealing in the midst of her struggles had turned into the impossible.

She got into the car without another word. Art closed the door. They were quickly on the move again, leaving behind an unknown stop and headed to an unknown destination. After a few curves in the road, then a rough patch that had the SUV rumbling on uneven dirt, the glass divider came down behind Art.

Again sunlight flooded her vision. Her eyes regulated to the harsh yellows and oranges of the bleak landscape outside the windshield just as the SUV drove through a gate in a beige cinder block wall. There was no way to tell where they were. California? Arizona? Mexico? It might've been Mars. Past a wide yard of dirt and rocks was a large house, looking at once brand-new and also like it had bubbled up from the hard ground. The exterior was brown and tan, like it was made of the same dry dirt and stone that surrounded them.

The driveway circled in front of the house, giving her glimpses of the three-story McMansion, complete with vaulted windows and a grand front entrance. And the men. Every exterior corner of the house had a man in dark clothes and sunglasses. Each guard held a gun. Some weapons were larger than others, but all shone like poisonous insects. She knew it would be hot outside but pulled on her jacket for extra armor.

The car came to a stop, and Art killed the engine. Her ears rang in the silence. The black box in the SUV that had been her mobile prison now felt like the most secure place to stay.

She came forward behind Art's seat. He didn't seem ready to get out of the car either.

"This isn't safe," she pleaded.

He turned to her, face dead serious. "No. It isn't. The safest place is with me." In a blur he spun away, getting out of the car. A second later, he'd opened her door.

The dry desert felt like a quick place to die. Art stood by the door with his grim expression. But his eyes still had light in them for her. Was he safe? Could she trust him? Beyond him was the house. There was nowhere to hide. Gathering herself with a breath, she stepped out of the SUV and into the harsh sunlight. The car door slammed behind her.

Art was right there with her. She'd seen his capabilities. The other men at this compound had guns, though. That might not make a difference to Art. It shouldn't matter to her, either. She strode to the back of the SUV for her bag. All these men were obviously trained fighters, but none of them were able to cook the way she did.

Art was close, and whispered, "You've got this, Master Chef."

A different heat moved through her. Art's reassurance carried more meaning than she'd expected, or wanted. Somehow this man of violence had the keen insight to understand her. And that made him a different kind of dangerous than whatever peril she was about to step into. He opened the trunk, and she pulled out her duffel, complete with her freshly sharpened knives.

"Yes." The bravado was for show. "I do."

Men with guns stared at her. Past them, somewhere inside, were Rolan and the other heavy hitters she needed to impress with her food. Art was behind her. Friend or foe, she didn't know, but he was her closest contact. Her ability to survive whatever danger the week would bring was inevitably tied to him. There were a lot of days and meals to get through before she'd be back in the SUV for the ride home to safety.

She hardened herself and walked toward the house.

FOUR

THE COMPOUND WAS a tactical nightmare. Easily defensible, with clear firing lanes from the house and almost no cover between the exterior wall and the bad guys. And at the center of it all, Hayley.

Art had recognized the small tremors of doubt in her and wondered how she'd get herself from the SUV to the house. His words of encouragement appeared to help. He'd watched her rally and sharpen herself enough to talk tough. He'd seen that happen elsewhere, from basic training to the wild hills of Afghanistan to knife fights in a crooked dry cleaners. She wouldn't let herself be overwhelmed. Her blue eyes remained bright and sharp. She tilted her chin up and walked toward the house. The desert heat seemed to bounce off Hayley like she was knife steel.

The woman was strong, determined. Somewhat surly and definitely sexy.

If everything went well, she could handle this gig.

But Art knew things weren't going to go well. She wasn't in on the plan. Rolan and the others had no idea. They were all sitting on a ton of C4, and Art was the trigger.

She was already a couple of steps toward the house when he slung his own duffel over his shoulder, then hefted her cooler and caught up. He'd learned scant details about the house while it was being planned and built, but this was his first chance to map the layout. The large propane tank peeked around the back of the house, on the southeast corner. The car gate was on the west wall; doors big enough for one man at a time were on the north and south walls.

He climbed the three steps to the wide front porch and glanced about for any high ground to attack from. The nearest hills were crowded toward the horizon. No sniper, not even his teammate "Bolt Action" Mary, could make the shot. The only way to get long-range fire support over the wall would be from a helo, but getting one close enough without alerting anyone before the ground team was in place would be next to impossible.

A guard Art didn't recognize stepped in front of the main entrance. He eyed Hayley's duffel and tipped his chin up as if it was too difficult to collect words into a sentence. She got his meaning, dropped her bag and unzipped it.

Keeping one hand on his submachine gun, the guard checked over her belongings. The gun was well used, brassed in areas, but maintained nicely. The man was a shooter. Right-handed. Patient. Art added him to the list of combatants.

When the guard pulled out Hayley's knife roll, she tensed a bit, protective, and put her hand on it. "Wait."

The guard stared at her, not liking being told what to do.

Art explained in Russian, "Tools of the trade."

With deliberate cool, Hayley unclipped the roll and expanded it. The blades flashed in the bright sun. The guard grudgingly nodded and motioned for her to roll it back up.

Art didn't wait for any formalities and placed the cooler down and opened it. The first blast of cool air refreshed him and brought faint aromas of the food inside. Hayley's food. Some of the vegetables were intact, but there were a lot of plastic containers of partially prepared ingredients. He saw her work, perfect cubes or long slices. She was as trained and practiced as the professional killer who blocked the door.

He'd given the guard enough time to check over the food, so Art slammed the lid shut and lifted the cooler. The shooter didn't move aside for a moment, and Art stared at him. If the hard-ass wanted trouble, Art could give it. He could pin the man's shooting hand to his body with a shove of the cooler. From there, knuckles and an elbow would make him bleed.

The standoff ended when the guard rolled his eyes with that bored, in-control attitude. He stepped out of their way, muttering in a thick Russian accent, "Second floor."

Art balanced the cooler in one hand and swung open the wide front door. Both he and Hayley fit side by side in the opening. Good. This entrance wouldn't be a choke point during the assault. But the firing lanes in the open foyer would be hell. Huge blind spot behind the door. Second-floor balcony could rain lead before the door breachers could get a shot off.

Hayley glanced about the room, then tipped her head back to the front entrance. "That guy was hard-core mad-dogging you. Thought you all worked together."

He replied under his breath as they walked up one

of the two curving stairways to the second floor. "I'm not full-blooded Russian. Never be part of the inner circle." Which shouldn't hurt his operation. He was close enough now. The Russians didn't trust him completely, not even Rolan, but they needed him. None of them spoke Spanish or had a handle on the Latino culture that surrounded them in the Southwest and West Coast. As long as they didn't suspect he was part of Automatik, every damn guard in the compound could try to stare him down until sunset. But that didn't mean he'd avoid giving someone a beating if a fool thought he was harder than Art.

"You're on the outside like me." But instead of the common ground bonding them, Hayley looked at him with wary caution.

They hit the second floor and started down a door-lined hallway toward Gogol, one of the nicer goons from Rolan's nightclub. His thick, wavy hair reached to just below his jawline, reminding Art of a European soccer player. And he almost always wore a tracksuit, same as today. The guard waved them forward, smiling like everyone was arriving for a ski trip.

Art murmured for Hayley. "No one here's on stable ground. From the top down. So you have to watch every step."

She slowed, and he kept pace with her. The hallway was a kill zone. A shooter with cover could easily pick off anyone trying to get from one end to the other. This area was to be avoided. All the doors must be the living quarters. He'd have to seek out alternate routes around the slaughterhouse.

Gogol motioned them toward him with increasing enthusiasm, speaking in Russian. "Today, Artem."

Hayley glared at Art out of the side of her eye. "Artem?"

So she had at least a basic understanding of the language. "But you call me Art."

They reached Gogol, and he swung a door open. Inside was a basic room: bed, side table, dresser. No window.

"This is you," Gogol instructed in Russian, nodding his head for Art.

Art put the cooler down in the hall and sidled past the man. The room smelled like paint and drywall. He tossed his duffel on the narrow bed. The wood creaked and settled. No one had even sat on it yet.

"And for you." Gogol stumbled over broken English, pointing Hayley one door farther. When she turned to look, the Russian gave her a quick glance up and down, then waggled his eyebrows for Art.

As far as Art knew, Hayley was the only woman on the compound. Even typical schoolyard bullshit like Gogol's display had to be killed quickly so Hayley wasn't always surrounded by mouth breathers. Art hit Gogol with the deadeye until the other man's smile faded. Shaking his head, Art made a quick motion across his own crotch, indicating there was to be no business below the belt.

Gogol put more professionalism in his posture when Art stepped back into the hallway. Hayley had missed the whole exchange. She stood, looking at her door. It was the last room on the hall. Art was glad he'd be next door and could keep an eye on her safety. Knowing she'd be just a wall away was another kind of thrill.

Private, the kind that made his blood run a little faster. Even though she was hands-off.

She was also checking out the proximity of their rooms. "Tell him," she said to Art, "that I want a room closer to the kitchen."

How could he explain all the reasons she needed to be as near to him as possible? Anything he said now would seem like a come-on. Which was a possibility he would've entertained with Hayley in entirely different circumstances. But it didn't mean he couldn't use the real spice of attraction he was feeling in the role he had to play with the Russians. "I'm your best translator here. Might want to stick with me."

She really was the master chef, keeping her jaw set against any arguments. "I'm not here to talk. I'm here to cook."

Goddamn, he wanted an empty after-hours restaurant and a table full of beer bottles to share with Hayley. She could talk tough, they'd share war stories, break glass and be invisible to the rest of the world.

All eyes were on them in the compound, though. And there was no chance of peace. He translated her request to Gogol.

The man screwed up his face and scratched at his temple. "There's only the room they built for the maid," he mused in Russian.

A maid? Art added another noncombatant to the list. So far it had just been Hayley.

Gogol continued. "But she just comes every other day and doesn't sleep here."

Art recalculated. He'd have to plan the assault for

one of the days she wasn't there. Too bad it wouldn't be that easy to get Hayley out of the line of fire, as well.

He told her about the maid's room.

She nodded. "That's what I need."

"Any way to change the master chef's mind?" He already knew the answer.

It was in the hardened steel of her eyes. "No chance."

He lifted the cooler again and told Gogol to lead the way to the maid's room. The three of them walked out of the hallway and into a set of wide-open rooms, like lounges, one with a pool table. On the other side of these rooms was another hallway, this one with only two doors across from each other. Conference rooms, Art remembered from the initial plans for the layout. He'd need to get inside for the best recon, but one should have a window, the other completely closed off except a single door.

Gogol turned to one side of the large, central rooms where a stairwell led down, then muttered to himself, changed his mind and walked back into the hallway with the guards' rooms.

One door looked like all the others, but it opened to reveal another stairwell turning down. Satisfied with his navigation, Gogol stepped down and encouraged Art and Hayley to follow.

Art kept bumping his knuckles along the narrow walls while he carried the cooler in the jagged descent. Another killing zone. Definitely to be avoided unless the team had the high ground.

But there was no immediate danger down there yet. Just Gogol, still smiling, though less sure. He stepped from the stairway landing and opened a simple door next to a laundry area in a service hallway.

Hayley didn't hesitate, walking into the room and placing her duffel at the foot of the small bed.

There was one high window and no lamp on the side table.

Art asked, doubtful, "This'll work for your quarters?" He revised himself. "Room?"

She peered at him, almost through him. "It's perfect. Soldier." There was a hint of victory in her quick smile, like she gained some leverage on him.

He was compelled to correct her. "Marine." Though he wasn't about to give her his entire service record. And while the Russians knew of his time in the military, none of them were aware of the specifics of his special forces experience with recon.

Her victory didn't waver. In fact, he'd given her more than she'd discovered on her own. He'd have to be very careful that she didn't have him spilling all his secrets into her pretty little ears.

And he couldn't take his eyes off her hands as she unzipped her duffel and pulled out her knife roll. Her skilled fingers were the perfect extensions of her direct confidence.

"Kitchen," she commanded and brushed past him, out of the room and back into the house.

Out one side of the narrow hallway with the maid's room, the floor plan of the house opened up. Couches and low tables, all brand-new, waited for men to lounge and drink, play cards and oil their guns. Tall windows were bright with desert sunlight. Past the dirt yard outside, though, the only view was the cinder block wall surrounding the compound. Parked on the northeast edge of the house was a large water truck, probably six thousand gallons.

The house windows would be easy to breach for the team, if they could get close enough.

It could be a night assault. They'd kill the generators as step one or two. Art searched for security lights but didn't see anything on battery power. There might be multiple generator backups. He needed to lock down all these variables before he could send in the shooters. Otherwise, the targets would escape and Automatik team members would die. Hayley would die.

There were already a handful of guards hanging out in the north living room. They eyed him and Hayley suspiciously. Four pillars broke up the open space, and they weren't large enough for one person to take cover, let alone two. He adjusted his grip on the cooler, imagining instead an M4 distributing bullets in choppy bursts. He felt how the lead would fly back in a deadly maze from the bad guys.

"No. This way," Gogol directed in Russian, waving his arm to the hallway with the laundry and maid's room. He said in English, "Kitchen."

Hayley didn't hesitate, turning back and walking off. Art took another sweep of the rooms, noting the broad French doors all the way at the other end, before following. He held back from warning Hayley she was moving too fast, not checking her blind spots.

He dismissed Gogol in Russian, "I've got it from here."

The other guard nodded, but also gave him a wink and repeated Art's crotch-blocking gesture back to him.

Gogol didn't wait for a response and ambled off into one of the large living rooms.

Hayley disappeared into the hallway to the kitchen. He hurried to catch up. To keep her safe. That was why he worked with Automatik: to protect innocents. But an extra burn of motivation flashed through his muscles as he strode faster toward her. *Hands-off.* The gesture had been clear. But he didn't want to follow his own rules.

THE HOUSE WAS a jumble, built, no doubt, by a man with a lot of money and short time. There was no corner of comfort, and any sense of flow was destroyed by choppy hallways and walls that seemed to cover secrets. And it was filled with gun-carrying men.

But the bedroom had suited Hayley fine. It had a lock on the door.

And the one room she really cared about was straight ahead of her. The kitchen.

From the laundry and maid's room hallway, she reached the side entrance of the expansive kitchen. The details were there: miles of granite, carved corbels, "antiqued" cabinets, a massive island with a deep sink. But it was slapped together. Sloppy paint edges. The drawer hardware didn't line up, top to bottom. Someone had rushed every step of this house, like the quality was inconsequential, as long as it held up for just one week. Whatever this meeting was, it didn't happen often enough to warrant a real, permanent house.

All that didn't matter, though. She turned to the stove and oven. A moan of pleasure escaped her throat.

Art was closer than she realized and murmured with an intimate chuckle, "You like?"

A deep pulse moved in her, connected with his laugh. "At least they got this right." The stainless steel appliance had six cast-iron burners and a grill grate above two ovens and a broiler. On the counter next to it were two large unopened boxes plastered with photographs of expensive pots and pans.

"You want the cooler by the fridge?" Art was already in front of the large stainless steel doors.

"Yeah." She knew from dragging it to the curb this morning how heavy it was. He'd been carrying it for how long now and it still seemed like nothing in his hands. "But I'll unpack it."

He placed it carefully by the refrigerator and took a step back. His gaze didn't rest, searching over the room, picking it apart. She felt that same attention on her. What had he discovered? He'd already understood her moan about the stove and was able to stir her up. Her blood pumped faster with the idea of his constant focus finding her hidden urges.

She'd pried things out of him, too. A marine. There was something about his bearing and efficient physicality that made him seem like more than just a goon. And she'd met her share of marines and sailors in San Diego. So she'd learned another piece of the mystery man, but didn't know how it all connected. He remained a bad guy, working for the bad guys.

Was it just this morning that he'd picked her up? She didn't even know what time it was now. There was a clock on the stove, but the numbers were arbitrary and remote.

"Do I need to cook lunch?" She hadn't even inventoried the pantry cabinets to see if there were any staples.

He pushed up his sleeve, revealing a rugged watch and his muscled forearm. "It's around that time."

"It's going to take a while to get the kitchen fired up." Usually she'd have at least one assistant. For all his skills, Art didn't seem like the sous-chef type.

Opening the tall pantry doors, he peered over the stock of canned goods and prepackaged food. "Fuck 'em. They can get by on this today. But they'll need dinner."

"I'll be ready by then." She placed her knife roll on the broad island and went to the cooler.

Art left the kitchen, glancing about at all the details as he went.

Even iced, the aromas of parsley, chicken stock and fresh cod gave her a small sense of stability. She opened both doors to the brand-new refrigerator. The factory-clean interior had basic condiments and a few loaves of bread. Bachelor sandwich fixings. Her ingredients joined them on the shelves and in the bins.

By the time she was done with the cooler, Art returned with all the other grocery bags.

She'd shopped for the best produce she could find the day before. Cabbage, carrots, apples. Some of it went into the refrigerator. Art didn't ask, but took the onions and potatoes and put them in the pantry.

He returned and stared at the produce she loaded into the fridge. "That's a big green onion."

"Leek." She held it up for him to examine for a moment before stowing it in the crisper.

"I've heard of those." He pulled a bunch of celery from a bag and handed it to her.

It was too easy. Too casual. She saw the scars on

his rough knuckles and felt herself harden. "There are tricks to cooking them, but I'll never tell."

The empty cooler blocked her access to the grocery bags, and she closed it with a definitive snap.

Art picked it up; it appeared just as light as when the cooler had been full. He found a storage spot for it back near the laundry room. Swaggering as usual, he returned like they were just getting set up for a catering gig.

But his eyes remained diligent. After glancing up at the ceiling light fixture, he turned his attention to the wide window in front of the sink. He leaned on the counter to examine something outside and his jacket rode up to reveal a heavy pistol in a holster on his hip.

She shut the refrigerator, and a chill continued to press toward her bones. He'd been armed the whole time. She'd seen how dangerous he was with his hands and a knife. With a gun, she imagined he would be quick. Death would be as simple as snapping his fingers.

He turned from the window and caught her peeking at where his pistol was under his jacket. "Everyone's carrying here." His face was serious and still.

"Except me." She'd gone to an indoor range with three of her girlfriends a few times and rented pistols, but was far from expert.

"So keep your eyes open and your head down."

She glanced again at where his gun was holstered. "Was that in case I didn't want to get in the car this morning?"

He shook his head and moved until he was completely backlit by the window. His expression disappeared into shadow. "I'll never aim this gun at you. If

I start shooting, you run in the opposite direction. Run until I tell you it's safe."

His voice was heavy with experience. The violence was in him, around him. But would he really protect her?

"You keep telling me how dangerous it is, but it was you who brought me here." She squinted, but his face was dark in front of the bright window.

"Did you have a choice?" He led her with the question.

"You know I didn't."

"Neither did I." His body was very still. The words barely reached her ears and wouldn't have made it out to the rest of the house.

The confession was for her alone.

Her combat had always been in the kitchen, battling past egos and expectations. She'd always had to protect herself. She didn't have a gun like everyone else in this house, but she had the tools of her trade.

Moving so the island was between her and Art, she unbuckled her knife roll and laid it out.

Art stepped forward as if the steel of her blades were magnetized. The shadows slipped from his face, and his gaze moved over the knife edges and points.

The metal of an eight-inch chef's knife hummed when she pulled it from the roll. She knew it was sharp and had taken care of all the knives before she left, but tested the edge along the top of her thumbnail anyway. It shaved a tiny curl that drifted down like snow.

Art's easy smile returned. But when he stepped around the island and approached her the smile faded. It seemed like all the light of the world dimmed with the darkness he brought. She replaced the knife in the roll. Art was more dangerous than the razor-honed edge.

"Keep them sharp," he said, gaze level on hers. A glimmer of light returned to his eyes. "Stay safe."

He rapped his knuckles on the island and walked away, that rhythm of his body taking over again. Instead of going through the service hall, he walked past a long eat-in counter that separated the kitchen from the rest of the house and disappeared around one of the strange corners of the living room.

The gravity of Art's warning spun the kitchen around her. There was no safety.

She'd been taken to a job she was forced to accept, countless hours away from her home and friends. And the one man who was her lifeline was just as gun-steel dark as the rest of this hazardous situation. She couldn't trust him.

But she knew she needed him.

FIVE

IT WASN'T EASY leaving Hayley alone, but he had work to do. And she wouldn't have been able to set up her kitchen with him hovering, mapping the quickest egress from the room and wondering if the heavy countertops would stop a standard NATO round.

He couldn't tell if whoever had designed the house had intentionally included blind corners and wide spaces with no cover, or if the architect had been just plain bad at his job. The designer must've had an Orel Group mob boss breathing down his neck the whole time. Or the architect could've been a woman. But Art couldn't imagine a woman putting up with the strange requests and bullshit needs of the bosses. The only reason Hayley was doing it was because she had to.

It took a moment for his eyes to adjust to the day when he stepped outside the house and back to the SUV. Opening the passenger door and rooting through the lockbox gave him an opportunity to steal glances at the house's exterior and get a better sense of the layout.

Not only were there guards on the two prominent doors he could see, but there were also armed men wearing a slow path beneath the windows. Walkie-talkies linked them all together. Submachine guns, assault rifles. Nothing with a scope, so their range would be limited.

The roof was too pitched for a sniper up top. The top-floor windows were the highest vantage.

He took Hayley's phone from the lockbox and closed up the car. A lot of the house's angles needed to be mapped. He'd have to take his time to avoid suspicion, but the clock on the operation was always ticking. It sounded in his head like the cylinder of a .357 spinning.

Back at the front door of the house, the shooter with the bad attitude didn't even glance at him. Fuck it if Art wasn't completely trusted. His goal wasn't to move up in the organization. His involvement with the Orel Group ended when the last shot was fired and the bosses were either dead or being handed over to the appropriate authorities.

The men who controlled the empire, who ran the guns, the drugs, the girls and intimidated or killed anyone who stood in their way, were literally at the top of the house. Art climbed the stairs to the third floor. The uppermost landing revealed a broad room and bright windows to the right and a wall of five doors on the left. These were the bosses' rooms.

It had already been arranged that Rolan would have the second door. As far as Art knew, only one other boss was there, Dernov. Three to go. When all five were in place, Art would call in and lead the strike.

He tapped on Rolan's door and was told in Russian to enter.

The silver-haired man sat in a plush chair by a far window. The room was nicely furnished. King-size bed, couch, matching lamps. Rolan took off his reading glasses, folded his book and motioned Art forward.

"Has the cook settled in?" he asked in Russian.

Art knew Hayley would never be comfortable in the house. "She's putting together the kitchen now."

Rolan checked his heavy, expensive watch. "But not in time for lunch."

"A bachelor's lunch today." Art held up Hayley's phone. "Do you want to hold on to her phone, or should I?"

"Give it to Garin, Dernov's man. They have a lock-box." Rolan put his glasses back on. His ice-blue eyes peered at Art over the lenses. "There will be times we bring you into the room to talk about the Mexicans, in America and across the border. Don't worry about the other bosses' bloodlines. You have something to offer, and I vouch for you."

"Thank you." Art smiled proudly, like he'd been given a gift. He knew Rolan couldn't see past the mask. If the boss could peer into the darkness within Art and see the black fury, he'd be screaming for the guards.

When the week was over, Art wouldn't have to pretend to like any of these sons of bitches anymore. He wouldn't have to give them slivers of information about the Latino population in San Diego. He wouldn't have to spend any more time with Rolan or the organization that had murdered his father.

Not that any of them remembered Tony Diaz. The Russian mob had just been getting a foothold in San Diego and had been on a mission to wipe out any competition. Art's mother had described Art's father as the mayor of their little corner of the city. He'd probably been running some social drugs, maybe a couple of dice games, but it was neighborhood business. The economy of the street, for and with the locals. He hadn't been a pusher and he hadn't shaken people down. He'd been a father to a five-year-old son, hustling what he could to keep his family afloat. Tony had been eliminated in a simple drive-by. To the Russians it was business. To Art is was his mother crying on the phone, aunts and uncles showing up, and a pain he still hadn't learned to understand.

Had Rolan pulled the trigger back then? Maybe he'd been the driver. They'd killed a lot of people to establish their power and continued to kill in order to hold on to it. And not just gangs and petty criminals. Business owners were beaten close to death if they didn't cooperate. And ordinary people who were unfortunate enough to witness a crime were also taken out. It wasn't until Art had been recruited by Automatik that he'd found out that the Orel Group was the organization that had eliminated his father.

"Just let me know when you need me." Art held up Hayley's phone again, indicating where he was headed.

Rolan nodded gracefully and resumed reading before Art had even turned away.

Art left silently and closed the door behind him.

Revenge would get him killed. This operation was tactical. Unemotional. The personal satisfaction would come when it was over and he'd chewed them up from the inside and broken their organization.

But emotions crept in. Hayley was already more than just a noncombatant. She was smart and fierce, and every damn minute he spent with her he learned new reasons he had to protect her.

The third-floor windows revealed additional miles of desert around the house. Past the cinder block wall were miles of dirt and rock and scrub. Far to the south, man-made shapes broke up the horizon. La Bota, the closest village. It was the nearest source for supplies, and it was the staging area for his strike team.

Somewhere between him and the team, invisible in the desert like a sidewinder snake, was Jackson. The former Navy SEAL pulled the rough assignment of relay man. Less than three hundred yards away from the house, he was positioned to receive Art's text messages. The app they used relied on proximity, not a phone signal, so they could always get through.

But Art would have to wait until he was alone in his room before sending relevant information from his initial recon. Any trust from the other guards was already hard to come by. The smallest lapse in concentration would get him iced. And Hayley would be dead soon after as they cleaned house.

"Where's Garin?" Art asked a lean goon in Russian as they passed on the stairway.

"Playing pool." The man waved back down toward the second floor, and in doing so revealed the two shoulder holsters under his track jacket. He was good for at least thirty bullets.

Art found the pool table past the long hallway where he and the other guards were roomed. Only one man circled the green rectangle, stalking the balls and holding the cue like a hunting spear.

"Garin?" Art could feel the man's attention on him, even though the thickly muscled guard stared at the table.

When he looked up, cold blue eyes tried to freeze Art. "I'm Garin." He spoke in Russian. Close-cropped blond hair covered the square brick of his head.

"I'm Art. With Rolan." Another standoff. Both men

remained motionless, fifteen feet away and separated by the pool table.

"I know, *denga*."

Art didn't know the word. Garin used it like an insult, but it must've been an obscure one. He'd have to look it up.

Instead of getting bloody and sweaty trying to establish who was the alpha goon of the house, Art stuck to business. "I need to get into the lockbox." He held up Hayley's phone. "The cook's."

A nasty smile crossed Garin's face. "The cook's a tasty treat herself."

Art reconsidered his hesitation to put his fist in Garin's throat. "She's not on the menu. She's doing a job here, just like us."

Garin carefully placed the cue on the table, not taking his gaze from Art. "You are not us, *denga*."

"Take it up with Rolan." The bosses were the last word, so if Garin didn't like Art being there, it was Rolan's business.

Garin blinked but maintained his confident, carnivorous grin. "The lockbox is in the conference room." He walked, deliberately brushing past Art though there was plenty of space to get around.

"Lead the way, *gilipollas*." Art knew Garin would never track down the Spanish insult. The hitter walked like he was bulletproof. But Art had seen too many times, no one was bulletproof.

The large, rectangular guard sauntered slowly toward the conference rooms, in control of the pace. His left shoulder was a bit lower than his right. Art imagined he'd broken a collarbone at some point. He wore a white button-down shirt with the sleeves rolled to just below his elbows. Tattoos of horses and swords and old Russian cavalry riders covered his forearms, the black lines interrupted only by aging scars. Knife wounds. Art knew that sometimes you had to take a couple of slashes in order to finish the other guy with the knife.

The shirt was tucked into pressed slacks. Where was this guy's gun?

Garin opened the door to the conference room with no windows and didn't even check to see if Art followed as he walked inside. Low cabinets lined one wall, complete with booze and water bottles. The main space was dominated by a large table surrounded by five chairs. This was where the bosses would do their main business in the dim light, figuring out how to best slice up the world around them.

With the element of surprise, the strike team could overtake the room quickly. Breaching the door would trap anyone inside. But the timing would have to be perfect.

"Maybe I should take your phone, too." Garin worked the combination lock on a four-foot safe that was built into the wall.

Without the phone, Art would be cut off from his team. "No signal out here anyway."

"I'm a perfectionist." Garin unlocked the safe and swung the thick door open. Inside were folders full of paper, two pistols, a magazine-fed automatic shotgun and a submachine gun. Extra ammo and other gear in a duffel were piled on a lower shelf.

Anyone hitting this room would have to hit fast and hard.

Art placed Hayley's phone on the top shelf, away

from any paperwork. But Garin didn't close the door. He put his hand out, waiting.

"Phone, *denga*." He maintained his mean smile.

"I need it for my music. Helps me sleep at night." Art stayed balanced on his feet, cool in his head.

"Russian lullabies?" Garin chuckled, made his open hand into a fist.

"Mariachi."

The smile flickered on Garin's face. He clenched his jaw and muttered, "Peasant," closed the safe and spun the lock.

The tension would only build if Art fed it. Instead, he turned from Garin and started out of the room.

The Russian's voice stopped him. "Don't think you have exclusive rights on the cook, *denga*."

Art turned. An ugly and playful smile creased Garin's face. They'd just met and there was already bad blood. The complications multiplied. Garin would be watching, waiting for an excuse to go after Art, making it harder to collect and communicate the intel he needed.

And this son of a bitch was a threat to Hayley. "Let her do her job in peace. Or there will be no peace for you."

Garin's eyes narrowed and he took a step toward Art, who stood his ground.

The goon laughed like a rusty razor blade. "I'm irresistible." He waved Art away like shooing a fly.

Art grinned back, not giving Garin the anger he wanted. But there would be no smiles if the guard made a play for Hayley. It might just be an excuse to ice the asshole without breaking cover.

Without another word or threat, Art left the room. The tension remained. Guards milled around the second floor, and someone had taken up Garin's abandoned pool game. Their eyes were diligent, though, checking out the windows for any threat. None of them knew the enemy was already in the house with them.

Art closed himself in his small room and sat on the edge of the bed. He pulled his pistol from its holster and felt the comforting grip in his hand. Secrets, guns, mob bosses, Garin, knives and Hayley. Art was at the center of it all. The only people he could trust were a text message away, and he had tons of intelligence to gather before he could pull the trigger.

This was the bleeding edge of his mission. But whose blood would be spilled?

Lunch brought a steady progression of rough and cruel-looking men into Hayley's kitchen. She alternated between restocking the sandwich fixings and bowls of chips, and washing the brand-new pots and pans for her real cooking.

Most of the men eyed her, the usual leering assessment. It didn't matter if she was a waitress, a cook or a chef. Too many men had thought if she was working, she was available. She stared back at some of the more brazen guards, telling them she wasn't an easy target. A couple of them met her challenge with aggressive confidence. The other men blinked away and preoccupied themselves with the food and paper plates.

Art's boss, Rolan, arrived and all the other men took a step back so he could go to the front of the line. He assembled his sandwich, gingerly picking up the meat with a fork like he wasn't used to doing any labor of his own. Hayley came over to the other side of the counter and took over, putting together a generous meal for the man who was overpaying her with untraceable cash.

"Spacibo." He nodded with the grace of a pope. "This—" he waved his finger in a circle, indicating the kitchen, "—okay?"

"Ideal'nyy," she replied, remembering how proud she would be when her aunt would use that word about her cooking.

"Good." Rolan gave her a light pat on the hand. Even his magnanimous gesture felt sinister.

She'd experienced the violence around him. He may not have participated, but it was his world and it felt like the underlying tension in the house could be unleashed if he gave the order.

Did he control Art that way? It didn't seem as if anyone could tell that man what to do, yet he followed the orders of his boss.

Art had been curiously absent during lunch. Part of her had been glad to be free from the dizzying spin he always produced around her. She'd focused on the work and less on the insane circumstances around her. But she also missed his presence and that sense that he was watching out for her, even though he was the one who got her into this.

Once Rolan's plate was complete, he moved out of the kitchen, and the steady flow of the guards resumed. It wasn't until the last one had built his meal that Art showed up. Relief and trepidation mixed through her, charged by the electric rush that Art always brought.

She stood by the counter while he assembled a sandwich. "The code of the lunch room?" she asked. "Art eats last."

He barely shrugged. "Some of them love to hate me. Some don't care. I keep to my business."

But she didn't understand that business. He wasn't just a ruthless bodyguard. Not like the others. She'd seen his brutality, but also his care. Was he as trapped as she was?

With a whisper, she ventured, "What are you doing here?"

His answer was in his eyes. On the surface, his look said, *"Don't ask,"* but beyond it there was a history of pain and determination. Battles fought and won, and deeper battles still ongoing.

"I'm here for lunch." He piled additional food on his plate and carried it out of the kitchen.

Instead of being shut down, though, she needed to know more. That was the real danger. If she continued to push, to seek, what truth about Art would she find? And what would he do if she discovered him?

Pulling away from the electrified chain that bound her to Art, she focused her attention back on the kitchen. Lunch was over, and dinner prep had to begin.

The new pots and pans were organized as they dried. She collected the ingredients for an adaptation of a stuffed carp recipe she'd learned from her aunt. But instead of carp, she was using fresh salmon steak she'd brought.

A few guards returned from lunch with piles of paper plates and other trash. Art wasn't with them. She pointed to where it should go and continued organizing the foreign kitchen.

Dried mushrooms were submerged in hot water. They'd come out two hours later. Meanwhile, she could work on the side salad of carrots and cucumbers. It was uninspired labor, but she was happy to have a familiar task she could throw herself into. Cooking had defined her for so long. She relied on that amid the questions and danger.

But her concentration was broken by a man entering her kitchen.

He smiled, but didn't look happy. His blue eyes were chilling. Broad and muscled, he seemed to block out the rest of the house from the kitchen. He put his hand out slowly, palm up. His forearm was drawn all over in tattoos. Rough skulls amid what looked like oil paintings. He glanced at her hand, then his, trying to direct her.

The last thing she wanted to do was touch him. His fingers would close like a trap.

"There's more lunch in the fridge." She busied herself measuring out cups of dry buckwheat.

Did he understand? The blond man didn't seem to care. "Dessert." His Russian accent was thick. He licked his lips. His hand remained outstretched and he flicked his gaze there, as if enticing her.

She picked up the large metal spoon she'd used to submerge the dried mushrooms and pointed with it to a large bowl of apples. "*Sladkoye.*"

His smile shrank to a thin line. He lowered his hand and took a step toward her.

Goddamn it. The son of a bitch wasn't going to quit. He'd played his power game, but had to take it further. But how far?

Another step closer, and she tried to blockade him with a stern, "No."

But this only made the smile reappear. His game. His rules, and he was loving it too much. Acid filled her stomach.

He came closer. She remained on the other side of the wide island. With a wiggle of his hips, he laughed, testing to see which way she would run.

"No." She repeated. Tremors of alarm ran up and down her arms.

He circled around one side of the island, and she moved away.

"Nyet. Nyet."

The man bared his teeth in a broader smile, like he was feasting on her anger, and the fear that pitched into her voice.

He lunged to one side of the island, and she scrambled to counter opposite. But he was too fast and swung back around to meet her.

His firm fingers slid over her hip. He tugged her forward, reaching with his other hand.

Words hadn't stopped him. Anger nearly blinded her. She refused to be one centimeter closer to this man. She swung the metal spoon, catching him across the back of his extended hand.

The impact echoed off the hard surfaces of the kitchen.

The man recoiled slightly, wincing and shocked. But he still held her.

"Nyet!" Rage overtook the fear. She attacked with the spoon again, hitting him on the knuckles and aiming for his face.

The expert fighter turned, taking the blow on his shoulder. She felt how solid he was and knew the odds of her finishing this struggle were against her.

He hissed, *"Suka,"* through bared teeth and lunged, knocking her backward into a counter with his chest.

Pain blazed across her back. She struggled for breath. The man was too big, too strong.

But she was cornered and wasn't going to make it easy on him. She was ready to gouge and kick at anything soft on the hard man.

The fighter puffed up to lunge again. Then he groaned, curling to one side. Art was behind him and had punched the man just below the ribs, in the kidney.

The larger man wasn't down, though. He spun, leading with an elbow that Art ducked. But it pushed Art back enough for the blond man to launch another attack. He jabbed out with fists, swung more elbows. Art absorbed what sounded like painful blows. Hayley struggled to regain herself. Was Art going to lose this fight? His face remained deadly calm, like when he'd taken on the men outside the nightclub.

Hayley saw something different in Art's eyes, though. A flash of rage.

He finally unleashed his own attack. The edge of his open hand caught the larger man in the throat. As he sputtered, Art slammed his elbow into the man's temple, knocking him into the island.

Off balance, the man kicked into Art's shin, slowing the next onslaught. Art stumbled into the blond fighter and locked up his arm, twisting it to an agonizing angle.

A strained snort shot out into the house. The open edge of the kitchen was already starting to fill with the other guards. None of them moved forward to break up the fight. She knew some of it was bloodthirsty curiosity. But there was also the danger that anyone who got too close would become a victim of the struggle.

She was frozen. Art had leaped in to defend her,

but she had no means of helping him. Her anger at the blond man doubled.

The large man gathered his legs and threw himself and Art hard backward into the corner of the island. Art bared his teeth and twisted harder on his arm. With his free hand, the other man reached for his ankle, where Hayley saw he had a small handgun in a holster.

Fear tightened in her throat. Art could be killed. The bullets could fly into her.

Art saw the man's gun, too, and quickly released his hold, sliding up and back and putting his hand on the handle of his own pistol.

"Stop!" an authoritative voice barked out.

The guards parted for Rolan and another dark-haired man to approach. From the way he carried himself, he was just as much a boss as Rolan.

Art and the other fighter were frozen, guns holstered, but so close to drawing them.

Rolan repeated, "Stop." This time softer, chiding. He shook his head, disheartened, then clipped out curt Russian sentences she didn't understand.

The words drained most of the tension from the room. Art and the other man moved their hands from their guns. The other guards dispersed, shuffling and disappointed there wasn't any bloodshed or murder.

Rolan and the other boss remained. The blond guard slowly stood up, his mouth twisted in a scowl as he eyed Art.

She still held the spoon. It would never be enough. Even if they didn't have guns, the way they fought was brutal and painful and to the death. Both this man and Art were experts in violence.

But they couldn't cook.

"Do you want to starve?" She broke the silence and didn't care who understood. The fear of the conflict trembled through her, but she continued to all the men in the kitchen, "Or cook for yourselves?"

With a curt tip of his head, the shorter boss commanded the blond guard to join him at the edge of the kitchen. The fighter didn't hesitate and was soon leaning down to listen to low words from his boss. The two of them left the area without looking back.

Rolan released a long sigh and glided out of the kitchen.

Art turned to her, the tension remaining in his body but a softer look was in his eyes. "You okay?"

She nodded and tested the bruise on her lower back from where the guard shoved her into the counter. "You?"

He rolled his broad shoulders. "Yeah."

"Thanks." Her legs wobbled as she moved back to her prep station on the island.

"Yeah." Art adjusted his jacket, covering his pistol. "That motherfucker is Garin. Dernov's man."

"Dernov was the guy with the dark hair?"

Art cracked his knuckles and twisted his neck until there was a small pop. "Another boss. Stay away from either one of them."

"I'd love to," she said, laced with sarcasm. "Keep them out of my kitchen."

"I'll do what I can, but things are going to get tighter from here out." His piercing gaze assessed the space again, lingering in the direction where Garin disappeared with Dernov.

"It's day one." She could hardly believe so much had happened already.

"Don't I know it." His piercing eyes turned back to her. "You sure you're alright?"

Needles of fear and anger pierced through her at the memory of Garin's hand on her hip. But there was also an electric hum, inspired by seeing Art stop the larger man's aggression and take him down. This surge urged her toward Art, with an ache to release all the energy pounding through her.

"I'm still cooking." She sifted barley through her fingers, bringing her back toward her usual world.

"You're amazing that way." He was dead serious.

The electric rush shocked harder up her legs and around her chest.

Neither of them moved. The charge could easily draw them together. Her blood rushed and she imagined his did, too. He was close, shielding her from the rest of the house. Long breaths rose and fell in his chest. His active gaze slowed when he stared at her. Their bodies were primed to clash.

But all the circumstances around them were twisted and jagged, making her feel very far away from this man who she knew only in fragments. He'd fought for her. Protected her. But he'd been the one who'd brought her into this world of violence.

He must've sensed her distance and took a step away. "Can't wait for dinner."

When he left, it wasn't with the usual swagger or roll to his walk. He was steady, grounded.

She missed him. His protection. She feared his violence. She didn't trust him. For the first time with Art, she didn't trust herself.

SIX

THE ONLY GOOD to come from the fight was that Art now knew where Garin kept his gun. Other than that, everything was a mess. At least Hayley hadn't been hurt badly. When he'd heard her calling out, *"Nyet,"* a dead chill had exploded in him. He'd been far, in his room. How many times had she called out before the furious and scared shout had hit him?

By the time he'd reached the kitchen, her conflict with Garin had blown open. She'd swung her weapon into his hand and tried for his head. Then the son of a bitch had shoved her. Art was armed and had almost put two rounds through Garin's center mass. The reaction would've been seen as too extreme by the others in the house. And Garin was Dernov's man. Art would've been killed before he'd gotten out of the kitchen. And Hayley...after she'd seen something like that, they'd never let her leave alive.

So he'd kept it to fists and elbows until Garin had escalated the fight to the pistols. Luckily they'd been stopped before the lead had started flying. But he would've liked extra time to make Garin's face uglier with the point of his elbow or the edge of the granite counter.

Things had diffused quickly once the bosses had arrived. Art knew the trouble wasn't over. The fallout was radioactive and would fester the whole time he and Garin were in the house.

Yet another complication for Art's operation with Automatik. He was back in his room, sitting on the bed, facing the door. His pistol was unholstered, resting on his thigh. He typed on his phone, while the app encrypted the information and sent it via the Wi-Fi connection between him and Jackson burrowed somewhere out in the desert.

He detailed the number of known combatants and the weapons they carried. As he relayed the layout of the house, he highlighted the blind spots behind the doors, the killing alley of the hallway on the second floor and the potential dead end in the conference room.

There remained three bosses left to show up, but the assault should be planned for when the maid wasn't at the house. Art reiterated that Hayley was not a combatant and needed to be treated as an asset to be protected. The wording felt too basic. It got the meaning across to Jackson and the others he'd bounce the information to, but Art's intent went beyond just strategy planning. He'd been damn close to killing for her, and it was only day one.

Jackson's simple reply, Received, disappeared on the screen shortly after Art read it. In case someone else got a hold of Art's phone, there would be no trace of this conversation. The app itself, unless a passcode was entered, looked like a simple number puzzle game.

Before ending the intelligence breakdown, Art sent a final request. Find out what the Russian word 'denga' means.

The message faded out quickly, and Art closed the app.

He'd been deep in country before, where resources grew thin behind him. The icy hills of Afghanistan had taxed him beyond his training and made him find new voices of inspiration. His dead father, who existed mostly for him in old, bent snapshots, had reached out of the past as a ghostly dream to tell him to keep enduring. His father had been a street-level hustler and had no business in the Middle Eastern mountains. But there he was, when Art was shivering and hungry and watching a specific rocky pass with his finger on his trigger. He'd spoken in Spanish, but the words had been muffled in the wind. Art had known the meaning, though. His father had died. Art had to keep going.

That man was talking again now, in the desert closer to where he'd been born. Art didn't need the words this time either. His father demanded revenge.

Instead of being cold, Art was consumed by fire. The organization responsible for his father's death surrounded him. The house could blow up any second. But he would dance through the flames, carrying Hayley to safety with him. And he'd let everyone else burn.

HAYLEY'S HANDS STILL trembled as she chopped the rehydrated mushrooms. The barley simmered in the former mushroom water, and dinner was progressing. She'd cooked this food before but couldn't grasp a sense of normalcy. After finishing the mushrooms and adding them to a bowl with thinly sliced shallots, she turned her attention to the salmon.

Every footstep at the perimeter of her open kitchen

snapped her attention away from the food. Guards milled about, looking out windows in the dining area and double-checking doors in the wide living room beyond it. None of them ventured into her kitchen, yet she couldn't focus completely on her cooking.

Garin had come on so fast, there'd been hardly any time to defend herself. Even his fight with Art must've taken just a few seconds, though it had felt like she'd watched each blow over the course of hours. If anything bad was going to happen in this house, it would erupt in an instant, and Art wasn't always going to be there to protect her.

He'd been absent for hours while she'd finished organizing the kitchen and continued prepping for dinner. What if something had happened to him? Punishment for his fight with Garin. Maybe that was why she was jumpy at every sound around her. She had to know he was okay.

But she couldn't go out into the house looking for him. That would've been asking for way too much trouble.

So she continued to work on dinner, distracted. Sectioning the salmon to individual steaks, she reserved the trimmings for a baked and layered fish-and-vegetable dish for tomorrow's lunch. If she was alive to cook it.

The bright yellow sky outside the window thickened to orange. Evening approached. They would want their dinner soon. She'd been rattled off her game and now worried she wouldn't be done in time. Usually she'd be able to call out to her assistant without looking up from her task. But she was alone.

A figure moved into the light of the window as it spilled into the dining area around the corner from the kitchen. Art flashed brighter than she'd ever seen him. Beyond even when he was in the stark day of the farmers' market. She saw the firm set of his jaw, the sleek shape of his shaved head. His eyes were more unguarded than ever, drawing her into their depths. A long breath escaped her as she discovered he was safe.

Suddenly, she was very exposed. He'd broken through the caution she'd built, and she didn't know where her defenses were anymore.

He'd regained his swagger and easily stepped through the invisible border of the kitchen into her prep area. "Need a hand?"

"Five big tomatoes from the bowl on the counter. Seven cucumbers from the fridge." Just having him in the kitchen seemed to balance the floor beneath her feet. And that worried her.

After a moment, he arrived at her counter with the produce she requested.

She kept her attention on the salmon steaks, laying them out on baking sheets. "You take orders well."

"I used to." He arranged the tomatoes and cucumbers on a cutting board. "It's getting difficult."

"Maybe you're in the wrong line of work." Was she pushing it too far, talking to him this freely?

"Maybe." The word resonated darkly through him.

"You could be my sous-chef." She pushed it too far, threading thicker intimacy between them.

He laughed, raspy. "I already am." Then he bumped the side of his fist on the counter. "What's next?"

"Fish goes in the oven." She pointed at the trays of salmon. "I'm sautéing the buckwheat and mushrooms. Then on to the salad."

Art moved quickly, sweeping the trays off the counter and into the oven. He turned back to her after closing the door. "No timer?"

She paused while selecting a sauté pan. "When you were fighting those two guys outside the club, did you ever forget where one of them was?"

"Never." He rolled one of his shoulders as if getting ready for another round. "And I knew where you were the whole time, too."

She didn't doubt that anymore. "I'm trained, too." She tapped her temple.

He saluted back. "Yes, ma'am, Master Chef."

For a moment she forgot where she was and who she was preparing dinner for.

Reality slammed back when a guard moved through the living room in the distance. She centered herself again and took the buckwheat and mushrooms to the stove.

The aromas of earth and body came alive as the ingredients hit hot butter in a pan. Sometimes cooking was work. The pleasure of the food could get lost in the math of portion sizes and the timing of getting everything done so it all hit the plate hot. But she wasn't simply a robot with spatulas for hands. The sensuality of food still lit her up. The edge of sautéed onions. Or even the orgy of boiling water.

Art's own energy near her in the kitchen fueled a different heat than came from the oven. But her aim had to be all about the dinner. Her body, those needs and the possibilities with this man would have to wait.

Wait until what? It could never be.

She continued to cook. Art stood by at the ready for the next task.

She poured the warmed buckwheat mixture into a baking pan and kept her voice low, just for the two of them. "I hope you helping me out with Garin didn't get you in any trouble."

He shrugged it off. "Nothing major from up top. He said he was just playing, but they knew he fucked up." Once she was done with the sauté pan, he took it from her and placed it beside the sink. "And that son of a bitch already didn't like me, so no love lost."

"Is he done 'playing?'" She put the buckwheat in the oven with the fish, which was coming along nicely.

"No," he growled. "But I'm watching."

She turned back to him, saw the tenacity in his eyes. "Thank you."

A smile glimmered on his face. "You've got to stop thanking me."

"You've got to stop saving my ass."

"Don't count on it."

She wanted to linger and find out just how determined he was, but instead slipped past him and back to the island, where the salad needed prepping. "It's just because I can cook."

"Damn right. Without you, I'd starve." He said it with a lightness in his voice, but again, a deeper intensity lingered beneath the surface.

She deliberately kept her eyes on the vegetables she chopped for the salad. "Grab the plates. This'll all be ready in a few minutes."

He jumped to the task and called in the other guard, Gogol, to help arrange things so they could expedite them to the dining room. She finished the salad and pulled the fish and buckwheat mixture.

Art stood at the ready. She told him to let the others know dinner would be on the table soon, and he got the word out in fluid Russian to one guard, who passed it to another, and she imagined so on through the house.

As the men started taking their places at the large oval dining table, she began plating the food. Slow movement at the edge of her kitchen drew her attention. Garin walked with a deliberate pace, throwing mean looks at her and Art until he disappeared into the dining area.

She asked Art quietly, "Does he speak English?"

"Assume everyone does." He took one of her completed plates and placed it on a large serving tray.

The other tray was already full, and Gogol started to lift it. Art interjected in Russian, making him pause. Then Art turned to her. "Are these good to go?"

She took one last check over the plate. Salmon, buckwheat mixture. Dressed tomato-and-cucumber salad. Chopped fresh parsley where it needed to be.

"Send it," she replied.

That got a chuckle out of Art.

"What?"

He hefted the tray of food. "That's what a sniper's spotter says before the sniper pulls the trigger." After speaking to Gogol, he and the other man exited the kitchen with the food.

She followed them out. This service would take care of the men at the table. The second shift's food would stay warm for a while.

Once she entered the dining area, all attention turned

to her. Garin smiled again without joy, showing teeth. His boss, Dernov, was there—dark and hunched in his seat, gazing disinterestedly at her. Rolan appeared satisfied, though he hadn't even taken a bite of the food placed before him by Art. The other guards at the table either leered a bit or just looked hungry and happy to be off their feet.

She defined the meal, and Art translated for her. "Baked salmon with barley and mushrooms. Tomato-and-cucumber salad with a sour cream dressing."

Dernov was eating before she'd finished. Rolan digested her explanation, then carefully dug into his food. The other guards ate unceremoniously.

Art sat and took his time getting into the food.

This part of her job was done. *"Priyatnogo appetita."* Her accent wasn't as good as Art's, but they all got the meaning.

Art finished swallowing before complimenting, "Hell of a good job."

Rolan smiled, equally pleased. Dernov made no expression but did hurry the food into his mouth. Garin was theatrically deliberate, glancing from the food to her. She brought her professional mask into place. He'd get nothing.

"Thanks for dinner." Art gave her a nod. He'd seen the leer from Garin.

"Enjoy." Art might've watched her on the way out. She didn't check. The living room was empty. The kitchen was quiet.

For a moment, she didn't have a pressing task to distract her. One dinner was done. Six to go. She thought she might use one of her paring knives to carve a notch in the wood of the cabinet next to the stove, marking her time like a prisoner.

She was getting paid, though she wasn't free. The guards weren't there to keep her in. But where would she go if she wanted to escape Garin and the other dangerous men? Endless desert surrounded the house.

If she fled, Art wouldn't be there. That dangerous man seemed like the only one who could keep her safe. The little loop of communication continued between them. Did he expect anything in return for his protection? She knew how her body responded to him. All that heat was going to burn. The idea of going up in flames wrapped up with his body was starting to feel like too much of a necessity. He was her safety, but dangerous in so many ways.

GOD, HER FOOD was amazing. So simple, but layered with flavor. And it gave him the feeling of being home. Eating it was almost as incredible as watching her work in the kitchen. She hadn't lied. She was trained and operated in her theater like a general in total control. He'd had to overcome the fog of war when he was overseas, but felt a bit of that disorientation in her kitchen, not knowing how she got everything done so expertly and on time.

He wished he could savor the meal but was on the clock and ate fast so he could help clean up when everyone was done. Rolan indicated he wanted to talk when he got up from the table. Art gave him a nod and carried a stack of plates to the kitchen.

Hayley wasn't there. The lights were off, and there were dirty pots and pans around the stove. Slight panic shook him, but he remembered that Garin remained in the dining room, and there weren't signs of any struggle in the kitchen.

Placing the plates down, he left the kitchen on the service side, past the washer and dryer. The light was on inside Hayley's room, revealed by a thin white line at the bottom of her closed door. It had been a hell of a day for her. He knew she needed the break and didn't speak through the door to check in on her when he passed.

Back up on the third floor, he knocked twice on Rolan's door and got permission to enter. Rolan was at his window, sipping an after-dinner liquor. He was like one of those elegant vampires, sucking the blood out of anyone unfortunate enough to be in his way or have what he wanted.

The man dressed Art down in smooth Russian, "Dernov didn't like you fighting with his man."

Art's anger rose at the idea of being dressed down for protecting Hayley. He tried to keep his Russian even and articulate. "But he knew why."

Rolan set his glass down and rubbed thoughtfully behind his ear. "Do you know who Garin is? His family?"

Do any of you fuckers know who my father was? Art would have to save that revelation. "No idea."

"It's an old family. History with other families, if you understand." This conversation was obviously tedious to Rolan.

Art did understand. Rich people had servants who they thought could never say, "No." But Hayley did. "I get it," he replied.

"This is not trouble I need." Rolan picked up his glass again.

Past the reflected interior of the room in the window, Art saw the desert stars. He would bring his own trouble to Rolan and the others.

The boss continued. "I have a very important week, and everything must run like a train. But not like your American trains."

"If Garin gets his way, then Hayley won't cook." Art shrugged, and felt the tightness in his shoulders with the thought of the blond guard shoving Hayley against the counter. "I was just keeping the train running."

Rolan sipped and nodded. "Yes, I appreciate that. And hopefully you won't have to go to such lengths again."

Art smiled. "Garin hopes not."

A small chuckle shook Rolan and his small glass of liquor. He glanced at the door, indicating they were done.

"Good night." Art walked out of the room.

Rolan answered the same while Art closed the door and moved back into the house.

Yes, there were guards everywhere, but security wasn't as tight as it could be. None of the shades were drawn while lights blazed inside. Anyone out in the night would have a perfect view of the men milling about the rooms. Art's teammate, Jackson, was too smart to break his cover and take a peek. But maybe there were other Automatik operators farther out there with spotting scopes, checking movement, confirming the head count Art had sent them.

It was good knowing he had armed friends waiting on the other side of the wall. In the house, he was very alone. The other guards now avoided him. Some just glanced away as he walked by. Others shot him mean looks. Garin had pull.

Even Gogol hardly acknowledged Art when they passed in the hall. Art knew better than to make the other man's life difficult by trying a conversation on him. Instead he closed himself in his locked room and turned out the light.

Same as before, he sat with his pistol resting on his thigh and opened the communication app. He sent the detail about the exposed windows, in case no one had seen it yet.

A message came back: 'Denga' means half kopek. Then it disappeared on his screen.

So the full-blooded Russian Garin had a problem with half-breed Art. He must've been super pissed to have been beaten by someone beneath him. The bastard wasn't going to give it up. He'd find a way to off Art without making too many waves.

Art had slept with his finger on the trigger before. He'd stay up all week if it meant keeping Garin from the satisfaction of ending him. But if it came to protecting Hayley again, Art didn't know if he'd be able to hold back before killing Garin. Which would throw off the whole operation. Once Art started shooting, he wouldn't be able to stop until he and Hayley were miles beyond the compound walls. The clock continued ticking a deadly countdown toward the first shot fired. Could he hold it all together until the rest of the bosses showed up and his team was in place?

SEVEN

SHE'D THROWN THE lock on her bedroom door, but Hayley wasn't able to get any sleep after dinner. Her nerves buzzed. Every muffled voice or creak of a footstep in the house had her eyes open and her legs wanting to run.

After a couple of hours alone and trying to convince herself to rest, she got back to work. The kitchen was hers. Even the ground floor was mostly vacated. A couple of the men were in the living room, sitting in comfortable chairs, facing the dark windows.

Most of the activity was upstairs. The crack of pool balls would startle her every few minutes. Low laughter filtered down the service stairs. Quiet conversations in Russian. Were they talking about her? Art? Were they planning something?

She had to stay busy. All the tension of the questions could overwhelm her. Ignoring the plates and pots from dinner that were piled in and around the sink, she worked on creating new food.

Her santoku knife easily lopped off the ends of an onion. Three others were already peeled. Paper stripped off the one in her hand, revealing luminous white. She knew if she skinned the secrets of what was going on in the house around her, the core wouldn't be so bright and inviting. The same must be true for Art.

Sweeping aside the paper, roots and stems, she

started breaking the other onions down into long curves. There wasn't a specific use for them, but it never hurt to have caramelized onions in the kitchen.

A silent chill swept through her limbs. A gust of icy fear. She spun, sensing a presence dangerously close to her. Had Garin come back to finish his game? The knife was still in her hand as she turned.

Metal hit metal. Art stood before her. She didn't know how he could be so fast. In a blur, he'd drawn a knife of his own and blocked her blade.

She froze, locked in his emotionless gaze. He was a hunter, a fighter.

He blinked, bringing the light back to his eyes, and took a step back, disengaging their knives. His black blade was shorter than hers, but thicker, with wicked serrations on the top edge.

What would he have done if she'd been an actual threat?

He squinted at the knife in her hand. "I think I fucked up your edge. Let me see it."

Was it safe to be unarmed with him just then? "Can I see yours?"

He hesitated, then glanced through the kitchen quickly, assessing. With a quick flip, he gripped his blade and held the handle out to her. It was all one piece of metal without any wood or plastic on the sides, and warm from his fist.

She presented her knife, and he took it, examining the steel. His fighting knife was well balanced and cleanly made. She shifted it to her right hand but couldn't quite get the grip for her needs.

"I don't know about cooking with this one," she said.

But it did make her feel safer with the weapon in her grasp.

"Never." He looked up from her knife to her. "It's not clean."

Now it was like holding a poisonous scorpion. "You've…used it."

"Whoever got it deserved it." His voice carried the same darkness as the deep desert night outside the windows.

She carefully placed his knife on the counter, far from any food. "I don't think I've ever had the authority to decide something like that."

Still holding her knife, he picked his up and replaced it into a slim sheath just behind the pistol on his hip. "Don't worry, I've never killed someone with this knife."

"But with a different one?" Why would she ask questions she didn't want the answer to? She was just begging to see how bad he was. Maybe that was her reasoning, so she could categorize him as evil and finally keep a safe distance.

He ignored the question, turning his attention back to her knife. "I nicked it here. Sorry." Turning the blade, he caught the artificial light from above. The clean line of her edge was interrupted by a jagged crescent, less than a quarter inch across. "Might be able to fix most of it. You have another one you can use for a bit?"

"Always." She pulled a shorter santoku from her roll but kept it in her hand instead of setting it on the board near the onions.

Their brief knife fight was over, but tension hummed like the echo of the clashing metal she'd felt all the way up her arm. It looked as if there were things on his mind, none of which he would say.

"I'm here for the dishes." He carried her knife to the sink along the wall and started to organize the dirty plates and pans from dinner.

"Try not to sneak up on me in here." She resumed cutting the onions but maintained a fraction of her attention on Art's broad back.

"I'll walk heavy. I'll knock on a tabletop." His knuckles hit a quick pattern.

"I don't know Morse code." Her knife through the onions made a slower, steady rhythm.

"Just two letters: Charlie Foxtrot." He chuckled. "Cluster fuck."

"Did you get your knife in the Marines?" Maybe that part of his past wasn't so dark. He obviously still held pride about his service.

"Couldn't afford it then, even in Recon." The water flowed, and he soaped up the stack of plates. "A lot of our gear there was pretty…primitive."

"Recon's like elite, right?" All her onions were chopped. She clanged a broad pan on the stove and kicked the heat up.

"We'd take whatever crazy ingredients the brass gave us and somehow make the missions work." He turned a knowing smile back to her.

She smiled back, then remembered how fast his knife had been drawn. The stove took her attention, and he resumed with the dishes. She put a knob of butter in the hot pan, letting it sizzle and brown down for a bit, then scraped in the pile of onions. With a shake of the pan, the onions were coated and on their way.

Art sighed. "Lord, that smells good."

"Sometimes the basics are the best." In order to bring the cutting board to the sink, she had to step dangerously close to Art.

Physical contact was common in a kitchen. Some spaces were so small, she'd been practically standing in someone's hip pocket in order to work the stove. But brushing her shoulder along Art's back was nothing like she'd experienced on the job before. Dark sparks tingled across her chest. Then lower. She'd never cooked with a hired muscle bad guy in the kitchen. And that didn't describe all he might be.

By the time she was next to him, placing the cutting board on the counter, he was staring at her. A hired goon wouldn't have the depth that he had in his eyes. His hands were firm on the edge of the counter, shoulders flexed, poised. She couldn't read all of him, but it felt like he didn't want to take his gaze from her. And she understood the hunger on his face.

It was her kitchen. She could be just as opaque as him. "I'll wash my own knives."

"Roger that."

But neither of them moved for a moment. Thousands of miles away, in a bar or restaurant in San Diego, she might think about taking it to the next level. Sure, he was good-looking. Lethal. He was a tough guy. And so was she. It could've been fun to wreck a bedroom. Under very different circumstances.

"I'm just here to cook. Remember?" She held his stare until he broke it.

"Loud and clear." He didn't sulk, though. A lot of

other guys would pout or get angry with rejection. Art maintained his energy, but didn't push.

She took the long way around the island to get back to the stove and the caramelizing onions. They sweated down nicely. Shaking the pan folded the raw strands down into the heat. Sprinkling a few pinches of brown sugar on them helped deepen the flavor and the sweet aroma.

The moments when she wasn't attending the food, she'd watch Art. His rhythm swayed, making the task of doing the dishes like a sultry dance. The black window reflected his face. Some of the time he was calm, but mostly his awareness continued to bounce from spot to spot.

After a while, the pile of pans and dishes were transferred from the side of the sink to the drying rack. He shut down the water. "I'm all done here, Master Chef." He made his way toward her, carrying a small pot full of soapy water and her notched knife. "Anything else you need?"

After organizing the onions just the way she wanted them in the pan, she took a step back from the stove. "That's all I can think of right now." Not true. She wanted a taste, just a taste of his potent energy. Her mouth watered for it. But she knew one bite wouldn't be enough.

Again their bodies got way too close when he leaned over to smell the onions. Sensuously, his eyes closed for a moment. Then they were open again, assessing his surroundings. "How long are you going to be working down here?"

"Probably another hour for the onions." If she had

the energy and focus, she might prep a bowl of quick pickled vegetables, as well.

"Go straight to your room when you're done. Lock the door." It wasn't a command, but his caution was clear.

"Roger that."

His low laugh rumbled through his chest. She could almost feel the vibrations. He moved past her and to the doorway. "You're a badass, Baskov." He didn't look back. "Good night."

"'Night."

Her voice echoed in the kitchen and service hallway, and he was already gone. The shadows had swallowed him, and she couldn't even hear his footsteps.

The onions sizzled and murmured like a group of approving girlfriends. Art had scared the hell out of her when he'd surprised her in the kitchen. Without him, though, the space felt less safe. She'd keep her head up. No one else would sneak up on her. Art had already gotten close enough.

HE'D NEVER HANDLED a knife as fine as Hayley's. Some master bladesmith had forged and shaped it, and now it was up to him to undo the flaw he'd notched in the edge. Hopefully that was the extent of the damage she'd take during the trip. Art mentally kicked himself as he opened what appeared to be a closet door in the service hallway to reveal a set of stairs leading down. He'd been giving himself orders on how to protect her, and his own damn knife had put her in danger.

Instinct had taken over, but it was his fault for sneaking up on her in the first place. She'd been so focused on chopping those onions, he hadn't wanted to distract from her Zen. He'd be more careful. And when he was back in his room, where her knife waited next to his sharpener, he'd do whatever he could to erase the flaw in the steel.

The house was quiet. The day-shift guards slept. The graveyard shift worked the perimeter with night vision goggles and sound amplifiers. Everyone was fed, and the dishes were done.

Art descended below everyone. The narrow staircase turned from the top floor down to a half basement that stretched out under the kitchen and a quarter of the dining room. He moved as quietly as possible, trying to keep the soapy water in the pan he carried for this stage of his recon from sloshing out.

His flashlight brightened the angles of the basement, which smelled like fresh-cut lumber. Plumbing ran all around him. Electrical wires were stapled to the joists overhead. He pressed deeper; the darkness closed behind him.

Desert spiders had already taken up residence in the corners of the construction. They were probably his only companions. Except for maybe a hired killer for the Russian mob.

But that's what you are, he reminded himself.

That was all Hayley thought of him. Because she had no evidence otherwise. Could he trust her enough to tell about his undercover work for Automatik? Would she ever trust him if he didn't tell her?

The woman was like her knife. Beautiful and purposeful, and with a wicked edge. She'd make a good asset. An ally. And knowledge of the real scenario might help her stay safe.

That, and he wasn't happy to know she thought of him as a leg breaker for one of the biggest crime organizations in North America.

She was above him, tending to the onions, which had blanketed the whole floor of the house with their comforting smell.

The joists and flooring of the building creaked with her footsteps. He could feel her, balanced and easy at the stove or focused on the cutting board.

Growing up, his home had been mostly filled with women. He'd watched his mother and sisters cook plenty of times, picking up enough tips and techniques to keep himself fed once he'd moved out. But Hayley's motion was so practiced. Like a sniper going through the routine and ritual of targeting, adapting, then firing. If she'd ever let him, he'd love to sit and just watch her prepare a meal.

There wouldn't be that kind of leisure time until the mission was over and he'd cleared the taste of gunpowder from his mouth.

He reached a concrete retaining wall that marked the edge of the house. Pipes and conduit from the kitchen ran over his head and out the wall near where it met the ceiling of the basement.

He set the pot of water on the ground and leaned close to the wall, feeling the concrete for the smallest flaw that an explosive charge could exploit. Jagged ridges on the surface bumped under his fingertips. This wall would go. It was just a matter of where to put the charge. Inside? Then he'd have to do it in advance of the assault.

He crouched low, moving the loose dirt at the base of the wall. If the concrete wasn't properly attached to its footing, the whole piece would buckle and take a chunk of the house with it.

Footsteps on the stairs to the basement interrupted the search. Art had his knife, his pistol, but that escalation of force wouldn't be necessary if he could maintain his cover. Looking like he'd been caught doing something he shouldn't would only rile things up, so he stayed low at the wall.

"Digging for your ancestors?" Garin sneered in Russian. He strode into the basement with his own flashlight, which partially illuminated that self-satisfied smile on his face.

Art picked up a handful of dirt and shone his light on it. He replied in Russian, "See how it glitters? Metal. Corrosion already." He swept the flashlight beam up to a pipe running along the ceiling. "Propane."

Garin came to a stop ten feet from Art. "You're a tradesman?"

"I do a lot of things." Art picked up the pot of soapy water and lifted it to a dark pipe near the ceiling. He poured water over sections that were lumpy with rust, watched and waited. "There." A series of bubbles marched out of one spot. "We have a slow leak. They used bad pipes." He'd suspected the work down here would be shoddy, and testing potential leaks gave him the perfect cover for investigating the basement space.

"You just want to be the only one who plugs the leak in the cook." Garin stepped closer, squinted at the bubbles, then moved back.

The two of them could dance to the death right then.

They both knew it. Whoever was left standing could tell any story he wanted. But the bosses had already gotten involved in their friction. Both men knew the big guns would be furious if anything else serious went down.

Art shot back, repeating, "I do a lot of things."

"Can you fix it, tradesman *denga*?" The large guard crossed his arms in front of his chest, indicating that he wouldn't dirty his hands on a job like that.

"Shouldn't be a problem. Just need to hit town for some supplies." The pipe would be the simplest fix in the whole mission.

"It's a slow leak. We'll figure out when we can spare you." Garin yawned in a broad gesture, then turned and ambled away the way he'd come.

The goon didn't have any authority over Art. Only Rolan could tell him what to do and when and how. But it wasn't worth getting in to a cockfight in the basement with Garin. The big man was baiting him. Art wouldn't give.

But when they did tangle again, because it was inevitable, there'd be no stopping until Garin was dead.

Until then, Art had to keep his real purpose in the basement secret. The flaws of the house, the weaknesses of Garin and any other guard would be logged and communicated and exploited when Art finally brought in the Automatik shooters. The endgame would have to come before he was compromised and Hayley was put in more danger.

EXHAUSTION WEIGHED ON Hayley like a lead coffin lid. But she couldn't sleep. Day one at the house felt like it had covered years. Her brain barely comprehended that she'd woken up in San Diego that morning. Her friends had been asleep when she'd left. Where were they now? Were they worried about her? She hadn't given them any cause to be and now felt even more alone and isolated in the compound surrounded by desert.

Hayley lay in the bed with a single, dim night-light on, staring at the uneven drywall work on the ceiling. She backtracked and tried to figure if there had been any way out of this. But Art had insisted, and Rolan's power had loomed behind him. She'd already accepted the up-front money, which she and her mom really needed. And the second half of the cash would help refill their bank accounts, as well. When Burton had pulled the plug, he'd fucked all the financial planning she'd put together.

Art had subtly promised consequences if she hadn't taken the job. What were the consequences of staying?

The door was locked. She'd taken Art's advice, going a step further to wedge a chair under the knob. But she still didn't feel safe and wouldn't rest easy until she was back in her bed in her old room in Kendra's and Julieta's guest house. Another imposition she'd placed on friends and family. This gig had better dig her out of this financial hole.

Not helping her sense of dread was the slow hiss of grinding metal echoing in the hallway on the other side of the door. It pulsed slow and steady, like a deadly calm heartbeat. In the ground-floor living room, Art sharpened her knife. He wasn't rushing the job. Every few strokes, the sound would stop and she imagined him checking the edge. Then it would start again.

Was he hunched over his work? Maybe in a tank

top. That would be a sight. She'd felt his muscles, had caught glimpses of what his T-shirt revealed under his jacket. She could imagine the definition of his deltoids and biceps. The cords of his forearms would flex as he handled her knife.

She let out a long breath.

Art would only be a possibility in a very different lifetime. No matter what she saw in the depth of his eyes, he was on the payroll of a bad guy.

But he wasn't a bad guy. He'd fought Garin. He'd kept watch on her. Even now, she knew he was sending a message by sharpening the knife on the floor where her room was. He protected her door.

It was as safe as she could feel in this pressure cooker of a house.

Tomorrow she'd be back among the guns and men. She had to sleep in order to do her job.

Turning out the light and closing her eyes, she tried to calm herself by going over a mental map of the kitchen. Counters and stoves and the sink and cupboards were all accounted for. The onions had cooked down well and rested in the refrigerator for whatever recipe she might work them into.

The steady rasp of the knife continued outside. In her imagination, it turned into Art's even breath next to her.

She must've fallen asleep. There'd been no dreams, but the next time she'd opened her eyes, the window high on the side of her room was brightening with daylight.

The cook had to be the first one up, so she hurried through her morning routine in her room and in the small bathroom down the hall, then brought the kitchen to life. There were about four different available ways to make coffee, from a large French press to drip to a stovetop espresso pot, and she fired them all up. If the rest of the house wasn't awake yet, this would get them going.

Rolan was the first to arrive. His silver hair was immaculate, and he glowed as if he'd already played a round of tennis, showered, then completed a crossword puzzle. He drew big circles around the kitchen with his fingers and indicated in broken English, "Breakfast here. We come to you."

She nodded understanding and started prepping for a buffet line. Bread, toast, butter and jam. Cold cuts and cheese if anyone wanted them.

Rolan collected his food and coffee.

Folding in what Russian words fit, she tried not to make it sound too much like an apology. "Lunch will be…bigger."

"This is good." It was almost like he played at being forgiving. Like he could lure someone in, then skewer the person with his disappointment.

Luckily, there was no way she'd get that comfortable in this environment. She was cooking in a minefield.

Rolan carried his breakfast away, and other men arrived for their coffee and toast. Dernov's hair was rumpled from sleep, and he didn't even glance at her while he gathered his food. A minute later, Garin arrived and selected his breakfast as if the whole process was entirely beneath him. That didn't stop him from making another leering smile at her before he left, though.

She was working on refilling the French press when someone knocked a quick pattern on the counter. Art stood at the entrance of the kitchen, her knife laid across his hand. The memory of the sound of his deliberate attention to the blade came back to her. The slow and steady pace brought a small sense of calm to her kitchen that morning.

"I wasn't able to get all of the notch out." He held the knife out to her as she approached. "But I straightened everything and put a new edge on the whole thing."

"I heard it." They were close now. She reached forward and took the knife from his hand, careful not to touch his skin. "Do you sleep?"

"Lightly." He busied himself with coffee and food while she examined the knife.

The edge was amazing. The small divot remained, but the rest of it was polished and razor sharp. "I could split atoms with this."

"A nice A-bomb would level this place." Unlike the others, Art stayed in the kitchen to eat. He leaned on a counter, sipping black coffee and crunching through the bread. Even this early in the morning, he wore a light jacket over his T-shirt. There was a pistol and a brutal knife under there. What else?

The flow of men slowed down then stopped. The house had been fed. Garin brought in dirty cups and plates, mumbling something to Art and glancing from him to Hayley. But Art ignored whatever it was and helped organize the dirty dishes in the sink, staring out the window at the already baking desert.

"There's a little propane leak below here." He moved from the sink to the back door, peering out the glass. "I can fix it, but I'll need to go to the nearby town."

She didn't know what state they were in, or if it was

even the US, but a small town always yielded interesting foods. "I'd like to go with you."

He turned to her, and they both paused with her bold statement.

She explained, "Local ingredients would round out what I've got here."

He nodded with understanding, then returned his attention to the window in the door. "There might be food out there." He swung open the back door.

Warm air swept into the kitchen. The land smelled dusty and dry, but not dead. A sharp mineral aroma on the breeze brightened Hayley's deep breath. She was drawn to the open door and stood just behind Art.

He pointed at several sprays of pale green that poked up from the cracks in the earth. "That's edible, isn't it?"

"It's green." Without thinking, she put her hand on his shoulder to move him aside. He stood solid. The resistance was charged. She could push harder. No doubt he could push back. They could clash together.

His eyes were heavy-lidded. Lips parted. Did she gasp a short breath?

Without blinking, he took a step back, giving her the space to pass.

Head spinning slightly, she needed all the fresh air she could get. The oven-dry desert wasn't as hot as it had just become in the kitchen.

A set of concrete stairs descended from the kitchen to the ground. Was she dizzy from the moment with Art, or were the steps uneven?

He followed a few paces behind her. The dirt was hard-packed under her feet. A lizard scurried for safety. She made a line for the closest plant, but Art took his time, always assessing around them. He turned, scanning the house, the ground, the wall surrounding the compound.

"Just because it's green doesn't mean it won't kill you." He thrived in the light. His broad hand smoothed over his bald head like he was knocking off a hat to soak it all in.

The air tasted wetter when she leaned low to the plant. The bigger leaves were broad and pointed, with jagged edges. Smaller sprays of thicker leaves reached higher.

"I think that's called shepherd's purse." Art's attention kept shifting from the house to the wall. A guard sauntered along the edge of the house but didn't linger near them.

Her hand hovered close to the plant but didn't touch it. "Edible?"

"Yeah. That's what they taught us in some of our desert training." He crouched next to her and plucked off one of the larger leaves. "Hardy things." He popped it into his mouth and chewed. "Like us."

They were both paid by the bad guys to use their knives. Could she judge him without judging herself?

She also pulled off one of the larger leaves and dusted it. Putting it in her mouth and chewing released a peppery flavor. It would be a good accompaniment on top of a salad, or cut into ribbons for fish or chicken.

For a moment, the house and guards and the compound walls weren't there. It was just her and Art in the desert. He watched her chew with a grin on his face. It was the same grin she felt as she'd discovered the food.

She grabbed the base of the plant and pulled it up,

roots and all. Art walked to another one nearby and did the same.

She asked, "When did you eat goat eyeballs?"

He knocked dirt from the roots and said, offhand, "We were making good with a village *malik* in Afghanistan. It was an important meal, but not something I'd order again."

The sunlight seemed to dim as Art's posture changed. The ready soldier stepped away from the area with the plants, eyes scanning. He cocked his head, listening, then glanced at her.

"That'll be Ilyin, incoming," he said. "Boss number three. Another mouth to feed." He was back on the job, walking with intent back toward the house, his shoulders swinging slightly with that badass theme song.

Their connection thinned with the distance. His game face was back, and she missed the unguarded truths they'd been passing back and forth.

After a few steps, he stopped and turned back to her. "You had zucchinis in your bags. Can you make zucchini cakes?"

The desert plant would give them a perfect kick. "The best you ever had."

His smile was more dangerous than his hidden knife. Even a few steps away, he could make her pulse kick faster. "Kill me with them." Then his dark edge came out. The serious eyes. He held up a cautioning finger. "With the boss comes a bodyguard. Another player in Garin's game."

She nodded, and he was off again. Maybe it would be safer if she ran off into the desert. She could eat the plant in her hand, but others were poisonous. Spiders, snakes and scorpions hid in the sand. The smallest thorn or fang could kill her.

The desert was just as deadly as the house.

Art was her guide. Only with him could she navigate the worlds of violence and danger. He was part of them, and as she drew closer to him, she became part of them, too.

EIGHT

THE GATE IN the surrounding wall opened and closed and the whole complement of guards around the house tensed. Fingers crept closer to triggers. The men coiled, ready to shoot and run. Art knew the guards might not be formally trained, but they were all experienced. Automatik's attack would have to take full advantage of the element of surprise.

Rolan and Dernov were already on the front porch, watching the cream-colored SUV arrive. Garin stood to Dernov's left, sneering at Art. Then his face drained of emotion when the SUV pulled up in front of the house.

The engine stopped, then ticked and settled from the long hot drive. Ilyin was the boss of the central wing of the Orel Group. He'd come in from Chicago or St. Louis or whatever big town he called the shots from up there. Art wasn't deep enough in the organization to get all the details, which made this operation so important. Automatik didn't have to go looking for all these criminals. The bad guys were coming to them.

Ilyin's driver/bodyguard got out of the SUV and strode around to open one of the back doors. The man was stone and concrete. Sunglasses hid his eyes, but Art knew he'd find nothing there. The guard's expressionless mouth told it all. And his veiny hands, fighter's hands, that showed from below his basic black suit.

The jacket bulged a bit. A submachine gun, or a sawed-off shotgun, hung under his left arm.

The man opened the SUV door, and Ilyin stepped out. His blue-gray suit remained perfectly pressed, despite what must've been hours in the car. This man was older than Rolan and didn't carry the same light as in that boss's eyes. Ilyin was a butcher. Art felt it. The man got his hands dirty.

With a subtle shift of his shoulders, Rolan caught Art's eye. A brief nod from Rolan toward the car told Art what he needed to do. Bellboy.

Ilyin approached the front steps of the house and Art moved opposite, into the parking area. Ilyin's guard eyed him for a moment, then dismissed him, pointing at the trunk of the SUV. After popping the latch, Art hauled out two suitcases, one heavier than the other.

The guard's luggage was probably filled with bullets. Ilyin's clean clothes had to be surrounding straight razors and bone-cutting cleavers.

After exchanging greetings and quieter words Art couldn't catch, Rolan, Dernov and Ilyin walked into the house. Ilyin's man was behind them. Then Garin. Then a couple of guards who Rolan had supplied as host. Art trailed the procession up the stairs, carrying the luggage.

Attacking up was a good possibility. Between each flight of stairs was an open landing with solid cover. It would take a little while, but anyone caught up top would have nowhere to go as long as the service stairs were covered.

He itched to communicate the information to his team. Three bosses were in the house. Two more to go.

Every firing lane and back exit had to be accounted for by then. And he still hadn't figured out the safest place for Hayley during the assault.

The group reached the top floor, and Ilyin eased into his room. The fourth down the hall. His guard went with him, checked everything out, then motioned Art forward.

He left the larger suitcase by the foot of the bed and considered lingering for a tip, but knew the joke wouldn't be appreciated. He wasn't full-blooded Russian. He was the second-class citizen in the house.

Like his dad had been. Easy for them to kill without a thought. But Art wasn't easy to kill.

Rolan kept him on the payroll for a reason. They needed him. And soon, they'd fear him.

But for now he was the *denga*, half-breed with unique information to share and a back strong enough to lift the luggage.

Once Ilyin was squared away with Rolan and Dernov, his guard and a few others broke away. Art followed with the guard's bag, returning to the second floor. Now that they were apart from the bosses, the conversations started flowing. The men knew Ilyin's guard, who they called Vasily. Their reverence for him was clear. He didn't speak much, but when he did, everyone fell silent to hear the raspy words.

Things were tightening up for Ilyin and the central wing. Asian gangs were crowding them. There had already been blood spilled, and Vasily had a taste for more.

The room he was given was on the opposite side of the guard hallway from Art, closest to the stairs. Art deposited the man's suitcase and extracted himself from the group. But not before hearing Garin speaking to Vasily, hissing something nasty about Art and throwing around *"denga"* again.

It was when Garin glanced downstairs, toward the kitchen, that Art's anger rose. If the high-level guards ganged up to make a play at Hayley, there'd be nothing short of bloodshed that could stop them. But Vasily didn't seem to care and remained stony in Garin's face.

The footing in the house continually shifted, always tipping toward disaster. Art was reminded of a helicopter pilot he knew. She said that flying one of those birds was like balancing a bowling ball on a marble. It was a matter of developing a touch for the equilibrium.

Going after Garin right then would've sent them all to hell. Art made no waves, walking down the hall to his room.

Once inside, with the door locked and the pistol on his lap, he sent the latest intel. The basement retaining wall was detailed, along with the stairway assault possibilities. He explained that Ilyin was there, as well as pertinent info on Vasily. Art consumed the house and the people in it, breaking them down to the smallest atom, then figuring out how to destroy it all.

Three bosses. Two to go. The countdown sped faster.

NEW FACES GAZED blankly at her while she described the lunch to the men at the dining table. Art, in the seat closest to the kitchen, translated. "Salmon baked in vegetables, zucchini cakes and a cucumber salad."

Art gave a secret wink, just for her, as he translated the zucchini cakes.

The men were already eating. Forks rang on the plates with quick rhythms. The food was going over well. She'd added the broader, peppery leaves of the shepherd's purse to the zucchini.

One of the new men was definitely a boss. Ilyin, Art had called him. He sat upright in his suit, eating with perfect manners. He looked like the kind of guy who wore an overcoat draped over his shoulders when it was cold.

His guard ate steadily, almost mechanically. She couldn't tell if he tasted any of the food or just fueled his ropy, menacing body.

And Garin was his usual slimy self. Taking his time, turning the plate and inspecting it. Then watching her as he ate.

She ignored him and turned to leave with a last glance to Art, her one friend in the place. And her biggest temptation. He smiled back gently, as if wrapping his arm around her shoulder and letting her lean on him.

The last thing she saw when she exited the dining room was a simple gold band on Ilyin's ring finger. He was married. These men had wives. Families.

She cleaned the pots and pans from lunch and tried to imagine these mob bosses with their wives. Or sisters. Children? Even as benevolent as Rolan pretended to be, she detected a cruel and manipulative interior. He always appeared calmly poised to lash out at someone if the person disappointed him. These men didn't seem human enough for family. They were killers and manipulators, destroyers.

But that didn't mean they couldn't do that to the people closest to them. What would their children become?

Art had talked about his family a bit. A mother, sisters. Did they know who he worked for? He hadn't completely lost his humanity. Maybe it was a matter of time among this organized crime. Perhaps for her, as well.

Then she wouldn't feel anything. The prickling anxiety that drew her shoulder blades together might go away. The cruelty of the guards and bosses would be normal. Emotions would seem like a weakness.

No, she couldn't live that way. And maybe Art wouldn't disappear into that world.

The food would save her.

After recovering the kitchen after lunch, she started on dinner. She needed to rest, but slowing down would only speed up her mind. The fear and sickening sense of dread would overwhelm her.

Carrots, jalapeños and red onions were chopped and bathed in a vinegar, sugar and water mixture to quickly pickle them. Once they were in the refrigerator to develop their flavor, she prepped the other elements for her kotlety-inspired meatloaf.

When she arrived at the salad, the process faltered. She needed something unexpected. Just parsley wouldn't transform the cut greens. The thicker, sweeter leaves of the shepherd's purse remained from the plant she'd pulled, but there weren't enough.

Stepping into the bright sun, she waited for her eyes to adjust before venturing onto the desert dirt. As soon as the kitchen door closed behind her, a guard came around the corner of the house, his shining machine gun tight in his hands.

He relaxed a bit when he saw her but maintained his

poise. She stepped away from the house, searching for plants, and his gaze remained on her.

Any shade would've been welcome. Or a breeze. Instead, the heated air sat on her back and shoulders. The sun burned into the exposed skin of her neck. It felt like the whole sky above the desert was trying to crush her.

A shallow crack in the earth led to one shepherd's purse plant, then another. She tugged them up, feeling what kind of determination it took to survive in that environment.

Deliberate footsteps crunched toward her, loud enough to be heard over the sound of the chugging generators. She knew the rhythm of the walk. It was disquieting how anticipation pumped her blood faster. She barely knew him, and he was able to change her heart rate with just a few steps. But she couldn't shut it down, or shut him out, and tested the temptation like a quick lick of a salt.

Art strode, his back to the sun. "Hottest time of day."

"I don't siesta." She searched out another plant and pulled it.

"At least find some shade." His shadow gathered around her feet.

She shook the plants, letting dirt fall from the roots. "I'm done now."

Art walked back to the house with her. The guard leaned on the wall and lit a cigarette, squinting into the sun.

As he strode, Art asked her, "What about dessert?"

"It wasn't requested. And I found plenty of candy in the pantry. Someone was thinking ahead."

"But do you make dessert?"

"I can handle a couple of things."

He opened the door to the kitchen. "I'm sure you can."

His surprising, deliberate sleaze and the cooler air in the house made a brief giggle bubble up through her. He closed and locked the door behind her, then glided out of the kitchen without looking back, leaving her alone. Wanting more. This taste of him wasn't quite enough.

She washed the plants off and rolled them in paper towels to dry. A siesta sounded pretty nice. A quiet room with a book, or just a window to stare out of for a while. With Art close by.

The excitement with Burton had always been about the future. Growing their skills and their careers. Cooking, analyzing.

Art was immediate. He lived and survived and inspired her to open her eyes to the moment. And they could share so many moments. Loud nights or quiet days. Together on a sunlit bed. His chest pressed against her back. His arm around her belly. Mouth on her neck, just below the ear. Her skin heated with the thought, and she shivered with the tease.

The fantasy shattered. Ilyin's guard entered her kitchen, his face emotionless, dark eyes remote. She didn't have a metal spoon in her hand this time, and a chill threatened to freeze her to the floor. Her knives were on the island, closer to the man than to her.

He extended his thumb and tapped it to his chest. "Vasily."

Okay, that was his name. What did he want?

The same thumb pointed at her.

She nodded understanding, the fear ebbing slightly. "Chef Hayley. Hayley."

He shook his head and turned his hand, wanting other information. There didn't seem to be a lot of patience in Vasily, and she didn't want to know what the coiled springs of his body would release when it ran out.

"Baskov." She hoped he was trying for her last name.

"Da." He tilted his head back and forth, considering.

Hopefully her family hadn't left behind too many skeletons in the old country closets.

Again, he tapped himself with his thumb. *"Moskva."*

The smallest of small talk. He was from Moscow.

She told him her family had come from Ufa.

With the narrowing of his eyes, her fear came back. She'd told him the truth, but it still might damn her. What were the consequences of not passing this test? Vasily didn't appear to enjoy toying with his victims the way Garin did. Even if she called for help, he could definitely do unthinkable damage before Art showed up.

She was ready to lunge for her knives.

Vasily nodded and repeated, "Ufa," back, seeming satisfied. Wired like a killing machine, Vasily walked out of her kitchen, leaving the air colder in his wake.

A long breath didn't release her tension. She hurried to her knife roll and pulled a paring knife and a chef's knife, placing them on different parts of the long counter at the wall. No matter where someone tried to corner her, she'd have a knife close by.

Her transformation continued. Kitchen knives were now for defense. She was accepted by some of the bad men. And she wanted one of them to be close to her. Not for protection, but so she could do bad things with him.

THE WINDOW OVER the sink was black with night and reflected the lit kitchen back to Art. Hayley moved about the counters and the stove, erasing the work it had taken to create that night's dinner while preparing for the next round.

He knew Jackson was out in the dark, watching. The wall around the compound was too tall for the hidden man to see into the ground-floor windows, so he wouldn't have firsthand knowledge of Art doing all these dishes.

Art finished the last of the large pots and broke the silence. "Dinner was a hit. Reminded me of my momma's kotlety." In the reflection, he watched her pause and lean on the kitchen island. "Overheard a couple of the guys reminiscing about their mothers and grandmothers. You've definitely got the touch if you can reach these bastards' dark little hearts."

She stepped away from the island. "What about yours?"

He shut off the water and turned to her.

Her eyes burned him.

Secrets weighed him down like a loaded gun. Every step might have a trip wire in front of it. He wanted to risk it, to tell her what he was really doing in that house and let all the mines go off around them as he pulled her close.

"No heart left," he said, staying by the sink. "Maybe I lost it in basic training, or at a forward base in Afghanistan, or back in the city."

She moved to the refrigerator and opened it. The door blocked her expression. "I don't believe you." When she reappeared, she held two mugs. A sly smile drew him toward whatever mystery she was holding. He was close enough that her whisper reached him. "Dessert."

She put the mugs down and pulled a couple of teaspoons from a drawer. The food was much less interesting than the crafty woman before him.

Their fingers touched as he took a spoon from her. They paused, and he soaked in the sensation of her skin. Smooth and strong. And charged with a quick spark, an electric thread that reached into him and drew him toward her. Then she eased away and dipped her spoon inside her mug.

He picked up the mug; the warmth from her touch couldn't be erased by the cold china. "Thought you didn't have anything for dessert."

She took a bite, still with that sly smile. "I'm never lost in a kitchen."

He had to know what taste she'd created. He spooned the creamy pudding from the mug and slipped it onto his tongue.

It was chilled, but the flavor was warm. Honey and vanilla. She would taste like that, if he kissed her. And she'd have something else, darker like smoke. The spark from her touch multiplied, gathering in his chest.

He kept eating, mesmerized, watching her lips close over her spoon as she slowly dragged it out of her mouth. The wicked smile was in her eyes. His blood sped, moving the electricity all over his body.

"Do you like it?" she asked.

"Never tasted anything better." And if he had, the memory had been erased by this moment.

"Honey custard." She shrugged small. "Easy to make for two."

"Thank you." He forced himself to take a breath and throttle back his pace so he could savor the custard.

"Better than goat eyeballs."

"Much."

The two of them leaned with their backs to the counter and looked out across the clean kitchen. Parts of the house were dark. Things were quiet.

Except in him. The thumping of his pulse marched quickly while he took in the taste of the dessert and the sight of Hayley in her element.

"What was that desert like?" She licked her spoon then scraped the bottom of the mug with the sound of distant bells.

"Cold. And hot. Different." He tried to remember what it had felt like when he'd first been helicoptered in to one of the remote outposts, but he'd spent so much time out there that he couldn't see it with fresh eyes. "We'd trained at Twentynine Palms. MWTC. It was desolate and helped get us ready. But it wasn't the same. Where we were training, like here, it's just desert for miles. There, it's people's homes." He finished the custard and was already greedy for more. "People live in those hills. Like they've been doing for thousands of years."

She set her mug down. "Hadn't thought of that."

He put his mug on the island, touching hers. "A lot goes on over there that nobody's thinking about here. I don't even think about half the stuff that happened."

"Really?" She didn't believe him.

"Maybe."

"Because you're heartless."

"Right."

He glanced at her, and she held the look for a moment. The darkness around the kitchen wasn't safe. He knew they were being watched. He wanted so much to damn it all and find out what her mouth really tasted like.

He needed to protect her from the danger in the compound, and also from himself. He wasn't what she thought. In this house, the undercover Automatik operator was more dangerous to her than the Russian mob goon.

He tore away from her gaze, wondering if she could see how difficult it was.

They both faced out again, quiet between them, the tension to move closer together remaining.

"Any tattoos?" She started unbuttoning her chef's coat.

He licked his lips, and they still tasted like honey. Her back arched a bit as she worked at removing the coat. Her breasts pressed out under her T-shirt, the fabric showing her shape. Her shoulders were firm and strong, just like her arms. The electric sparks gathered around his beltline and lower.

She pointed at her left biceps. "Octopus holding a cast-iron skillet." It was beautifully drawn in an old nautical style.

He tugged at the collar of his T-shirt, revealing part of the tattoo on his upper left chest. "Mexican eagle."

Her lingering eyes drew heat to his skin.

Taking off his jacket would've been liberating, but he was on the job. Both jobs. And who knew where the two of them would stop if they took turns removing articles of clothing. He tried to slow his blood and keep it from shooting to his cock.

Though they were covered, he pointed to different areas on his body. "Flintlock rifle. M60 machine gun. A few knives."

She put her thumb on the back side of her upper hip. "Pomegranate."

"That's weird." The fruit didn't seem too appealing. But seeing her butt in jeans was very nice.

Her hand curled at the hem of her shirt and almost pulled it up. She slowed herself down, though, and turned so her back was again at the counter and she faced the kitchen and the rest of the house. He was happy to know that she understood there were eyes everywhere.

"It's a good fruit," she informed without getting defensive. "Historic. Legendary."

"Like you."

She scoffed. "Not yet."

"Hell yeah, you are." He took her in. Even without the authority of her coat, her strength was clear in the set of her chin and clarity in her eyes. "Look what you've survived. Look how well you fight."

She was silent. Her posture was straight, unbroken. She stared down, through the floor and way beyond. Then she looked up at him, revealing the slightest gloss of emotion in her eyes, as if she was thanking him without a word.

The pull between them grew stronger.

Overt footsteps came to a stop just outside the kitchen. Garin glared at Art and Hayley. His mean gaze bounced between them, then he glared at the mugs and spoons. "I want dessert," he spat in Russian.

Art translated for Hayley. Garin was already mad, but it was a pissy pout. Both he and Art knew there wasn't to be any additional trouble. The bosses had laid down the law about the kitchen.

Hayley gathered her coat, ready to leave for the night, and didn't back down from Garin. "You do the dishes, you get dessert."

Garin didn't understand, his brows knitting over growing anger. Art had the pleasure of translating what she said with a chuckle.

Garin turned red. Hayley strode to the switches on the wall and turned out the lights in the kitchen, leaving the guard behind. Art walked her out of the kitchen and to her room. She was definitely legendary. Garin had made his play, scared her good, and she'd bounced back. A lot of people would be cowering whenever that asshole showed up. But she was someone unique. And amazing. A fighter who hadn't lost her heart beneath the steel.

"Spokoynoy nochi." She stood in the doorway to her room.

They hung on a moment. It seemed like he studied her face forever. And it seemed to go by too quickly when she smiled with a bit of sadness and turned into her room.

"Spokoynoy," he answered, not wanting to leave. Wanting another spoonful of dessert, or the taste of it on her mouth. Wanting to see all her tattoos and show her his, naked and unguarded. Wanting to learn how she stayed strong against the odds.

Her door closed and the lock latched. Good. She could be bold, but she still had to be careful.

Art walked back into the rest of the house. Garin was gone from the edge of the kitchen, but him or someone like him was out there, in the dark. Just like Art. Waiting for the perfect time to attack.

NINE

A SHOUT WOKE her from deep, exhausted sleep. Hayley's body jolted, all muscles locking for a moment. She must've dreamed it. The building stress needed an outlet and had shocked her awake. Starlight filtered in through her high window, carving the elements of the room in dark pitted stone. Day remained a far way off.

She tried to breathe out the tension from the dream. Why couldn't she have blown off some steam in a pleasurable fantasy with Art? That would've been a welcome relief.

Another shout split the air. It was real, not a dream, and the cold urge to run flashed up her legs. A loud thump echoed through the house. The walls creaked with an impact.

The shout was joined by another voice. Men growled and hissed in a conflict. Scuffling and banging sounds came from the second floor. She imagined Art in a fight for his life with Garin.

Clouds of sleep blew away as she hurried out of her sweatpants and into jeans and shoes. She was at the door, hand on the lock, when she paused. The struggle continued upstairs. What was she throwing herself into? But Art had come to her defense before, and she couldn't just let him fight alone now.

Drawing the lock and opening the door, she stepped

into the service hallway. Most of the lights were off, so she used the sounds of the fight to navigate to the utility stairs to the guards' room hallway. Blows were landing on bodies, making the men grunt. She hurried, thinking about the punishment Art might be taking. If the other guards took Garin's side, there would be no hope for him.

Halfway up the stairs, she slowed. The silhouettes of several men loomed at the top of the steps. They were turned away from her, and must've been watching the ongoing struggle. Startling them could mean taking a bullet. How could she get through them if Art was in trouble?

The trouble came to her.

A man wrapped impossibly strong arms around her from behind. His hand covered her mouth. Terror jolted through her. Her back and neck stiffened. Her arms and legs tightened in a frenzy to fight. He was below her on the stairs, but she still didn't have any leverage to push off or away. Fear and rage boiled within her. Any breath to scream was choked deep in her lungs. She tried to bare her teeth to bite him. Or to twist just enough to kick him in the balls.

"It's me, Hayley," a voice whispered in her ear. "It's Art."

It took a moment for the meaning to reach past her thundering blood.

He continued, "You going to fight me?"

This was not at all how she imagined being coiled in his arms.

She shook her head, and immediately the pressure released around her.

Art's face was serious in the dim light. His eyes glittered with awareness. He pointed back down toward the stairs, and they moved as silently as possible. All the way, he remained close, his arm or his leg touching her. His ready gaze shifted up and down the stairs.

They paused at the bottom, where she backed against a wall, trying to catch her shaky breath.

"Did I hurt you?" His hands hovered over her shoulders.

"I'm fine." She winced as the fight continued upstairs. Other voices started to join in.

"Garin and Vasily," he explained in low tones. He loomed close, hands fixed to the wall she leaned on, bracketing her. "Some kind of bad blood between their families. Probably goes back hundreds of years."

"Vasily came to the kitchen, asked questions about my name and where my family was from. Guess I passed the test."

He peered up the stairs, but she had no idea what he could see in the dark. "I don't rate. Vasily didn't even ask about my family."

The fight reached the next level of violence, with a piece of furniture breaking. All the voices came up in a chorus, and footsteps swarmed. They were breaking it up.

Art's mouth was close to her ear. "You've got to stay safe. Don't be running around alone out in the house. There's stuff here you can't see."

She whispered back, lips brushing his stubbled cheek. "I heard the fight. I thought it was you."

"You came out for me?" The surprise appeared to shake him.

"You've helped me." Her pulse rushed. "I had to help you."

His chest was close to hers. His breath was hot on her ear. "You've got to be more careful."

"Yes," she said, gliding her hands over his shoulders and around his back. "I do."

They were so close, and barely had to move for their lips to meet. The kiss was a shock. Gentle. Hesitant. As if to test and see if all the tension that had been growing between them was real. And how much potential charge remained after the initial touch.

The kiss deepened, revealing their connection went beyond what she'd imagined.

His lips were firm, commanding. Stubble on his cheeks rasped on her. He surged closer, and she opened her mouth to him. He tasted of his own spices. Cumin. Smoked paprika. Salt.

Their tongues teased, probing out and sliding along each other. The skin at her throat heated, and she felt the blush on her face.

His muscles were firm under her hands. She ran them farther down his back until she bumped on his holstered pistol and sheathed knife.

He cupped the sides of her neck, incredibly tender. The rough pads on his fingers were more of a reminder of his danger than the gun on his belt. He didn't need tools. His whole body was a weapon. But he didn't use it for that just then.

The passionate intent was clear.

His body leaned closer, pressing her onto the wall. He smelled of yesterday's soap and sweat and gun oil. His breath rumbled through him and vibrated her skin. She was pinned and loved feeling all his strength around her. It was for her. He'd shown that by fighting, and now he showed it by coiling himself around her, taking her mouth with his and running his fingers through her hair.

The cold fear that had wakened her burned away. Hungry need bloomed through her. Her legs still wanted to move, but not to run. She could wrap herself around his waist. He'd hold her up, and she could grip his shoulders.

She kissed across his jaw and down his neck. He growled low and skimmed a hand along her spine, resting it on her hip. His lips found her collarbone, just at the base of her throat. She lost her breath. Need centered between her legs, wet. Her breasts pressed forward, rubbing against his firm chest.

His hands moved down around her ribs, under her arms. He picked her up, held her tightly. And he started to carry her away. Caution tried to stop her, but she ignored the impulse, needing to go wherever he was taking her. She had to find out what they could do together, unleashed.

The lights turned on in the stairway. Stark reality blew apart the fevered moment between her and Art. He set her down, his breath rushed, eyes heavy-lidded. And his mouth was turned down in a frustrated scowl.

Half a dozen faces stared down at them from the top of the stairs, including Rolan. Many of the men leered; others' expressions were blank or confused. They had just been witnessing the fight upstairs, now they'd stumbled on her just before she was about to try to tear into Art's clothes.

Rolan wore a small, knowing smile. Like a father who'd caught his son with a girl, yet approved. He drifted to the back of the group and disappeared. The other men weren't so fast to disperse.

Standing so close to Art, she felt him try to contain all that energy that had been focused on her. With his careful hand on the small of her back, he urged her back toward her room.

Together they turned away from the men and walked down the hallway. She drifted backward into her room, not knowing if he would follow. Wanting him to. Though caution was blaring louder now that her blood didn't thunder so much. The moment had broken. It might be best that he stay away. She couldn't involve herself with him. He was one of the criminals in the house. She was just there for a job.

But her body wouldn't listen to all that rationalization. She needed to know what he felt like, naked, against her. In her hands and under her teeth. Inside her.

He was so close. Coiled. Looking at her like he could pick her up and smash the both of them through the house, through the wall around the compound and to their own secret spot in the desert.

Art reached forward and put his hand on the doorknob. He growled, "Lock me out," and closed the door.

Cut off from the light in the stairway, she was blanketed in darkness. Only a line of illumination came under her door, broken by the shadow of Art's feet. He was still. She wanted him back against her but didn't open the door. He was right. Damn him. He was the wrong man. Damn him. She locked the door and he walked away.

LITTLE SLEEP, HIGH STRESS, the constant threat of violence. That old, strung-out feeling of operating deep in enemy territory came back to Art. He'd learned the rhythm years ago and had figured out how to pace his energy so he could always be ready. But he'd just been a marine then.

Now he was undercover for Automatik. His secret was like another munition. It could help him take out the enemy. Or it could blow up in his face.

Mission failure didn't just mean the death of combatants anymore. He had to protect Hayley at all costs. She was innocent. He'd helped put her in harm's way. Every second he was apart from her was too long. And every second he was with her wasn't enough.

Making his compulsory rounds through the house in the morning, he avoided the kitchen. Rolan hadn't asked him to walk the perimeter and check security, there were other guards for that, but he had to look busy and useful. It was also an opportunity to collect intel. He estimated 70 percent of the shooters were getting lax, even leaning their weapon on a wall at times. But they had plenty of attention for Art. Some waggled their eyebrows. Others scowled. Gogol made a broad show of shaking his head in mock disappointment.

They'd all had their breakfasts and made their way into the day. Art couldn't clear his head. Coffee in the kitchen wouldn't help. Hayley in the kitchen might be the answer.

Last night's kiss still shook him. He'd just been trying to keep her from a bad situation. Then the closeness of their bodies, the insulated intimacy of the dark stairwell, her concern for him—it had all stripped away his good sense. It had seemed like all the blood had drained from his head to find every spot she'd touched. Not a lot of time for thinking when he'd been hollowed out by animal hunger, and her chest had risen and fallen with his. With her mouth so close. Or maybe kissing her was the best idea he'd ever had. Though it wasn't entirely his choice. She'd pulled him in, as well. The most delicate touch of her hands on his shoulders could move him miles.

Her soft lips, quick tongue and the taste of honey were overwhelming. If the lights hadn't killed their privacy, he might've carried her off to her room to see how well they really fit together.

Leaving her at the door had felt impossible. Everyone had been gawking by then. The safest place for her was behind a lock. Safe from the leering eyes. And safe from Art.

He couldn't go any further with her. He couldn't stop.

Garin crossed in the living room in front of Art, slowing his pace. A couple of small bandages taped over the cuts on Garin's face from his fight with Vasily. Blood crusted the corner of his mouth, turning his scowl deeper. He glared death at Art, who gave him nothing back and pressed through the living room.

More than just the hunger in his stomach moved Art toward the kitchen.

Was what he'd done with Hayley compromising the mission?

Garin's menace continued on his back. The whole house was cocked, safety off, making Art realize that Hayley *was* the mission. All the innocent people who were threatened or manipulated or hurt by the Orel Group were consolidated into her. It was Art's job to protect her.

While he approached the kitchen, he tried to wrap his mind around the best strategic approach. Did he let her think he was just a hired guard until the assault started? Or was there a value to revealing Automatik and its mission to her?

Art rounded through the dining room and arrived at the edge of the kitchen. Hayley was back in her chef's coat, wrapping up the space after the breakfast service. Another woman, who must be the maid they'd hired from the local town, was also there, handling the dishes. He had a moment to observe Hayley undetected. She was expert, but not removed. Her attention lingered on details.

Memories of her body, so close to him, her mouth on his, woke up all kinds of new heat in his limbs.

The first advantage he saw to letting her know his real mission clanged in his mind as purely selfish. He didn't want her to think he was a bad guy. Chef Hayley and goon Art had no chance. But if she saw him as the operator he was? The idea cooled his building fires. A black ops shooter wasn't a stable kind of guy for a girl.

But there were tactical advantages to telling her. She could be ready. Safe.

She moved her attention from her task at the stove and caught him staring at her. Her intensity deepened. This woman was not shy and didn't look away.

The thundering energy that had brought them clashing together last night resumed. Along with the hunger. He stepped toward her. She stood her ground.

Questions played out on her face. Maybe the same ones within himself. Had she closed the door for good last night? Could they start over? Or pick up where they left off, like diving out the back of a C-130 wrapped in each other's arms.

He cleared his throat enough to talk and asked, "Any breakfast left?"

The ordinary task of collecting a plate and food loosened her. She brought it to the island, and he joined her there.

"Coffee?" She tipped her head at a half-full pot near the stove.

"Hell, yeah." Knowing the kitchen, he found a mug while she pulled the pot.

The middle-aged maid glanced warily at him. She was shorter than Hayley, with dark hair pulled back into a tidy ponytail. She didn't shrink with fear but was aware that this was no ordinary vacation home. What a terrible place for her to work, this house full of criminal foreigners. Art reinforced his plan that Automatik's strike would happen when she wasn't there.

He nodded and said, *"Hola,"* to her.

She smiled cautiously and returned the greeting.

Art and Hayley came back together at the counter, where she poured the cup nearly full.

To his surprise, she spoke pretty good Spanish. "This is Martha. From La Bota, a little more than twenty miles south of here."

"Hola, Martha." He understood if she didn't trust him and kept things as casual as possible. *"Soy* Art Diaz."

"Gracias," she replied with less guarded eyes and returned to her work.

Art sipped the coffee, turning his attention back to Hayley. "Good accent." And she was a crafty field operator, even if she didn't know it. Using Martha as her asset, she'd figured out where the nearest town was. He admired her subtle talents, hidden like a pocket pistol. A born survivor who kept surprising him.

"I grew up in San Diego and have worked in kitchens

for years. If I didn't speak a little Spanish, I wouldn't survive."

Maybe she was the undercover operative.

"Any other skills I should know about?" He ate and knew he wouldn't be satisfied.

"You'd like to find out." She sassed him easily, not hiding and slipping right past his guard. Making him want to tell her all about how hungry he was to learn everything about her.

He put away more of his coffee.

"Sleep?" she asked.

Just a grunt was his answer, and a shake of his head. "You?"

She pulled the end off one of his breakfast rolls and ate it. "I hate going to bed hungry."

A dark edge of regret cut into her flirtation. The uncertainty lingered in her eyes.

"Rough night." He almost put his hand on hers, hoping just a touch would communicate everything he was thinking and didn't know how to say. But he kept his fingers around the mug. "Not all of it," he amended.

"Not at all," she whispered.

"And at least we didn't need any stitches." The lack of answers thickened the air too much. He tried to bring them back up. "Garin's face is all taped up today."

"I saw." She glanced over Art's shoulder, but he knew there was no one there at the moment. "He looked pissed."

"He's too busy licking his wounds from Vasily to make trouble." The ticking time bomb continued. "But he will once he gets his strength back."

She took a long, shaky breath. In the kitchen, she

ruled, but there were things bigger than dinner that could affect her. In very bad ways.

Hayley was already a player in this deadly game, but she didn't know the real rules. The tactical advantage of telling her was to transform a victim to an asset. The real reason was that he didn't know how to lie to her anymore.

"You need more shepherd's purse for dinner tonight." He shot a glance toward the kitchen's back door.

"I hadn't thought of using it…" Her sentence trailed when she caught his gaze.

He insisted. Gently.

"Sure," she said, somewhat louder. "I like the peppery bite it gives."

The guards in the house watched Art and Hayley leave through the kitchen door. He knew they thought they understood what was going to be discussed outdoors. Hayley probably thought so, too.

SHE'D BELIEVED SHE'D locked him out. He was a criminal, though. Of course he knew how to pick locks. But he hadn't forced his way in. Anything she'd done to keep him away had been just for show. For him. For herself.

When Art came into her kitchen that morning, she could've served him hot coffee and kept herself cool. She knew how to protect herself. Seeing him, though, brought back the rush of their moment in the stairway. His caution as he'd approached had reinforced how caring he was, despite his rough exterior. It wouldn't have been right to let him in her room last night. The whole house had been watching. But the idea of keeping him out forever didn't seem possible anymore.

It was so easy to talk and flirt and test the tension that strung between them in the kitchen.

Then his eyes got so deadly serious as he silently insisted they go outside.

Another warning? Was he going to try to tell her again to keep away? Or did he have an underground hideaway beyond the wall where they could be together in peace?

She followed him outside, feeling the looks from the other men until Art closed the door. Sunlight bathed her. There could be no secrets in the desert. Or they would have to be so dark that they hid in the crescent shadows beneath the rocks.

They went through the motions of tracking down the shepherd's purse. On his exterior, Art seemed as calm as ever. He strode easily, kicking up small puffs of dust, gaze moving over the house and territory around it. Something grave was on his mind. She was tuned to him by now and sensed deeper gears turning.

He asked in Spanish, "How much do you understand?"

"A little," she answered in the same language. Seeing his surprised and impressed expression in the kitchen when she spoke Spanish had been a small victory she savored.

A slow breeze stirred the hot air. Art moved farther away from the house, where they were exposed to view, but private and alone in the middle of the dirt yard.

The growl of a car engine invaded the desert stillness. Every development at the compound was like a new opportunity for things to get terrible.

Hayley didn't waste time joining Art out in the yard and asking in English, "Another boss arriving?"

He squinted toward the parking area and shook his head. "It's Garin on the way out."

The black sedan kicked up dirt. Two armed guards rolled away the metal gate in the wall, letting the car pass. As soon as it was outside the compound, the engine screamed and the tires spun, spraying rocks before digging in and sending the car speeding into the wasteland. Garin must've stood on the gas to get it to go like that.

Art's gaze remained on the gate until the guards muscled it back into place. "Cool-off period after last night's fight," he said. "He must be headed into town."

"I doubt he'll ever cool off." She wished he was just running away but knew he'd be back and bringing the trouble with him.

"This looks like a good one." Art nodded toward a plant farther toward the wall and away from the front of the house. He was quick to it, and she hurried to catch up.

They both crouched low over it.

"But we're not here to look at plants, are we?" she whispered. Talking about what had happened the night before would blanch all the flavor from it. She didn't want to discuss things like that with Art; she wanted to take advantage of the protected moments they had. Too much analysis would only strengthen the doubts that lingered. And after everything that had happened with Burton, she needed to live first and think later.

Once she and Art were settled over the plant, he murmured serious words in Spanish while he pointed out leaves and stalks. Her brain revved high, trying to keep up, but translated only fragments.

"...soldier...secret organization...this week..."

She reached forward, stopping him with her hand

clasping his wrist. Without looking up, he leaned closer to her. His presence shaded her from the sun, pulling her into his shadows.

He whispered, quietly and directly, in English, "Keep your eyes on the plant." His free hand separated a few of the leaves, as if examining them. "I'm undercover. A soldier on a secret team."

Her grip tightened on him. It took all her will not to stare at his face. But she'd already seen how serious his eyes had been in the kitchen. He told the dead truth. It resonated in his steady voice. And it shook her. Her foot dug into the hard earth, trying to find something stable. Or gain traction to run.

He bent over a high stalk of the plant and pointed at it. "We're here to take out or bring in the heads of the mob who are meeting at the house this week."

It was English, but she still had trouble understanding. She tried to take the Art she knew and put all this new information in him. Undercover soldier? She'd always seen more in him than just a crook's bodyguard, but could this be the truth?

"Secret team?" Her quaking voice felt far too loud, but it was a whisper.

"Pull it up." He exposed the edge of the plant's roots.

She tore it from the ground, keeping her other hand tight on Art's arm.

He helped her brush dirt from the roots as he spoke, as if he simply explained other parts of the plant. "I was recruited by Automatik when I was on the way out of the Marines. They knew I was multilingual, and with my combat experience, it made me a perfect fit for the mob. The team got to me before the goons reached out."

He dug through the hole the plant had left behind. "Automatik is all kinds of military. Global. Delta, SEAL, MI6, Spetsnaz. But the decisions come from the operators, not the brass. Special forces run by special forces."

"You can't be fucking serious." It was like a bad movie she tried to wrap her head around. Her brain spun in an attempt to tie together everything he was saying.

"We're doing good, supported by an intelligence network. Going after deep crime." He brushed the dirt from his hand on his jeans and pulled a leaf off the plant she held. "Special forces is a career killer in mainstream military. I chose this so I can keep making a difference."

He bit off a piece of the leaf and held out the other half for her. She shook her head. Her body was so tight it was hard enough to breathe, let alone eat. Nodding, Art popped the rest of the leaf in his mouth and stood, taking her with him.

Walking casually to the next plant farther from the house, he kept talking. "I've got a guy on the other side of the wall, conveying all my intel. Team is standing by beyond him, waiting for my call. We don't move until all five bosses are here."

She dropped the plant from her hand next to the one in the ground. They stood over them, their backs to the house windows.

"This can't be real." She tried to think back to any clues but couldn't lock on to anything.

"But making lunch and dinner for a bunch of Russian mobsters makes perfect sense?"

She pulled her hand off his arm. "It didn't. And

it doesn't." Anger choked her, and she hissed, "But I wasn't given a choice. By *you*."

"This is for show." He ran his hand across her lower back and wrapped his arm around her. The men who were watching from the house would see a stolen intimate moment.

She barely resisted the need to yank away from his grip. "Was it all for show?"

"None of it." His voice was a low growl. A vow. "But if I hadn't gone along with what Rolan wanted and pulled you into this gig, then the whole operation would've been compromised."

"I was just part of the setup?" She shivered in the heat. "I'm collateral damage."

His hand tightened on her hip, and he moved her closer to him. This wasn't for show. And his voice wasn't for anyone but her. "You're the master chef." He turned toward her, revealing the unwavering light in his eyes. "Protecting you is priority."

She wanted to believe him. To believe that she was safe. "There are soldiers with guns out there?"

He nodded. "And in here. With you."

"Last night?" All the events with Art were cast in a different light. The shadows remained, they were just in different places. The charge in her attraction to him hadn't diminished. Knowing this new side of him chipped at her defenses, putting her on slippery footing.

"I meant it." His grip eased. "I understand if you don't trust me."

"I didn't trust you before."

A smile lightened his serious face. "I knew you were smart."

She fell back into his lively energy. "Why should you trust me?"

"You're safer knowing." His eyes narrowed again, taking in the top edge of the wall. "Things can change real quick here, and now you'll be prepared. But we don't talk about it. Unless we're absolutely alone. They find out, it's over." He then whispered a confession. "And I didn't like you thinking I was a criminal."

Some of the ground leveled out beneath her. It was a hell of a twist to think of him as a secret soldier, but Art the man became much more real. She wasn't just a piece of his operation. His need for her to see his truth struck her deep in her chest.

"But that's why I kissed you." She waited until his gaze snapped to her face before flashing her own small smile. Anything to convince her she had a sliver of power in this newer, extra fucked-up scenario.

He grinned with her. The Art she'd known wasn't an act. The same man stood before her. A dark edge remained in his eyes. "I wish it wasn't like this. But it is. And we're going to get through it."

The reality threatened to suffocate her. She was in the middle of a secret war zone. "Convince me."

He turned to face her, both hands bracketing her hips. He dipped his face closer to hers. "I will die keeping you safe."

There was truth on his lips as he kissed her. Unafraid. Exposed. Confident.

She kissed back, demanding, hard. Yes, they were being watched, and she was in a whirlwind of secrets, yet her heart beat harder and her nipples tightened as she held on to him. She punished him with a bite to his lip.

"I get it." He pulled away, their faces remaining close. The understanding in his eyes darkened to regret. "You've got to know, I never wanted this for you."

"You never wanted to kiss me?" She balled her fists in the lapels of his jacket and pressed her knuckles into his chest.

"I've always wanted to kiss you."

He did again. His hunger fed hers. They opened for more, tasting and biting. Last night's passion flooded back and hit the new revelations like gasoline on fire. She could burn in a second, twisted up with Art.

Several encouraging whistles came from the house. She and Art pulled apart to see a group of men crowding the windows. They sounded like fans at a soccer match. Art sneered a mock grin and flashed them a rude hand gesture.

She picked up the plant and uprooted the other. "Back to the game."

The swagger returned to his motion. It was a testament to his skill how quickly he reabsorbed himself into the world of the criminals. She'd have to learn that dexterity. Fast.

Yeah, she could strut, walking next to Art. The leering men thought they knew her, but she ruled in the kitchen with talents none of them could match. And she now had secrets no one could suspect. The secrets could kill her, but they also made her stronger. Art, an undercover soldier, had trusted her with his operation. The control had been shared, and she was honored, awed to now have his life in her hands. They had to rely on each other now. With Art, she had a fighting chance.

TEN

THERE WAS NO shortage of sly, knowing looks from Rolan and Ilyin. Dernov didn't seem to care about anything except the ice melting in his vodka as he hunched over his glass at the conference table.

Art sat in the room with no windows, facing the three Orel Group bosses. At no point had anyone brought up Hayley or Art's involvement with her, but it was clear that everyone knew what had gone on in the stairwell and out in the yard.

But these sons of bitches had no clue what Art had actually told her when they'd been outside. The days where these men were free to hurt others, scheme money from abuse and destroy lives were numbered.

Rolan had called the meeting, a preliminary to start the discussion before the other two bosses showed up. If they covered the setup, then there would be less time wasted when everyone was at the compound.

Art knew there would be no time for talk once the house was full. He itched for action, yet kept his face calm. Part of his attention stretched downstairs, trying to reach Hayley. It would be impossible to hear anything in the kitchen from this distance, but he tried to stay as tuned as he could. She wore the burden of the secret now. In a way, she was undercover, though she didn't have a specific objective other than surviving. Art would take care of the rest: tactical planning, prepping the house for the assault, calling in the team, firing the first shot. But how was she holding up under that weight? He knew she was strong, but this was a completely new frontier for her.

Ilyin brought Art's focus back while he boasted for a bit about his interactions with the Mexicans and Central Americans who bordered his territory in Chicago. Art faked interest and respect. Just because the Russian could order off a Mexican menu didn't mean he knew anything about the people. The boss thought he had a handle on them, their "traditional" ways and the "honor" that came from the gang lifestyle.

But Art wasn't going to set him straight. He could've told him about how the street gangs had formed alliances in order to consolidate their power, and these were now the big rivals. That information would've been too valuable to the Orel Group. So he gave up vague details about the gang colors, or the symbols of their tattoos.

The bosses appeared to like the intel. Even Dernov raised his eyebrows in consideration.

Art's stomach churned. Handing them bullshit felt like a betrayal. It shouldn't have worried him. If the operation was successful, then all these men would end up behind bars. He could deliver them the best intelligence and it would be for nothing. But he knew better than to assume the op would be perfect. There were always contingencies to plan for. If one of these men slipped through Automatik's noose and used Art's data to hurt others, then the crime would be on Art. As the Orel Group grew in power, it sank deeper into the community. They weren't just interested in taking over a pusher's territory. If the mob got the kids hooked in the first place, they'd have their own loyal customers.

Rolan tapped his fingers on the table thoughtfully. He explained that this was the kind of thing they needed from Art. It was to make Art feel good and useful, but it was also a gold star for Rolan, who was responsible for bringing Art in. Rolan told Art to create a list of the gangs he knew about, especially ones with national memberships. The list should be illustrated with all the reliable identifiers, so anyone in the Orel Group could pick them out.

Art nodded, said he had a notebook in his room and would take care of it. He wouldn't. Ever.

It was probably in a meeting just like this one where the men who came before these bosses made the decision to kill Art's dad. It could've been as casual and offhand as Ilyin saying he wanted to take care of the Mexican gangs on his territory, but without shutting down the restaurants. He had a thing for quesadillas.

Art hoped the perfectly dressed boss would choke on one.

And he couldn't wait to have these men on the fire-breathing end of his gun, with the other Automatik operators behind him, and to tell Rolan and the bosses that the son of Tony Diaz had come to take them in. Tony Diaz didn't die quiet.

If Art was a cowboy, he'd draw his pistol right then in the room and take out all three of these assholes. Three out of five was a good average. Then he could die fighting his way out of the house. And that would get Hayley killed, too.

Unacceptable.

Rolan continued to explain what he wanted in Art's notes. How the Orel Group could reach out to threaten gang members' families in order to influence them. Border crossings, coyote routes. Ways to get into the US and out if they needed to. Art said he could work on what he knew, California and most of Arizona, but didn't have much insight on Texas.

The boss accepted Art's shortcoming with benevolence. The white-haired man thought himself a father figure to his men.

Art was all smiles and his stomach knotted tighter. Even when Rolan dismissed him, saying he knew that Art was eager to get to the kitchen to sample what was for dinner. Ilyin chuckled, and Dernov showed yellow teeth in his leering smile.

Art absorbed their attention and nodded back, smug, without apology. He left the room and closed the door behind him. The bosses didn't know it, but they were already sitting in their cells. Or their tombs.

HAYLEY SLICED A head of cabbage into fine ribbons using the knife that had clashed against Art's blade. He'd repaired the edge to near perfection. Anyone else wouldn't have noticed the minute catch in the cutting rhythm created by the small notch.

She and Art were the only ones who really understood what was happening in the house. She didn't regret having the information. Knowing Art and his team would sweep into the house and clean up the dangerous situation gave her a little reassurance. Though she realized that the guards and bosses wouldn't happily lie down once attacked. That inevitable conflict dug a sense of dread deep into her belly.

And all of her joints ached with the new tension her knowledge brought. If anyone other than Art had told her that there were undercover, secret soldiers, she wouldn't have believed it. But it all made sense, all the links he'd explained. And she'd seen what it had taken for him to tell her. He'd been carrying a secret burden. Now the weight burdened her shoulders, too. What if she slipped up and said something? Or gave it away without knowing, without a word? The criminals could be looking for signs she didn't know to hide.

She figured if she just kept cooking, no one would know. These motions were practiced, second nature. She could control the kitchen and had to trust that Art could take care of the rest.

He certainly seemed capable of running a team of soldiers. His precise violence finally made sense. And that extra depth in his eyes. Protecting her had been part of his job, but the connection, the attraction, had that been faked?

Her knife now moved through a tart green apple. It would add just the right brightness to the warm cabbage salad she was serving for lunch. Her attention glanced off the routine action of peeling and slicing.

Two kisses took over her mind. Two different Arts. Before he'd told her the truth, and after. Which Art was real?

The answer didn't arrive. Instead, Gogol came into her kitchen, shaking his head and waving his finger in denial. *"Syrniki?"* he said with concerned disbelief. *"Syrniki? Nyet."*

"Da. Syrniki." She put the knife down and raised her hands to calm him. The guards had started the habit of asking what she was cooking for the day at breakfast, then spreading the word. Obviously Gogol had an issue with the farmer's cheese pancakes she was planning for lunch.

He rattled off a quick burst of Russian she didn't understand. Imploring, insisting. He even put his hands together in prayer for a moment, gazing at the heavens.

She said in English, "I don't understand."

So he explained slower, the same Russian sentences, forming his mouth around each word, in an attempt to get the point across. The one word that she picked up, over and over, was *mat.* Mother.

From the way he kept saying *"nyet"* and the worried look in his eyes, like she was doing black magic in a holy place, she guessed he had a problem with someone other than his mother making *syrniki.*

"It's okay," she told him over and over.

But he remained unconvinced and started to move deeper into the kitchen, toward the plates and bowls she'd laid out.

She blocked his path, and he pulled up. "Don't fuck with my ingredients." Maintaining her calm, she glared at him with all her authority.

He may not have understood all her words, but he got her meaning. Now that Gogol had cooled to a simmer, she tried a gentler approach.

"Odin." She held up one finger. *"Odin."* If she could make one she might convince him.

His lips twitched and he gazed skyward again. She

imagined his dearly departed mother somewhere up there, scolding and clicking her tongue.

Hayley moved slowly so she wouldn't startle him. He watched, wide-eyed and nervous, as if she was assembling a bomb. Instead of massing explosives, she mixed farmer's cheese and eggs with measured doses of flour and sugar.

Firing up a skillet, she cautioned Gogol, *"Zhdat."* Wait.

He barely held himself together, one hand gripping the edge of the granite countertop.

The olive oil was just shimmering in the pan when Art stalked into the kitchen. He must've seen Gogol hovering close to Hayley and thought there was trouble. His focus was laser sharp on Gogol. One hand curled into a fist; the other was open and ready.

Gogol saw him coming and grunted with a sudden shock. Worrying about his dead mother's recipe was one thing, but Art approaching like that surely made him wonder if he'd live to see lunch.

"We're good." Hayley tried to diffuse Art before he blew up and wrecked the kitchen with Gogol's body. "It's all good."

Art slowed and his intensity lowered, though she knew it never went away. "No trouble?" he double-checked.

She shook her head to reassure him, wondering if they needed some kind of secret signal. "We're just cooking *syrniki.*"

For proof, she took a scoop of the batter, dredged it in flour and put it, sizzling, in the pan. The smell brought both men closer to the stove. She held the scoop out for Gogol. He shook his head, no, and looked like he wanted to cross himself.

Art took the scoop when she offered it. He was hesitant at first but picked up on her direction and soon had a pancake browning next to hers. Gogol still wasn't willing, so she made a third and set it to cooking.

In a couple of minutes, they all had a single *syrniki* on their plate. Art ate first, nodding as he chewed slowly. She tried hers and was happy with the result. Creamy center, but cooked through, and a nice brown edge.

Gogol hesitantly used his fork to separate out a bite. He chewed, then smiled, then guilt brought his gaze to the ground. But the secretive smile persisted. And he took another bite of his pancake.

She asked cautiously, *"Priyatnyy?"* Meaning, good?

He was ready to tear up. *"Da."*

Art agreed, saying, "They're fantastic."

"Tell him," she said to Art, "that I wish I could've tasted his mother's *syrniki*."

She watched Gogol while Art translated. Emotion welled deeper in the guard's eyes.

He set his cleaned plate down and said with an appreciative smile, *"Spacibo."* With an appreciative bow, he left the kitchen. She heard him clearing his throat as he moved down the secluded service hallway.

To her surprise, the shadows of emotion moved across Art's face, too.

The dangerous situation in the house, her new knowledge of what Art's true purpose was, as well as the charged blasts of attraction that kept her coming back to him, all took her down to a raw edge. Fear or hopelessness could take her over. She didn't deny her emotions, but she wouldn't let them dull her focus.

Now that she was alone with Art in the kitchen, she placed her hand on his forearm. "I miss my mom, too," she confessed. "This feels a hell of a lot longer than a few days. It's hard not to worry that I'll never see her again."

Art put his hand over hers. "You will." His palm was warm. "Keep cooking. Keep sharp."

He gave her a small squeeze, then released her hand so he could finish his *syrniki*. Hayley joined him. Once they were done, he took the plates to the sink. As he washed them, he gazed out the window. Now she understood what was out on the other side of the compound wall. His soldiers.

Art's words were nearly swallowed by the sound of the running water. "I was missing my dad. Don't remember much, but there was always the kitchen. My mom cooking for him and the rest of the family." His face remained stoic. "He always had a bottle of beer, shining gold, like he was some kind of wizard with a mustache."

He laughed with nostalgia, and she saw a bit of tension shimmer away from his shoulders. It pulled her worry away, too, at least for now. She put her hands under the running water for a moment, then dried them.

Art could still surprise her. He wasn't a criminal, he was a soldier. But he was always looking out for her. That was evidenced by the way he'd charged into the kitchen when he'd thought Gogol was giving her trouble. Now she knew more about him. A fragment of his past and family. Closer to his heart. He'd already revealed so much dangerous information to her. He trusted her.

Once the dishes were done and the water off, they heard a car pulling up to the house. Art gave her a reassuring nod and eased out of the kitchen. She busied herself with the *syrniki*-making supplies, making sure everything was in its place for the lunch rush.

Art returned with an eye roll and a scowl on his mouth. "Garin's back."

The goon strutted a few paces behind Art, with a collection of guards around him like groupies. The bandages on his face didn't restrict his huge grin. He boasted in Russian, making sure to toss sticky-sounding words and a smarmy wink into the kitchen as he passed. Thankfully he disappeared into one of the living rooms, where he held court with the other guards.

Art stayed behind, dark and angry. She knew he was waiting for a specific moment to spring his operation. But he appeared to be barely restrained for the moment.

He kept glaring into the living room and told her, "Garin had a good ol' time in town. That should calm him down for a bit." His expression brightened when he looked at her. "Thanks for the *syrniki*. Looking forward to lunch."

He left, but was back before long. Gogol was the first guard to arrive in the kitchen, ready to help plate the food and carry it to the dining room. Art pitched in, and soon the house was fed.

She did her job, cooking for the criminals. And she had to trust that when Art's real job as undercover soldier started, she would survive the fight.

Lunch was fantastic, as usual. Art had wished for all afternoon to savor it, eating *syrniki* after *syrniki* and drinking cold beers while talking to Hayley about cooking or guns or music or whatever the hell they wanted to.

But he was back in his room. Was this what it was like to fall for someone? He'd jumped out of helicopters, swum through freezing rivers, been shot at, but had no experience with something like these consuming thoughts and sensations. Relationships had lasted a few dates, a few hookups. Special ops in the Marines didn't make for a very stable lifestyle. He'd never gotten to know a woman beyond her most superficial compatibility. And they hadn't tried to pry too deep into him, either.

Hayley pierced right through him.

He considered texting Jackson for the finer details of getting caught up with a woman. That SEAL had a track record but might not know much about the profound issues. He was a quick strike man.

And it wasn't the best use of resources during an op to ask personal questions when there remained tactical planning to do. Art sat at the edge of his bed, pistol out, phone in hand. His notebook was also open, pen on top, as if he was working on the details Rolan wanted.

Somewhere out in the dirt, Jackson received his messages. Hayley, the one regular civilian in the compound, had been informed of his mission.

Jackson responded, wondering if that was best.

Too late, Art wrote back. She won't compromise op.

She compromise you? The message faded away, but Jackson's burn didn't.

Affirmative.

Art was glad to have the distraction of genial shouting coming from outside the house.

He texted, Over and out, shut down the app and holstered his pistol.

Without a window in his room, he had to venture out to the second-floor common room to peer down. A group of about eight guards kicked a soccer ball back and forth on a pitch crudely marked out with lines scratched in the dirt. Two larger rocks on each side indicated the goals.

Heading downstairs, he made a mental note to tell Jackson that the guards had fallen into a sense of security. Diligence would tighten up when additional bosses arrived, but the shooters were already inclined to think themselves safe.

The day remained bright and hot outside, but a new breeze lightened the air enough to breathe. It tasted damp and woody, like the distant mountains.

Art hung out on the sidelines with a couple of other guards, watching. The guys kicking the ball were pretty good and had probably been going at each other since being kids in some old country apartment block.

The catcalls started when they saw Art. They mocked being afraid of him, saying that the Mexican in him would dominate the pitch.

He moved into the field to intercept a pass and kept a foot on the ball. "If you're too embarrassed to lose to a Mexican, you can pretend my Russian half is beating you."

Without waiting for them to set themselves, he was off, dribbling through the dirt toward a goal. After all the pent-up tension, it felt great to go at these guys, taking their contact, avoiding their attempts to strip the ball. Everyone played fair enough. The goalie's eyes were wide when Art reached shooting distance. He put everything into the kick, and the goalie didn't have a chance.

One person clapped. Hayley stood on the sidelines, nodding her approval. She wore her chef's jacket but stood relaxed. He backpedaled for defense, giving her a flex.

She laughed and stepped onto the pitch. Shouts of surprise and encouragement came from the other guards. One of the opposing team deliberately passed her the ball so she could go against Art.

The rest of the men cleared back for the one-on-one. Art bodied up to Hayley, slowing her attack on his goal. Because of his size advantage, he could've knocked her to the ground and taken the ball. But fouling would've been bad play. And it felt good to run alongside her, feeling her quick, nimble muscles. Her body on his during the kiss had set him on fire. Now his pace raced faster, getting this taste of what she was like full speed.

He did try to steal the ball with his feet, though, not making it easy on her. She dribbled well, avoiding his attempts while continuing to press forward. Attacking and defending kept them clashing on each other. Her leg along his. His arm around her lower back. These impacts woke up his hunger for all of her, naked and stretched out with him.

"You've got skills, Baskov." He blocked her path. She tried to sidestep, but he was there again.

"And elbows." She proved it with a sharp jab in his side, just below the ribs.

It was more surprising than painful, but the move worked. He stalled for a moment, and Hayley spun around him. She booted the ball through the goal rocks and put her hands in the air, victorious.

The guards whooped for her and jeered Art. He held out a fist for Hayley, she bumped it and they walked off the pitch together. The game resumed behind them.

He draped his arm around her waist, feeling the sensuous curve and wondering if that part of her skin had a slick of sweat on it. She bumped her hip on his and swiveled suggestively while they kept moving toward the house. The breeze continued, cooling the perspiration he'd collected on his head and neck.

They paused before the steps to the kitchen. His blood raced and it wasn't from the game. Not too many people were watching them anymore.

He stole a moment, leaning close to her ear. "You have a sunny window in that guest house you live in?"

"Yeah," she breathed back. Her cheek was warm on his.

"Private?" he asked.

"Very." Her fingers lightly scratched at his stomach, above the waist of his jeans.

"I want you in that sunlight." He had to let her know what he was feeling, what she inspired in him. "All day with you."

She tugged on his waistband and pulled him closer. Her breath was shaky and her words were stained with sadness. "I want that, too."

It was enough to hold on to. She needed him as much as he did her.

She released her grip on his jeans. "I have to work on dinner."

He moved his hand from her hip. "And I have to go sharpen my knife."

Her small smile lit him up. They parted, her going up the stairs into the kitchen and him walking back past the soccer game, past the propane tank and around the east side of the house. No one would wonder why he'd step off alone back there. Any guy would want to savor the glow.

Art did, clutching the memory of Hayley's warmth to his core. And he tracked the lines of the generators into the house. There were two, no backups. Because of the noise of the motors, they were kept near the perimeter wall. Knocking them out would have to be one of his first moves.

And where would Hayley be, then? With him? Somewhere safe? But there were no safe places. The only way he could keep her safe was to be between her and the bullets.

ELEVEN

ALL THROUGH THE prep and cooking, Hayley had been distracted. Undercover life bit at her. She was able to remain at least friendly with some of the guards in the house. After the soccer match, she'd gained a handful more of their respect. Was it a betrayal that she didn't warn them about Art and his assault team?

Hayley pushed that concern out of her mind. No matter how much the men had cheered during the game, if their bosses wanted her dead, they would pull the trigger. But she continued to smile and accept the praise of the guards who made the extra effort to bring their dinner plates into the kitchen and thank her for the meal.

Martha did not smile. She helped with the cleanup and dishes, cautious of the men around her. Even Art didn't warrant much trust. Martha spoke around him but remained guarded.

When it was time for Martha to leave, she wanted Hayley to come with her. She said there was an extra bed in her house and that she had a son who could bring her back to the job in the morning. Hayley thanked her and declined—a few times, as Martha continued to insist.

Eventually Martha got into the car with a Russian driver for the drive back to town and Hayley stayed behind, watching her go from the front steps of the house. The sun had long set. The sky grew darker and the stars disappeared.

"Rain." Art stood at the bottom of the stairs. He'd lurked just out of the shadows at the corner of the house.

"Dessert." She watched the gate shut behind the car, then turned and went back into the house.

Art's energy was her other distraction. Since their soccer game, she kept remembering the first impact of their bodies as he'd moved to block her attack. The kiss at the bottom of the stairs and them pressed close had been charged with potential. Some of it lived out when they'd clashed together during the match. They were both strong, but he was a rock. He could move her, and she could hold on tight.

He beat her to the kitchen. The space was lit by the under-cabinet lights, throwing shadows high and low. Art's face was obscured, but she felt his intensity and it sharpened her awareness of him. Each shift of his torso and legs made her move her own in a slow grind. Like they were dancing, despite a distance between them.

She collected ingredients and directed him, "Bring me those peaches."

"Last two." He carried them to her.

"They're ripe now. We have to eat them tonight." She halved and pitted them quickly, then turned her attention to the pan on the stove. Brown sugar dissolved into butter, warming the room with its aroma.

Art came close, his hip on hers. "I don't know what you're doing, but I like it."

"Stand back." She waved him off a bit so she could grab a bottle of bourbon from the island. But it was also because of the dizzying effect he had on her. When he was that near, she just wanted to tilt the floor and have them both tumble onto it together.

The bourbon whooshed into flame as it hit the pan. Art's face was lit by the fire, making him appear almost demonic. A lusty devil, from the way he gazed at her. And her own lust answered with hurried, hot breath through her throat.

He started coming forward again as the flame died down.

She held him at a distance. "Do you have a girl back home?" Need had been pushing them closer to each other. Once he touched her again, she would want it all. But that depended on whether she was just a convenient body to warm him while he was undercover.

"No one." He glanced into the dark house, then back at her. "I have a hard time…connecting with people."

"Not with me, though." She placed the peach halves, cut side down, in the brown sugar mixture.

"You're different." Stepping closer again, Art watched her cook. He whispered, "I can be myself."

She'd seen how hard he'd worked to maintain his cover. For him to be this unguarded with her was a rare gift. They had to keep each other safe.

"Who are you?" she whispered back.

"I'm the guy you're making dessert for." He left for a moment and returned with two plates and silverware. His voice was low, molten like the bubbling mixture in the pan. "I'm the guy who's going to eat that and taste you."

Her mouth watered. Her hunger wouldn't be satisfied in the kitchen.

She killed the heat on the stove and still felt the

flames. He held out the plates, and she slid the peach halves onto them. The caramelized brown sugar pooled luxuriously around the fruit.

"Thank you." Art looked her over with a savoring gaze, then moved his attention to the dessert.

She ate hers, feeling the vibrations of his appreciative growls and moans as he consumed the food. Each sound he made warmed her nerves. Her nipples hardened, wanting the touch. Wet heat gathered between her legs.

The house darkened around them. The night shift of guards came on, and voices dropped to low murmurs. Only the most necessary lights stayed on.

"There's the rain." Art stared out the dark window.

But he was wrong. There was none, not yet. After a moment, though, a streak like a shooting star moved across the window glass. Other drops arrived, hatching the window in the angled direction of the wind. She heard the drops hitting the dry dirt outside. It grew to a stampede.

She carried her dessert to the back door and gazed out the window. Art joined her. His large shadow blocked the kitchen light, and they were able to see outside. The faint illumination from the living room revealed the silver rain. Steady. Unhurried.

The top edge of the cinder block wall was already dark from the moisture. It looked like it was crumbling, but she knew it was just a trick of the colors.

Her dessert was finished and she placed the plate on a counter. Art continued eating.

"How'd you know the rain was coming?" She wanted to feel it on her face, to run in it and not to worry about who saw her or what she'd do with all her wet and muddy clothes.

"Smelled it." The handle of his spoon rang on the window glass. "Not a lot of wind. It parked over us. It'll last." He took her plate, stacked it on top of his and took them to the sink. After hurrying through the dishes, he returned to the windowed door. Focusing outside, he asked, "You like camping?"

"I've been a couple of times. Mostly I just remember trying to keep the beers cold."

"I kind of lost my taste for it, but…" He double-checked the lock on the door. "I might like it out there with you."

That kind of peace and solitude was impossible. And she wanted it so badly. "Do we get to cook, or will we only eat what we can catch or kill?"

"Car camping." He chuckled. "You can cook gourmet if you want to."

"But—" she turned to him and he peered into her eyes, "—you'll have to cook, too."

His shoulders tensed with the prospect. "I hope quesadillas are okay."

"Doesn't matter what it is, as long as you make it."

He relaxed and ventured to put a warm hand on her hip. "We'll go. And if it's raining, we'll get wet. And if it's hot, we'll be sweaty. And we'll be okay."

"Let's go." They couldn't. But she could turn herself harder into his touch, inviting more.

"Anytime." His murmur reflected what she knew: not yet.

His hand slipped up to her waist, held her there. She caressed down his chest and lingered at the top button of his jeans. The room darkened as she closed her eyes. He leaned down and kissed her, tasting of the burned sugar peaches and sharp bourbon.

Her body responded with new need. Close to him, her breasts grew sensitive. She held his arms, fingers curling into his jacket to urge him deeper into the kiss. Harder against her so she could find where her delicate flesh was shimmering with heat. Hours alone with Art in the wilderness wouldn't be enough isolated time for what she wanted to do with him. How could all her urges be satisfied? Denying them was starting to tear her apart.

She felt frayed when Art ended the kiss and slowly pulled away.

"Anytime," he repeated.

All the things she wanted were reflected back from his gaze. Heavy lids hung over his eyes. Long breaths moved his chest. He seemed ready to tear away any barriers between them.

She licked her lips, thinking about what they could do if they both let themselves go.

He made a small growl, watching her mouth. His hand tightened on her waist. Baring his teeth with frustration, he took another long breath and released her.

She understood and she hated it.

"Good night," she said.

He shook his head and stepped away from her. Sliding along with the shadows, Art left the kitchen.

She shut down her space, trying to distract herself with tomorrow's meal planning, but all the pent-up urges continued to gnaw at her. The rain persisted outside, sometimes streaking along the black window. The

slow pace of the drops was too sensuous to be medita-
tive. It was as if nature was taunting her with what she
couldn't have.

THE WARM PEACH and hot bourbon on Hayley's lips
haunted Art. He'd never been so shaken by a woman.
He forced his fingers to cooperate while he sat in his
dark room, texting with Jackson.

Tactical details were communicated curtly: the
placement of the two generators. How their lines ran
behind the wheels of the water truck. No backups for
either resource. Extra fuel for the generators was kept
in an unsecured shed near the eastern wall.

And all the while, Art cursed himself out for letting
temptation erase his better judgment. After the soccer
match, he'd asked her about where she lived, and he'd
imagined her lying naked on the crumpled sheets of a
sunlit bed. Then he had to taunt himself with the idea
of camping with her. Just the two of them, listening to
the rain hit the tent all around them, would be heaven.
The prospect of camping hadn't been at all appealing
after being exposed to the extreme hot and cold of Afghanistan, but Hayley in his world changed that.

He texted Jackson, Loving the mud?

The return message appeared quickly. It's all good.
I was getting thirsty.

The app faded the conversation out, erasing evidence,
but Art knew that Jackson was out there, hidden in
whatever ditch he'd dug, getting rained on.

Art typed, We owe you a bottle of the good stuff.

Shots after the shooting.

That was how they had to do it, knowing they'd all

make it to the bar. Art convinced himself that he and Hayley would survive to find that tent out in the mountains. But he couldn't wait. She was here, in the house.

Now. A voice echoed inside. His body responded, bringing him to his feet, hurrying his pulse. *Now.* He was still alive. He had to live.

Most of the guards and bosses slept. The rain continued. Drops pattered in what was now mud around the house. He knew the clouds would probably blow out by morning. The ground would be baked dry again at noon.

He navigated the dark hallway to the service stairway. At the bottom of the stairs, he passed the ghost of his first kiss with Hayley. The atmosphere there remained sultry and humid.

Down the hall, past the laundry and cabinet of cleaning supplies, he found her door. The sound of the rain was stronger on this edge of the house. It drummed on the roof eaves.

He knocked, trying to be louder than the rain but not to pound on her door.

Hayley's voice came from the other side, "Who is it?"

"Art."

The door opened. Only one dim lamp was on. She wore sweatpants and a T-shirt. And caution on her face.

"I thought I was supposed to lock you out." Part of her body was protected behind the door.

"You can." He remained on the outside of the threshold.

Her hesitance burned away, replaced by a deeper look that slowed the world around him, putting her at the center. "I don't want to."

"Then let me in." He had to live. With her.

Hayley stepped back, swinging the door wider, allowing Art inside. She shut and locked the door behind him.

THE SOUND OF rain surrounded them, making Hayley feel insulated from the house. She turned to Art and ran her hands over his firm shoulders, down his thick arms. He slid his fingers through her hair and down the back of her neck.

Her nerves rushed to collect every touch, the feel of him close, his warmth and the dark want in his eyes. It was all too much. She'd needed so much that everything hit her at once and she wasn't able to savor the tastes that made up this man before her.

She glanced at the door, indicating the full house beyond it. "Can we?"

He nodded. "Whatever we want."

"Because they expect it?" How deep did Art's cover go? Was he able to manufacture all this desire just for show? She certainly didn't. It was about to tear her apart.

"Because I need you."

Cupping her head, he drew her into a kiss. It wasn't an act. None of this was. He was here, real before her. She kissed him, revealing how much she wanted him, as well. Their mouths opened. Their hands moved over each other's bodies.

He wore too many clothes, so she started by tugging at his jacket. His hands left her for just a moment while he shrugged off the jacket and let it fall to the ground. Stripped to his T-shirt, he felt so real and firm under her hands.

Breathless, she pulled away from the kiss. She had to see him. The dim table lamp carved his ridged muscles with shadows. Many of the tattoos he'd mentioned were revealed on his dark skin. Guns and knives. Skulls. And a flower.

He saw her examining it and smiled.

She traced a finger around the perimeter of the petals, feeling the muscles of his forearm jump. "What are you doing with a rose?"

"It's pretty like me." He deliberately flexed his biceps as he reached up to stroke his chin. "And we both have thorns."

She chuckled and put her hands in his waistband, pulling him forward. His pistol and the knife handle on his belt jabbed her belly.

"Do you take off your thorns?" she asked.

"For you." Quick hands undid his belt and pulled it from his pants. His holster and knife and a couple of clips for the gun were placed on the seat of a chair, which he moved so it was easily reached. "Your turn."

"I already took off my chef's coat." She teased him by pulling down the neck of her T-shirt.

His gaze was fixed on the top of her chest. "No hidden knives?"

"Not on me." She put her arms out, as if he would search her.

He held up a hand, pausing them. "But I do." Tugging up his right pants leg, he revealed a long knife in a sheath strapped above his ankle. Once removed, he placed it on the floor closer to the door. Then he pulled another knife from his back pocket. The blade was obscured by the sheath, but she saw that the handle formed a T so the knife would stick straight out of his fist.

"So many thorns." The violence of his world came with him. She was in it now.

He placed the last knife on the small bedside table. "We'll have to get you one."

"I have knives."

"You have cooking knives." He returned to her. "You need something less…clean."

"Later." At last, she was able to pull him to her chest without any of his weapons' obstructions.

"Later."

His hands caressed down her back, over her waist, along the outside of her ass. Even beneath her clothes, her skin tingled for his touch. He surged and lifted her up. Her legs naturally wrapped around him. Hungry, she kissed and bit his neck, wanting him in her mouth, wanting him to fill her. He held her close, pressing deep kisses into her neck and the top of her chest. She raked her nails over his back and shoulders.

And they moved, finding their rhythm. She ground against him. He pressed up to meet her. The heat in her pussy grew and she felt how wet she'd become. His cock was firm in his jeans. More of the man was made real. It wasn't enough yet.

He swept her shirt off. While he held her, she released her bra and dropped it. He took a moment to gaze at her face, her breasts. She felt his attention and grew ravenous needing his touch.

"So beautiful," he murmured and brought his free hand to her neck and along her collarbone.

She arched her back, inviting him farther down. He

palmed her breast, and she sucked in a breath. He was still for a moment, his warm breath splashing across her chest.

"So smooth. So fine." An almost reverent expression crossed his face. "But you're not delicate."

"But I am sensitive." She brought their hips closer together and moved her breast across his palm.

"To this?" His hand continued rubbing hard pads along the edges of her tight areola. Rough sparks of pleasure spread over her chest.

"Yes," she barely breathed.

"And this?" His fingers circled her nipple, then pinched it.

She moaned and bit her lip.

His mouth swallowed her louder sounds as he continued to tease her nipple to a firm point. Their tongues tested along each other. Her hand smoothed over his shaved head and clutched the back of his neck.

The rhythm of their bodies quickened. He thrust up and she ground down. Through all the layers of clothes his firm length slid against her wet lips.

She broke the kiss to breathe out, "Too many clothes."

Art turned them and leaned her down onto the narrow bed. The wood and metal of the cheap frame creaked out in loud protest of their weight. Still holding her, he picked her off the bed and placed her standing on the floor.

They both stared at the bed for a moment. Her body ached to be closer to Art again. Just that one second apart was too long after all the tension that had been building between them.

He gripped the mattress and muscled it onto the floor

with one swift move. Then he was back with her, helping her down to the rumpled sheets and blanket. They kneeled, facing each other. She tugged at the hem of his T-shirt, and he obliged, reaching back and pulling it off over his head.

More tattoos came into view, along with more muscles. And scars. A long one across his ribs and a series of small ones on his shoulder.

She traced the Mexican eagle tattoo on his chest, then trailed her fingers down to the scar on his ribs. "You're not delicate either."

"But I can still feel you." His low voice was almost reverent. He tilted his head back, eyes closed, as she continued.

Her hand skimmed farther down, over his defined abs and to where his narrow waist disappeared into his jeans. When she undid the top button, his eyes snapped open and his gaze fixed on her.

He stepped to her again, pressing their naked chests together and inspiring harder sparks in her sensitive nipples and breasts. He leaned her down onto the mattress, resting her head on his shoulder as he curled an arm around her back. They kissed, supporting each other. Her hand found his jeans again and moved over where his cock strained in the fabric. He growled into her mouth.

While she touched him, he slipped his fingers along the waistband of her sweatpants. Every inch of her skin blazed. The top edge of her panties was so flimsy in contrast to him. Pulling down his fly, she slipped her hand into his jeans. His cock jumped in his boxer briefs when her palm glided along it.

She made low moans of her own as his touch dove under her sweatpants, under her panties and along her waistline. She rubbed her thighs together, her pussy wet and flushed. His palm smoothed over her ass, then came forward while she lay back and spread her legs.

His fingers slowly skimmed down her lower belly; she ventured under the waistband of his boxer briefs. The firm length of his cock filled her hand. He surged forward and pressed harder into her grip.

She stroked along the warm, tight skin of his shaft, his whole body rocking to her rhythm. Every muscle, every part of this capable man, was under her control. He'd always been tuned to her, focused, and now she found out how much they were connected.

Heat raced through her. He chased it higher, his fingers just at the top of her sex. Then he paused, letting them both feel the building tension. She urged him to touch her by running her fingernails in light lines along his cock.

He hissed a breath and dove down along her clit and pussy. She moaned as he parted her slick skin.

"Oh, God." His voice vibrated in his chest, moving her.

She repeated his words back again and again. He slid along her folds and gathered her moisture and swirled it around her clit. Jolts of electric sparks shot up her body and down her legs, and she bucked against his hand.

Their mouths met again, open and hungry. And their bodies moved in unison. Need tightened through her. Even this wasn't enough.

She released his cock and tugged at his jeans. The two of them parted for a moment, hurrying through the process of him kicking his socks and boots off and her helping him out of his jeans and boxer briefs.

Art lay naked before her. She leaned down and kissed his ribs, up his chest to his neck. He ran his fingers through her hair and across her back. She swung her leg over his body and straddled him. His smile was ravenous.

She braced her hands on his chest and rocked. His cock pressed through her sweatpants and panties, grinding with her pussy. He locked her in his grip and leaned up to lick at her nipple. Then he took it in his lips and nipped it with his teeth. Her fists curled onto his shoulders. An orgasm started climbing through her, tight like an electric coiled spring. Ready to break. She sped her rhythm, rocking back and forth on him.

And he surged up with her pace, giving her plenty to spark with. Commanding but not forceful, his hands cupped her ass, moved along her legs, grabbed her ankles.

She was so close to coming, but there was too much fabric holding them back.

He must've understood her frustrated sigh. Turning them both, he soon had her on her back. He kissed her jaw, her neck.

With his mouth at her ear, he whispered, "I'm going to taste you."

She might have pleaded or demanded he do that, but wasn't sure what words she made.

The naked shape of Art moved down her body. His fingers skipped along her sensitive skin until they hooked into her panties and sweatpants. She arched up, and he eased the last of her clothes away.

His hands smoothed back up her legs. A wicked little smile curled on his face. He nodded and tilted his shoulders in that rhythm she'd seen in him since the beginning. And he moaned with appreciation like the first time he'd tried her food.

He leaned close, scooping her up to turn her slightly. "There's that pomegranate." His mouth found the tattoo on her lower back.

She arched for more. Having his lips on her that low rushed her blood faster. He carefully turned her back onto the mattress and leaned back.

With his hands on her thighs, he parted her legs. She spread for him, pulling her knees up and placing her feet on the mattress. His broad shoulders moved her legs farther apart and he leaned closer to her sex.

She ran her hand over his shaved head. He held her hips and his mouth found her pussy.

Was her gasp lost in the sound of the pounding rain?

It didn't seem like there was enough air in the room. She was caught up in the rush while Art licked deliberate circles around her clit. His tongue slicked lower, through her lips and into her. Then back up again, more firmly.

One of his hands reached up and palmed her breast. She writhed to rub her nipple on his rough skin. Searching for something to brace herself, both of her hands stretched over her head and grasped one leg of the bed frame. Now she could buck harder against Art's mouth as he continued to drive her dizzy, moving up and down.

"Oh, fuck," she thought she whispered when she tasted the first sweet edge of the climax, but her voice was breathless and hoarse.

Art paused for a second and smiled up at her. "You taste like peaches."

"You've got to be kidding—" Words failed when he brought his lips back down around her clit.

He sucked her lightly into his mouth and played along the most sensitive tip of her bud with the point of his tongue. A few flicks, then the flat of his tongue ran over her clit and back down again. Her heels dug into the mattress. The orgasm surged closer. She gripped the bed frame and thought she'd snap the wood in half. Her back arched and she pressed hard into him. He did not stop.

She came, trying to swallow her cries and not knowing how loud she was. Her legs squeezed his shoulders. He remained still, letting her move on him to savor all the sensations.

Her hands tingled as she released the bed frame. Blood rushed through her. The air thickened and she caught her breath.

Art crawled up next to her and encased her body in his arms and legs. She held him. The pulse in his veins matched hers.

There was a smile in his voice. "You do taste like peaches."

She kissed him for proof, but only detected her own musk. Once she found her voice, she asked, "Was I loud?"

"The rain was louder." He stroked along her back and ass. "Barely."

She licked her hand and rubbed it along his rigid cock. "Let's see how loud I can make you."

He growled. The need in his eyes was downright

animal, adding to the thrill of having him in her touch and moved by her will. He thrust with her strokes. She'd seen him fight, knew his power. His muscles now moved for her, because of her.

"I have to have you," he rasped.

"Yes," she gasped back.

For a quick moment he pulled away and rustled in his jacket. He came back, unwrapping a condom.

"You knew before we left San Diego?" she asked, almost coming again with just the sight of him rolling the condom on.

He took her leg and pulled it over his hip. "I also brought twenty feet of rope, water purification tablets, spare flashlight batteries and a fire steel."

"Kinky." She put her hands on his rib cage, directing him over her.

"I can be. We can be." His face grew serious. "Another time. I just…need you now."

"I'm yours now." The meaning of her words sunk in. A deep blush rushed through her. Her connection with Art changed every second.

She laced her fingers behind his neck and leaned him down for a kiss. He returned it, then they parted and breathed together as his cock lined up with her opening. Deliberate and slow, he entered her.

When he filled her completely, he stopped. They gripped each other. The rain continued, protecting them with blankets of sound.

Art slid out and returned. The pace increased. She hooked her other heel over his leg and tilted her hips up to invite him deeper. And faster. Her breath rushed with him. Her body sweated and slicked and opened to have as much of him as she could.

His brow pulled low over intense eyes. He licked his lips and bared his teeth and kissed her. His arms curled around her back and his hands climbed higher to wind into her hair. She held on to his shoulders while his thrusts continued, moving both of them.

Another orgasm started to glow deeper than the first. Every time he entered her, grinding their sex close, it grew in intensity.

"Yes," she told him. "Yes," she commanded. "Yes," she promised.

He returned the promise with his lips on her mouth, on her cheek, on her throat.

The climax took her.

She bit into his shoulder to keep from calling out too loudly while the release swept up and down her body. He moaned with her and his pace increased. Her orgasm swirled with his energy.

Faster. He thrust harder. His breath rasped while his muscles tensed. She held on with all her strength. Deep inside her, he came. She felt his cock pulse as he spent, and she wound herself tighter around him.

For long breaths, they remained motionless, coiled together.

Art turned to the side, pulling from her and lying next to her. He blinked slow, staring at her. *"Mi reina."*

An intense blush heated her face and the top of her chest. He had called her his queen.

Quiet air settled on them. The patter of the rain slowed outside. Time shortened.

Art rolled off the mattress and removed the condom,

folding it into one of the facecloths stacked on her side table. She sat up, noticing now how the sheets had all been pulled from edges and bunched in the middle of the mattress.

Still naked, she and Art reassembled the covers and tugged the mattress back on the frame. When they were done, they both stared at the narrow bed.

"A little small for two." The chill of reality started to invade the room and her bones.

"We could make it work." Sadness darkened Art's smile. "But I can't."

She nodded. "I get it."

He dressed, collecting his gun and knives and re-attaching them to all their hiding places. She put her sleep clothes on, not wanting the night to be over and knowing it was.

The rain had receded so much that she could hear the drips of water from the roof. Even the metallic rasp of her door's lock echoed in the room. Too damn loud.

Art kept his hand on the door, face dark.

She moved to him, and he kissed her.

His voice was thick with emotion. "I'm still right here with you."

They kissed again until he eased the door open. They parted. He slipped out the door, and she closed and locked it behind him.

Quiet chilled the room. She turned out the light and got into bed, trying to preserve the warmth she and Art had created. It faded, but she wouldn't let it go. The house full of criminals had become her world. And Art was the only good she'd found. Those few minutes of pleasure might be the last she would ever feel.

TWELVE

INSTEAD OF SLEEPING with Hayley's arm draped over him, Art had spent the night in his windowless room with his pistol in his hand. Light sleep had taken him to morning. His mind had swirled with the tactical details of the house. Every time the floor plan emerged in his imagination, the map moved to Hayley's room.

Instead of satisfying the built-up need between them, he was left wanting to know every inch of her. His body ached from how they'd thrown themselves together. It wasn't enough. The image of her naked and writhing on the mattress on the floor haunted him.

Art rose from the bed, knowing he was done with sleep, and pulled his supplies together for a shower. Sunlight already blasted through the second-floor windows. Yesterday's clouds had been erased by the bright blue. Traces of moisture remained outside in the long morning shadows.

He was the first one in the bathroom. There were three shower stalls, and he took the one farthest from the door. If someone was coming, he would have a second of extra time to know. He had his soap, towel, change of clothes and his push dagger. It was stainless steel and held up fine in the water. Because of the T-handle grip, he didn't need to worry about soapy hands mishandling the knife.

This morning, he showered in peace. Though his mind churned with thoughts of Hayley. She trusted him. She'd let him into her room. She'd let herself go with him.

And he'd let himself go with her. He couldn't remember the last time he'd been that honest with someone.

Never.

He finished his shower and dressed, wondering if trust was a mistake that would get him killed. The stakes of the mission rose every second he was with Hayley. His judgment, his aim, needed to remain clear.

After kitting himself back up with his pistol and knives in his room, he emerged while the others were waking up. There was the usual dirty look from Garin, and Vasily was stone-faced. If anyone knew Art had been with Hayley the night before, they didn't indicate it. And he knew they wouldn't have been able to keep from making lewd comments or gestures. The secret was secure.

So was Hayley. He watched from the first-floor living room as she exited her own bathroom, dressed after her shower and headed straight for the kitchen. Her chef's coat was already buttoned over her, like a flak jacket. But he knew how she was curved beneath it. How silky and responsive she was.

Before she immersed herself with work, she looked up to where Art leaned on a pillar in the open living room. Her smile for him was private, knowing, and it built a warm glow in his chest. He gave her a small wave back but couldn't approach. That floor of the house was too quiet. He wouldn't be able to keep his hand from her hand, his mouth from hers.

She hurried together the walking breakfast, then

prepped other things, presumably for lunch. The men started filtering into the kitchen, collecting their coffee and rolls, while looking a bit weary of the guard detail in the compound. How crisp would they be when he called in Automatik's strike?

Rolan approached Art in the living room, interrupting a count of which guards carried extra submachine gun magazines. The boss revealed in Russian, "Krylov is delayed."

He ran the northeast territory of the Orel Group. Art didn't know the arrival times of the bosses, which was one of the complicating variables to the mission.

Rolan went on, "We might push the meeting longer once he arrives. But be ready with all of your information."

He nodded back and gave a small thumbs-up.

The clock for the assault changed. All the springs stretched tighter. They could break any second.

He glanced to Hayley, who maintained the supplies while the men continued to gather their breakfasts. She didn't betray her secrets and remained in control of the kitchen. But for how much longer? He'd put some of the pressure of the operation on her, a civilian.

And he was balanced with just enough tension on the trigger to get the shot off before anyone else.

Time wasn't his. But he wanted more. Extra seconds and minutes and hours with Hayley. Before the explosions. Because after that, it was all unknown. His mother had lost his father in an instant. What would he or Hayley lose?

WITHOUT THE PROTECTION of the night or the rain, Hayley had to hide her secrets on her own. Art was with her, always watchful, but he wasn't in complete control of this world. She'd seen how he'd had to adapt to things changing all around them.

The biggest change had happened last night. Was it just the delirium of the situation that made it okay to let him in? Was she just seeking safety? God, no. Art was not safe. Not with the way he stole her breath, heated her body. Not with the way he allowed her to see the man beneath the knives, inspiring her to reveal herself, too.

Hayley laughed to herself, probably making the guards in the kitchen think she was crazy. *Good, they'll keep their distance.*

Art, though, approached. He plated his breakfast, stealing glances at her and not afraid to show her that light in his eyes. And the swagger in his hips. She tested her response. Her body warmed in the spots he'd touched. But she was able to keep cool, too, and not let everyone in the house know what had happened the night before.

Luckily, Art didn't get too brash. Rolan was with him, and the two of them were chatting in Russian. Garin had already finished his breakfast but stood to the side of the kitchen, sneering as he listened in. The stone-faced Vasily also gathered up the conversation.

When Art and Rolan had moved to the end of the breakfast counter, Art waved her over.

He explained, "There's a delay with someone's arrival, so the trip might be extended. How are you for food?"

She did a quick tally of how much she'd gone through and what else was planned. "I could always use extra. We want everyone to be happy, right, and not just getting by?"

Art translated to Rolan, who nodded sagely. The conversation continued in Russian without her. But it had something to do with her. The nearby guards were curious, glancing between her and Art. One man started to complain to a nearby guard, who tried to calm him, gesturing subtly toward Rolan. The upset guard left, but his darkness remained. Garin gathered the ill will like a dark coat over his shoulders.

After a minute, Rolan patted Art's shoulder with paternal approval, nodded at Hayley and left the kitchen.

Art leaned toward the center of the island, and she moved to meet him there, creating a sliver of privacy. "We're going into town," he said. "I need to get supplies to fix the propane line."

"Thanks for getting me out of the house." Any time away might relieve the pressing sense of suffocation. And it would be with Art, with the possibilities...

"You'll be working, too." His finger found a drop of coffee on the island and drew it out into a long, curved knife. "Extra days means extra food. Do up as much of a new meal plan as you can. You're going to market." He wiped away the image of the knife with the side of his hand.

Leaning back from the island, Art's awareness swept back through the area, including Garin's dark stare.

Art brought his attention back to her. "In about an hour, if that works, Master Chef."

"Affirmative."

A small wink from Art was like striking a lighter in a room full of explosives. She savored the burn.

He left the kitchen, and she immediately started taking stock of what ingredients she had remaining and what she needed to stretch the menu out a few extra days. Talk about her circulated through the guards. She understood what they were saying, even without the vocabulary. Tilted heads, knowing sneers.

Fuck them. They judged out of jealousy. She had a job to do in the kitchen and outside of that, her life was her own.

For now. Until the real danger started.

She dove back into the meal planning, trying to ignore the bigger trouble that lay in the unknown territory ahead. Maybe going to town would be an opportunity for escape. Or at least to take an unguarded breath with Art.

But until she was outside the walls of the compound, she remained on alert. She made her wish list for ingredients, knowing that local markets would yield only what they wanted to.

A sudden sense of missing something slivered under her skin. Trouble shook through the house, though she couldn't see anything from inside the kitchen. Something bad was happening. Footsteps hurried. She didn't know where Art was.

Leaving her arena was dangerous, but she ventured out, past the dining area and deeper into the living room.

Before her were the backs of men. The guards all focused on a corner of the room that had been hidden from the kitchen.

Hayley choked back a shout.

Art had death in his eyes. He stood coiled, black knife in his hand, facing off with Garin. The other guard had a brutal chisel-looking blade in his grip. The two men had obviously hated each other since the fight in the kitchen, but what had set this off?

They were next to a tall window, with nowhere to run. The other guards blocked any exits. Vasily watched, interest on his stony face, thirsty for blood. His hand rested on the handle of a knife in a sheath on his belt. Hayley knew that he wasn't getting ready to step in and help Art.

She had to.

One step forward. She was ten feet from the first line of guards. Would she be able to get through them? And then what?

Another step.

Art's intense eyes quickly flicked to her, then back at Garin. The brief glance told her everything. "Not another step. Stay away."

But she couldn't.

Now she was only about five feet from the line of guards.

Garin flinched a fake attack, then chuckled when Art recoiled, balanced and ready to strike back. They didn't have much space for this dance. The next lunge with a knife would be deadly.

Hayley was just behind the guards and tried to figure out the best way to press through them. Whatever she did would have to be as far away from Vasily as possible. He poised like he'd love the opportunity to unsheathe his knife.

Garin hissed something in Russian. Art didn't answer, but remained ready. Blood was about to be spilled.

She had to act.

A gunshot exploded behind her. She ducked on instinct, and the guards in front of her spun, drawing their own weapons. When they saw who'd fired, they immediately lowered their barrels to aim at the ground.

Rolan stood in the living room. His face was calm, but the small black pistol in his hand represented his dangerous rage.

Hayley's heart pounded in her chest. She couldn't hear her speeding pulse because the ringing of the shot continued in her ears. Standing, she searched for Art. He remained ready, with his knife in hand, though the tension of the fight had been drained.

Garin was a few paces back, nervous and glancing from Art to Rolan. A precise bullet hole marked the wall above the window where the two men had faced off.

Rolan's steady commands were lost on her, but the guards cleared out of the room in an instant. The acrid gunpowder smoke swirled. The boss still held the gun out when Dernov and Ilyin arrived.

Art fixed her with his look again, adamant. When she hesitated, he nodded, trying to reassure her.

Rolan didn't spare her any attention as she backed out of the living room. But she stopped at the edge, watching and not willing to leave Art.

Russian commands and conversations flew about the room. Art sheathed his knife, and Garin put his away. Rolan lowered his gun and holstered it so he could gesture with his hands to the other bosses. For a moment, Art and Garin were forgotten. They glared at each other, and she wondered if the fight was about to start over. Rolan's next shot wouldn't be a warning.

Before things got messy, Rolan clipped short sentences to Art, pointing him toward the front of the house.

"Da, da," Art replied, striding that way. He caught her eye and motioned her in his direction with a quick tilt of the head.

Garin watched, scowling like he had a mouthful of acid, as Art met up with Hayley and the two of them made their way to the front door.

"What the fuck happened?" She wanted to put her hand on Art's arm, but he radiated so much malice from the fight she thought he might explode.

He growled, "Garin said things about you I didn't agree with."

"Like what?" Though hot anger was already brewing in her and she didn't know if she needed more fuel.

"Things he should bleed for." He slammed out the front door and continued toward the SUV that had brought her there, keys jingling in his hand.

The sun washed him out for a moment. She adjusted, coming down the stairs, and saw him waiting by the side of the car.

Care emerged in his eyes. "That shot was close. You handle it okay?"

"Scared the hell out of me…but yeah." A tremble in her hands reminded her. "Are you hurt? Cut?"

"It's all good."

Tension hummed through him while he stroked the side of her neck and pulled her toward him. They rested for a moment, forehead to forehead. She felt his breathing slow.

He kissed her cheek and whispered, "The car might be bugged."

She answered with a slight nod.

Their mouths met. The connection overrode the fear from the fight. But the danger remained, and she knew people were watching.

Art clearly knew it, too. He glared at the house, stepped away from her and opened the back door of the SUV.

"I have to ride there?" Her stomach dropped at the memory of the black isolation in the back of the SUV.

"Safer that way." He put out a hand and helped her in. "And it makes you look like a VIP."

"But you're not my chauffeur." The intense darkness of the interior already worked on her nerves.

"Personal security." He closed the door and moved around the car to the driver's side. Climbing in, he continued, "With benefits."

The car started with a hum. Air-conditioning knocked the desert back a bit.

Art turned in his seat to glance back at her. "It's just for a minute." The dark partition glass rose, taking Art away. Taking everything away.

The SUV moved, and she was lost in disorientation. Backward, forward. Slow and fast. She was finally out of that house but didn't feel free.

After an unknown amount of time passed, the partition dropped. Art drove them down a dirt road that carved a line through the desert. The landscape was almost featureless, like any minute, they'd drop right off the earth.

"You have your shopping list?" he asked as casually as if they'd just had brunch and were headed to weekend errands.

"Wish list. Who knows what we'll find?"

"I just hope I can find La Bota. My map is a little crude." He held up a piece of paper that had only a scribbled line connecting two circles.

"You'll just have to put all that Marine training to use."

"Aye, aye."

She sat as far forward as she could and leaned her arms on the back of the front divider. "What rank did you get to?"

"Sergeant." He patted his shoulder, where his insignia would be. "I wasn't really political. Just a specialized grunt. Never thought about climbing the ladder into the brass." He glanced back at her. "You have ranks in the kitchen, right?"

"Yeah, gotta work your way up."

"What was your first gig?"

It was strange to think back, like trying to unlearn everything she'd fought for. "High school. I was a busboy and dishwasher at a semi-fancy Italian place."

"Earning your stripes." He patted his shoulder again.

"Learned a pretty good marinara there. Built on it since then."

"You cook more than Russian?" His eyes were surprised in the rearview mirror.

"All kinds." But right now, all the flavors she could think of were bitter. "The place I was supposed to open was going to have a few influences. It was a menu for traveling."

His gaze grew sincere. "You'll open that place." And determined. "And I'm going to eat the first motherfucking chimichanga that comes out of that kitchen."

Her laugh bounced along the rough road. "I wasn't planning on chimichangas."

"Well, you are now." He scowled tough for a second, then broke into a smile.

"I suppose I owe you that much."

"You don't owe me anything." His face was unreadable and distant.

She reached over the back of the seat and put her hand on his arm. "Not your decision to make."

His fingers laced with hers. "Then just let me know when that chimichanga's ready."

She wanted to say, "Soon," or, "Anytime," or, "I'll always have a table for you," but none of that was certain. She couldn't will it to be.

The road became choppier, and Art released her hand to steer over deep ruts. She stayed close, not wanting to recede into the darkness at the back of the SUV. The tires rumbled, and small rocks chattered along the bottom of the car.

Exhaustion pressed into her shoulders and burned her eyes. The farther they got from the house, the more pressure was released. She'd been revving high for too long and felt how tired she was once she spun down.

Art's voice came from a great distance, snapping her to waking. "Yeah, shut it down for a bit. I'll get us there."

Sleep sounded like the sweetest dessert, but it wasn't how she needed it. Gathering what energy was left in her muscles, she pulled herself over the divider and into the passenger seat next to Art. It would've been better if she could've leaned along him. She put her hand on his thigh and leaned back to let the fatigue take her.

The desert drifted in and out of darkness. The car thundered all around her and from hundreds of miles away. Art was always there. And when she woke, he smiled at her.

"Power nap."

"How long was I out?" She groaned and stretched.

"A few miles." He pointed down the road. "La Bota's out there."

The dirt road carved toward low buildings collected into a town a bit closer than the horizon.

"Have you been there?" The atmosphere of human life hung lower over the buildings, but she couldn't get a sense of the mood of the place.

"Not yet." Small bits of ready tension collected around Art. "But it's got something for everyone if Garin left there with a smile on his face."

That smug son of a bitch continued to needle her. "I wish he'd gotten mugged there."

"If he keeps pushing, he's going to get dead." His fist was tight on the steering wheel.

"Can it…? Will it…?" She'd seen the deadly intent of the men with the knives outside the club. The smell of gunpowder remained in her clothes. "It's inevitable."

He remained focused ahead. "The trigger's already been pulled."

Their silence blasted into the desert when Art rolled down the windows. Hot, dry air scoured her. She removed her chef's coat and tossed it in the back of the SUV, leaving her in a T-shirt. Art kept his jacket on. She'd seen all the weapons it hid.

Another dirt road intersected theirs. It brought power lines that then marched beside them on the way into town. A flatbed truck passed them going the opposite direction. Thicker dust rose around the road as other cars moved about the edges of town.

Various warehouses or small factories sucked trucks in and spit them back out, increasing traffic. Hayley saw faces. Men and women living lives completely apart from the pressure she'd been under.

The noise built. More intersections. More cars. The road was now asphalt.

"This is Mexico, right?" she asked. It was unsettling to be in a foreign country without a passport or any legal safety net. To the outside world, she was riding with the Russian mob, and didn't cross borders like normal people.

Art nodded, staying alert while he drove them into the thick of the town.

She could've guessed the answer anyway. All the shop signs were in Spanish. It was a medium-sized place, a few thousand people. Satellite dishes bloomed on the sides of buildings. Small construction crews kicked up clouds of plaster. A school struggled to contain the boisterous children in its yard.

Art took them farther into the center of town. They passed a couple of carts lined with produce, and she turned in her seat to try to see what they offered. When she brought her view back around to the front of the car, they were in the town square.

A church and three government buildings held down the corners of the square. Inside was a small park with fountains and benches. And the market, with tables and carts full of produce. Hayley could already smell the onions and the moist bitterness of the greens.

Skirting the edge of the activity, Art took them onto a side street and parked the SUV.

"I spotted a hardware store just off the square." He shut down the car and gave her a questioning look, asking if she was ready.

"Let's go."

Free from the oppressive pressure in the house, she felt alive again. And to be out, under the sun with Art in a new town, discovering the local produce, felt like a fantasy.

Reality cut in when she felt Art's caution in the street. He was next to her, moving with purpose and scanning the surroundings. She tried to learn his awareness. Rooftops and sunken doorways were noted. She tracked the flow of traffic and found herself easily moving through it.

"Can we run?" She imagined disappearing into the town, cloaking herself with the ordinary life and commotion.

"They'd find us." His voice was steady and grim. "Or we'd be running forever. And anyone left behind… family…would suffer. We need to end them before they end us."

The hope of escape choked off, and she tried to resign herself to a prolonged struggle.

Art stopped at the edge of the market and carried his steady gaze over the place.

She restrained herself from sprinting to the nearby tables. "Those beets are calling to me."

He smiled warmly and clasped her hand. The food became less interesting as she absorbed the care of their connection. He turned her palm up and pressed a wad of folded peso bills into it. "I'm going to the hardware store." His gaze flicked to a stall at the middle of a row. "Start with the tomatoes."

"Tomatoes?" His instruction was too specific. A cloud passed over the glow of freedom. There was some kind of business here.

"Tomatoes," he confirmed. "Meet you back here. Happy hunting." He gave her hand a squeeze and headed off to the edge of the square.

Was she walking on a minefield? She tracked her slow steps while she passed tables of carrots and peaches and unknown greens, on her way to the tomatoes.

Maybe Art just had a great eye for produce. The piled tomatoes were beautiful. Deep color. Perfectly odd shapes. She picked one up, feeling how thin the skin was, delicate and not overengineered.

"Bueno, si?" A woman with dark hair tied up into a bandana stood behind the table of tomatoes. She nodded knowingly, looking at the tomato in Hayley's hand. There was something else in her eyes, a steely glint.

Hayley had seen the same edge in Art.

"Si," she replied, cautious.

"You're the chef." Surprisingly, the woman's English had no accent. She casually scanned around them; no one was within earshot. Then she busied herself prepping a shopping bag.

"Hayley." Mimicking the everyday activity, Hayley went through the business of selecting the best tomatoes.

"Mary." The woman was around Hayley's age, but built like an athlete. "Friend of Art's."

"I was glad to find out he had friends."

Mary laughed. "I'm sure." She took the tomatoes and put them in the bag. "That wall around the compound, is it reinforced cinder block?"

Hayley tried to remember any detail she could about it. "I don't know. Sorry."

"That's okay, sister." Mary winked at her. "Is there a little mound on the top of the wall, or is it flat?"

"Flat." That much she knew.

Mary nodded to herself. "They rushed it. Doubt they had time to reinforce. A fifty will do it."

"Fifty dollars?" Hayley was lost again.

"Fifty caliber." This time, when Mary winked, she kept her eye closed, as if sighting down a rifle. "You ever shoot a gun?"

"Couple of times, at a range." If they could just talk about the produce, then she'd be in control.

"Stay with Art." Mary watched Hayley's face when she said this.

Hayley felt a slight blush betray her. She tried to keep the heat down, but all the need and attraction always pushed so close to the surface.

Mary didn't judge, but she nodded with understanding. There was even a slow small secret darkness, far away in her eyes. "He'll get you out." Mary leaned forward, dead serious. "But watch your six. If you pick up a gun, don't point it at anything you don't want dead. And if you have to pull the trigger, do it." She took the tomato from Hayley's hand. "Stay alive to say your Hail Marys to me later."

"I will." Though Hayley couldn't imagine herself with a gun in her hand. "Thanks, Mary."

"But I ain't full of grace." She handed over the bag of tomatoes. "Gratis."

The produce wasn't nearly as heavy as the advice.

But knowing that Mary was part of Art's team, and there were others like her out there, gave Hayley a touch of extra confidence she might make it through whatever was coming.

She paused before moving on to the next stall. "What's your comfort food?"

"Lebanese."

"I can work with that."

"No backing down now that you owe me." Mary extended her fist, and Hayley bumped it. "Stay awake out there."

Hayley smiled a thanks and headed into the market. She was out of the house but still in the action. By the time she made it one stall over, Mary was gone, replaced by an older woman at the tomato table. The market was Hayley's territory, but stable footing was hard to find. Art could only lead her so much. No one was what they seemed. Not even Hayley.

THIRTEEN

AUTOMATIK WAS READY. All Art had to do was call the shot. He didn't see any of his team in the hardware store but knew they'd been there. The tools he needed to fix the propane line had been supplemented by them, stashed in a spot high on a shelf. It would've taken an employee a year to find the secret gear in the crowded aisles of the hot, cramped shop. And even if they did, it would've just looked like oily thin cardboard used for packing machine parts.

Art knew what it could do, though, and carefully tucked the sheets in the paper bag with the rest of his supplies. He chatted in Spanish for a bit with the older man behind the counter, thanking him for the hardware, commiserating about the heat and taking in other details about the town.

Back in the square, Art stalked through the market. Hayley wasn't hard to spot under the makeshift umbrellas and awnings. She could not be rushed and stopped at each table to pick up the food, test it and think about it. Some she bought, some stayed behind. Among her bags were the tomatoes. Mary was gone from the market and was probably in the field, zeroing in the scope of her rifle.

Hayley turned to see Art before he reached her. Good, she was aware and her radar was up. But her open smile was bright, nothing like a hardened merc or shell-shocked private.

He stood close enough to take a couple of her bags, smelling the aroma of greens fresh from the dirt, and lean into her a bit. She shifted her weight, pushing back. "You met 'Bolt Action' Mary." He kept a casual appearance. No one was close enough to hear them.

"She has great tomatoes." Hayley started to turn in the direction of the tomato table but stopped herself. "Glad to know she's out there."

"Me, too." He quickly negotiated the price of bell peppers and paid the person at the stall. Just by putting them in the bag, he could tell how sweet and spicy the bright red peppers would be. As he and Hayley walked to the next table, he told her, "She's a sniper."

Hayley acknowledged him with her eyes and turned her attention to piles of carrots. For a few minutes, they were normal. People out shopping. He was just a guy hanging out with a woman who was a chef who found inspiration in a red onion.

She was confident and comfortable in the square, even though she'd never been to this town before. And if she didn't speak all the Spanish, she spoke food, and everyone else there understood her.

At the end of a row, she sorted what she'd collected in the bags. "The last time we were at a farmer's market, you kidnapped me into this job."

"It's going to look great on your résumé." He held open the bags he carried so she could inspect them.

"Do you have a résumé?" She appeared satisfied with her haul and peered up at him.

He barely moved his lips to speak, deepening his voice. "Graveyards are my résumé."

Her eyes went wide, and he saw doubt tremor through her.

"I'm kidding," he reassured, laughing at her slow realization.

"Jesus Christ." She sighed a relieved breath, then burned him with her eyes. "You sounded like a fucking killing machine."

He admitted, "I did shake down the hardware store owner for the most important intel."

Her jaw set, anticipating trouble, but he quickly reached forward to give her arm a reassuring squeeze.

"Lunch." He turned her so she could see a tiny restaurant tucked under a taller building. "Best *machaca* in town. At least, that's what the shop owner's last words were."

"If it's a final confession, it must be true." She hefted her bags, and the two of them walked away from the market.

People watched them. The town was small enough that strangers were noticed. Garin's trip in had probably caused a stir, and now here were Art and Hayley marketing like locals. But they weren't local. Curious gazes followed them across the street to the restaurant. Women talked, unashamed to stare. Men were wary, protective of their space. Open hostility blazed out of a few of them. Art marked them in his memory: worn boots with an exposed steel toe. T-shirt with a soda logo on it. Rust-red car.

The owner of the restaurant, who was also the waiter, lit up like family when Art and Hayley came in. When he spotted the bags of produce and found out that Hayley was a chef, the holiday started. The owner refused to bring menus and said he would serve the best.

To show Hayley and Art how authentic food was cooked, he escorted them from the dining area, with only about five tables and a TV in the corner, into the kitchen. The man's wife abandoned her post at the cash register to join them, crowding the already small space.

Every surface was dangerous. Boiling water, open flames on the stove, searing-hot griddles. Hayley was at home, grinning and taking it all in with an expert gaze.

He asked over the sound of sizzling meat, "Are all kitchens like this?"

"Some are bigger." She stepped around the owner to get beside the hurried young cook. "But this has everything you need."

The cook continued with his business but took extra time to show her the process. She nodded appreciatively, asking a couple of questions in decent Spanish and getting terse answers. Art watched her bank the information. She was so alive, in the moment. And he could see that she was itching to jump into the dance.

When the cook expertly spun two huge tortillas on the griddle, she turned to Art, eyes wide and drawing him into her enthusiasm.

He braved all the burning surfaces around them to step closer and whisper in her ear, "You're so beautiful, *mi reina*."

She reached forward and caressed her hand down his forearm. Her gaze stirred his blood. But there was a touch of sadness in her eyes, and he understood. Feeling good only made the inevitable battle that much more terrible. He should've stayed away from her. The way he'd avoided too much close contact during his military career. And during his work with Automatik. But there was no escaping Hayley.

Licking her lips, her words were for him alone. "I'm starving."

"Let's eat." He repeated the idea to the owner, this time in Spanish.

Plates clattered while the owner and his wife collected lunch. Art and Hayley were swept out of the kitchen and back to their table. *Machaca* burritos. Roast chicken. Cactus and corn salad. Art had seen most of it being cooked and knew how fresh it was.

He sat with his back to the kitchen so he could watch the front door and sidewalk outside.

Hayley hadn't even picked up her fork. She stared at the food, turned the plates for different views. Her analysis was far from unemotional. She breathed in the aromas, closed her eyes for a moment, then came back to his world with a smile.

The owner and his wife monitored them from the edge of the small dining room. Even the other people at their tables watched and waited for Hayley to eat.

Her fork continued the discovery. Pieces of the food were lifted, exposing the layers below. How could she not dig in? Art was starving, poised to attack his food, and she took the smallest bites of everything on the plates.

Watching her experience the taste made him hungry for other satisfaction that tortillas and chicken couldn't bring. She closed her eyes, chewed slowly. Her shoulders swayed, like she danced to a slow song. He'd felt her rhythms through him and wanted her again. More and more.

His cock tightened in his jeans and he wasn't even touching her.

She opened her eyes after savoring a bite and looked at him. "Aren't you going to eat?"

"Aren't *you*?" The fork almost bent in his clenched fist.

"I am." To prove it, she took a large bite of the roast chicken and salsa. When she groaned with pleasure, he wanted to smash the table to splinters so he could reach her. "It's so good," she said after finally swallowing. "You're missing out."

"I'm just…making plans."

That slowed her. Her wicked, knowing smile licked a new frenzy into his blood.

"There's got to be a room to rent in this town." She tapped his shin with her toe.

"I'll break us into a house if I have to." His head spun with the idea of her and him in a cool, quiet living room with the shades drawn.

"I thought you were one of the good guys." She resumed eating and gave the restaurant owner an appreciative nod.

"I'll be bad for you."

She shook her head, sober. "Be good for me."

Could he? He'd protected her, but only because he'd put her in this terrible situation in the first place. "Until I've got nothing left."

No one had ever dedicated that much sacrifice to her. Hayley saw that he meant it. Burton had bailed when things were just getting real and she'd needed him the most. But Art didn't run. Every time the crisis tightened, he came closer.

She couldn't let him die. Not for her or any other cause. Art had to survive.

He must've seen her concern and smiled to lighten the mood, then attacked his food.

Every taste and texture was excellent. Rustic and refined. The chaos of the small kitchen was tuned like a race car engine, and the cook was a driver. She tried to identify unknown herbs and suspected they grew only in someone's backyard in this very town.

Art appreciated the food, too. He nodded with each bite and rapped his knuckles on the table. The owner and his wife watched, satisfied, then returned to their duties in the restaurant.

The food disappeared from the plate. Hayley grew full. But she wanted to order the food she hadn't tried. Anything to keep her and Art there. Their time was stolen. They were outside the crisis, and she didn't know if she could handle going back into that pressure cooker of a house.

The restaurant owner returned to the table, oblivious to Hayley's dark thoughts. He was all smiles while he cleared the empty plates to the back. When he returned, he was joined by his wife and the cook. Art helped translate the parts of the lively conversation that whirled around them. Many compliments were given, and a couple of the cook's secrets. She thanked him twice for the technique of smoking avocado leaves before seasoning the chicken with them. He credited his mother and smiled warmly.

Plans were made to visit her kitchen, but she had to explain that her restaurant was a distant possibility. She understood the Spanish when Art told them that it wouldn't be long. Was he saying it to make her seem important in their eyes? Or did he believe in her that much?

After many handshakes, Art paid the bill, they collected their produce and stepped back into the heat of the day. The car was somewhere off the square to their left, but Art started walking right.

He'd been navigating her through a twisted maze ever since they'd met. She had no choice but to follow again.

But she could still school him. "Do you know how hard it is to start a restaurant?"

"No." He shrugged, keeping his gaze moving along the street and checking any intersection.

"There's permits and insurance and cash, cash, cash. And that's just above the table." Merely operating a steam cart outside Rolan's club had gotten her into this situation. "A lot of palms need to be greased to make it all come together. And that's before publicity, word of mouth, exposure."

"You had a plan for all that." He wasn't daunted. "You had a plan for the place you almost opened."

"Burton and I had come up with it. He was better at PR, front-of-the-house stuff." Son of a bitch. "He had more contacts than I did. That's why it all fell apart so fast."

"I don't know how hard it is to open a restaurant, but I do know how hard it is to walk into a house full of Russian mobsters and hold your head up and excel at your job." He stopped at a corner and turned to her. "That's what you've done."

"With your help." Yes, he was partially responsible for pulling her into this world, but how terrible would things have turned if he hadn't been watching out for her since then?

"That's my job." An undercover secret soldier with a gun under his jacket, and he managed to look bad-ass holding bags of produce from a farmer's market. "You're doing yours."

His confidence always found its way through her doubt.

"Thank you." She brushed her free hand down his chest.

He took a long breath with the touch. "Thank me in private."

Impossible. Luxuries like privacy and safety were unobtainable.

With all his experience, he must've known what she was thinking. A secret glittered in his eyes, and he purposefully scanned up a side street. She followed his gaze to see a small four-story brick hotel tucked between apartment buildings.

"But first," he said, holding the bags of produce, "I need you to reach into my right front pocket and pull out the pesos."

She started for his jacket.

He redirected her. "Pants pocket."

"Oh." She stood close, rubbing her thigh on his, and slipped her hand into his jeans pocket. "Nasty boy."

He feigned innocence. "I'm just trying to get some cash to buy sodas from that cart." The street vendor was between them and the hotel.

"Is this the cash?" Her fingers moved along his pelvis, over the top of his thigh. "Or this?" She did feel the money but passed it so she could brush the side of his hardening cock. "I think I found it."

"Yeah. That's it." He swiveled to press his length into her touch.

Before they made a scene on the corner, she retrieved the money and stood back to catch her breath.

He angled his pelvis to adjust.

"You hard?" she teased quietly.

"You wet?"

Just watching his mouth saying the word pushed a tremble down between her legs.

She couldn't answer his question without moaning.

Nodding slowly, he walked up the side street toward the hotel. He paused at the street vendor to get four sweating bottles of cold fruit soda, and she paid the man from the wad of pesos that were still hot from Art's pocket.

The man kept throwing them curious looks from beneath the brim of his straw hat until they moved off to the hotel.

Limp air-conditioning in the dark lobby helped Hayley breathe again. Art did all the talking at the front desk, where the middle-aged woman pulled a key and waited for payment. Art told Hayley what they owed, and she handed it over.

"Gracias." The woman made the money disappear quickly and slid the key across the desk without any judgment in her eyes. Long black hair framed her wise face. *"Tres, cero, tres."*

The brass fob on the key was hand-stamped with the numbers 303.

"No elevator." Art tipped his head toward a wide set of stairs that climbed out of the back corner of the lobby.

Fans blew on every landing, swirling the heat. Sweat dripped down the small of her back and soaked into her shirt by the time they reached the third floor. The room was thankfully close to the stairs.

She threw the heavy lock and opened the door. Inside, a small air conditioner made a set of gauzy curtains dance lazily. Gold light bounced off the simple bed and dresser. She and Art entered and put their bags down on a table in a corner. He immediately returned to the door, locking it and placing the lone chair in the room under the handle.

He took off his jacket and tossed it on top of the dresser. Sweat on his shirt defined the lines of his chest and upper arms. He dug through the produce bags until he found two of the soda bottles. Quickly popping the tops on the edge of the table, he handed her one and held out the other for a toast.

After a short deliberation, he toasted, "This room is ours."

"Ours." She clinked her bottle's neck on his. Their gaze didn't break while they drank the cool, sweet soda. The tart orange cut through her thirst. Other needs pulled stronger. The tremors continued deep in her, sensitive. She placed her drink on the table and approached Art.

His bottle joined hers, then his hands were free to smooth through her hair and tilt her head back. Hot sugar skimmed across their lips. His tongue found hers. More sweat covered her. More moisture collected between her legs.

The room was theirs. Time wasn't. She needed him now.

ART BURNED HIMSELF on Hayley. He gripped her slick, strong arms, pulled her close so he could lick at the salty sweat on the side of her neck. Her moan brushed his throat, followed by her fingers. She caressed him, then tugged his shirt collar down so she could kiss his chest.

The room was as secure as possible. They'd be expected back before long, and the mission and the clock would continue. He wanted weeks with her and had only minutes. But each second was absorbed slowly as he welded it to his memory.

He took a step back to undo his belt and remove his weapons while she sat on the edge of the bed, smoothing the sheets with her palms. His pistol and knives were placed within reach, each in a different area depending on where a threat might intrude.

When he started to take off his shirt, she held up a hand.

"Take your time." She leaned back on her elbows, watching from beneath heavy eyelids.

He reached back and eased his shirt over his head. "I've never stripped for someone before."

"You're not stripping." Her eyes moved over his arms, his chest. "You're getting naked."

Seemed like the same thing. He undid his pants and stopped. Each of his tattoos was examined by her slow gaze. She looked at his scars, too, eyes squinting, trying to determine the cause. He turned, revealing the tattoos and marks of history on his back. And he understood what naked meant.

He didn't hide from her.

"I'll tell you all their stories." He rubbed at the scars on his left shoulder, remembering the bloody pain. "Another time."

She smiled wistfully. "I'll trade you my stories."

"And pour the tequila." Another night that might never be.

"But for now…" Hayley signaled down with her finger. "The pants."

She brought them back into the now. Art didn't want to keep her waiting. He pulled off his boots and socks, then eased his jeans down. Once he stepped out of them, he was nude except for his boxer briefs.

He did another slow turn for her. There were scars on his legs and a couple of tattoos for her to examine. Her gaze rose to his. She curled her fingers, gesturing him forward. He was in her grip, moved by her smallest motion. She didn't even touch him, and his pulse thumped harder.

She remained on the bed, and he stepped to her. Her fingertips traced his tattoos and skimmed around the perimeter of his scars. The gentle contact woke up old nerves, those that had been dulled by pain, and now they tingled with new awareness. He smoothed his hand over her hair and closed his eyes to savor the quiet attention.

When she tugged at his waistband, his eyes snapped back open to see her lean forward and kiss his stomach. She dragged his briefs down farther, moving her lips along the exposed flesh.

He shivered in the heat, anticipation growing. She got his underwear all the way down, freeing his cock. Her steady breath breezed across his erection. Everything she did moved him.

His knees almost buckled when she wrapped her fingers around his length. Slow strokes glided up and down him. She looked up, catching his gaze and revealing the wicked light in her eyes. He snarled back at her with the same raw intentions.

Her grip became firmer as she brought him closer. He stepped out of his underwear. The fact that she was fully clothed made his nakedness even starker. But hunger on her face was unguarded and let him know he was protected because they were both exposed.

She licked her lips. He was hers for the taking. She licked the underside of the head of his cock, and he lost his breath.

Her lips kissed along the edge of his length. She opened her mouth and took him in. He had to close his eyes to completely concentrate on the hot, wet feel of her around him. Her hand stroked him and her mouth began to move.

He opened his eyes to see himself disappear through her lips as she sucked him deeper and deeper. Her free hand ventured up his thigh and caressed down his belly. All the fires she lit in him joined into a steady blaze. The burn wasn't enough. He started moving his hips, testing how he and she fit together. She moved down his cock and he pressed forward. She encouraged him, holding his hip and guiding him closer.

Her fingers and lips continued to stroke up and back around him. He pumped in and out of her mouth, his pulse charging harder. His moans bounced off the plaster walls. Her sounds of pleasure vibrated up his cock and shook him completely.

It was almost agony to feel this good. The danger always came back. There was no safety. Walking away after their first time together was probably the right thing to do. But impossible. Their possibilities wound them back together again. This was theirs. No one could take it away.

His hand clutched hers on his hip. Raking his fingers through her hair, feeling the back of her neck, holding her shoulder, he collected more of her around him.

She took him from her mouth and ran her fingernails lightly down his shaft. "You don't taste like peaches." Her raspy voice stroked over him.

He reached down and helped her out of her T-shirt. "What do I taste like?"

Arching her back in a languid stretch, she undid her bra and removed it. Thoughtful, her head tilted to one side. He took in the curves of her flesh, the artful tattoos, the rosy nipples hard at the ends of her breasts. And her moist lips, smiling.

She said, "Cumin." And she brought him forward again with her hands on the sides of his thighs, then on his ass. "Turmeric." She kissed the side of his cock, took it in her mouth, then released it before he had a chance to ease deeper into her. "Mesquite."

Seeing himself in her hands, along her lips, was almost enough to make him come.

Before she could draw him into her again, he leaned down and claimed her mouth in a kiss. She stood and held herself to him, skin against skin. Her breasts were soft. Her muscles were hard. He ran his hands up her naked back, and she sighed, murmuring things he couldn't understand.

"I have to undress you," he said, turning them so the bed was now behind him.

He sat and urged her toward him with his hands on her hips. She quickly removed her shoes and socks. Undoing the button of her jeans was like taking the first bite of her food. The zipper dragged down tooth by tooth so he could take in every second of this experience.

She wiggled to help him remove her jeans. Sleek and simple black panties stood out on her pale skin. His dark hands also contrasted against her when he hooked his fingers in the flimsy underwear.

He stared up at her and she back at him. Trust balanced between them, allowing the hunger to take over. Pulling slightly on her panties, he walked her closer to him. She rubbed her hands over his head while he kissed her ribs and smooth belly. The desert dust had found her skin, as well as the flavor of her floral soap. Her fingernails raked his scalp then dug into his neck. He dragged her panties down.

Taking his time, he felt every curve and turn of her legs along the way back up. Her eyes were closed and her head tilted back slightly. She steadied herself with her hands on his shoulders when he ventured to the silk between her thighs. He climbed higher and higher, rewarded by her delicious little moans.

The heat from her body consumed him. She was an oasis of fire in the desert. And she was wet. His fingers stroked along the edge of her pussy, finding her moisture and making her lean harder on him.

She rocked slowly and drew the edge of his hand along her lips. His knuckle rubbed her clit, and she froze for a second, shivered, then started again. They sped up, and her breath rushed faster. He wrapped his arm around the small of her back, supporting her, giving her something to hold while her body bucked.

But he needed more of her. He moved his hand from her, and she protested with huffed breaths. His answer was to place his hands on her waist and turn her so she faced away from him. Coiling his arms around her chest, he brought her down to sit on his lap.

Their bodies lined up; he adjusted so his cock slid

up between her legs without entering her. Her unbelievably smooth thighs surrounded him. She leaned her head back and turned so he could kiss her. Their mouths were joined and he breathed her in.

And he swallowed her moans while he palmed her breast and thrust with his hips. His cock ground up and back along her pussy. She gripped his thigh with one hand and used the other to press his length harder along her.

He was wet from her, slipping back and forth. Her ass moved on his lap and lower belly. The back of her neck was salty with sweat, and he licked it up. She rasped a quick breath when he bit lightly into her shoulder.

Her moans grew louder when he reached around her and rolled one of her tight nipples between his fingers. She dug her fingernails into his thigh. He pinched her nipple harder, and she arched her back.

Their skin was so hot he didn't know where she ended and he began. Teeth clashed, mouths open. Their tongues teased and searched each other.

Between rushed breaths, she said, "I…need you… in me…"

He stood and brought her with him. Keeping one arm around her, he stretched to where his jacket hung on the chair and searched the inside pocket for a condom. Their bodies parted for only the shortest possible time when he put it on.

The urgency of her words still shot through him. He turned her away from him, and she understood, leaning down so her hands rested on the mattress. Moving behind her, he ran his hands down her ribs, around her waist. She arched her back, and he gripped her hips.

Because she was shorter than him, he coiled his body

lower, bending his legs so the tip of his cock could slick at her wet opening. Anticipation grew, and he savored the hunger. She hummed approval and tightened her fists in the bedsheets.

He entered her, warmth surrounding him. He eased deeper, she pushed back, taking him all the way in. Then she swiveled her ass, tight moves that pumped his cock back and forth within her and made bigger shock waves up through him.

The pace started to speed. Her moans rushed. He reached down between her legs and circled her clit with the tip of his finger. She bucked and slammed harder. He met her, thrusting as their voices joined.

She pulled the sheets off the mattress. Her legs shook. She tilted her head up and stared back at him, lips parted, eyes heavy-lidded. With an almost surprised gasp, she closed her eyes and leaned back, her body locked to his.

Her climax shuddered through her, and he supported her with her back to his chest. And when her legs felt like they were giving out, he helped her to the bed and sat on the edge next to her.

She smiled, breath rushing, and climbed onto his lap, facing him and twining her legs around his waist.

"You're...relentless." His own blood was rushing.

"I'm taking...what I want." She reached back and held his cock to guide it into her. She spoke through her teeth in his shoulder. "When I want."

The when was now. He knew that. Only a few moments. Safe and stolen.

Hayley lowered herself onto him. They coiled their arms around each other. He protected her, and she protected him. They clutched those rushing seconds tightly, contained within their circle.

She arched and he ground with her. Her breasts rubbed on his chest. Her breath heated his neck. Each of her moans moved him. He joined them with his, not caring if they shook the bed, the walls, the whole damn town.

Her rhythm sped; she widened her legs to take him deeper. He thrust harder when their bodies slammed together.

"Coming… I'm coming," she chopped out between breathy moans.

"Yes." He held her stronger, wanting to feel her climax all around him. "Yes."

"Come with me," she demanded. "I need you with me." She kissed his mouth and jaw and neck. "I need you with me."

"I'm yours," he answered, then ran out of words.

She called out and curled her arms tighter around him. He thrust up one last time and released himself completely with her. They both shook and shuddered, searched for breath and searched each other's body for places to hold.

They eased themselves down onto the bed. Their legs untangled and he pulled out from inside her, but they remained as close as possible. She rested her head on his arm, and he curled it around her back. They hoarded the heat of their bodies, keeping it between them and away from the deadly cold reality that was always just inches away.

FOURTEEN

THE THIN CURTAINS glowed white-hot. Hayley may have slept. Or just slipped into her mind as her body lay satisfied next to Art. She'd thought about the produce in her bags and what to do with it. The beautiful tomatoes. And Mary, the woman behind them with the sniper's eyes.

The room's atmosphere turned sere with the desert; Hayley pulled herself closer to Art. Their sweat ran between their skin, joining them. His breath was slow and steady, but he didn't sleep. His eyes were open and he'd look at her and smile for a moment before glancing about the space, the windows and door and corners where the walls met the ceiling. There was always a plan in him, a motion. Escape? Attack? She imagined he strategized for whatever might happen next. He knew that world, could anticipate it. Hopefully he was prepared, because all she could do was keep reminding herself not to let her guard down.

With Art, though, she was out of defenses. When she'd thought he was a crook, she'd had ammunition against the attraction that bound them together. Now that she knew his true purpose, she wasn't able to fight the connection. And she didn't want to. His caring went beyond the mission. Their need for each other was clear and hungry and devastating and deeper than she'd imagined.

That was what scared her. A fight to the death was

coming. Would he be hurt? Was he compromised because he had to protect her?

Art took a long breath, his body shifting the sheets and mattress around her, and got up from the bed. He returned with the remaining two sodas. Condensation dripped from the glass. They'd been sitting in front of the air conditioner, but that hadn't kept them very cold.

Still, she drank, welcoming the sweet liquid and the sight of Art, naked with the soda in his hand, in the bright sunlight.

He swallowed and thought and swallowed again. "Maybe that's why my mom doesn't keep these in the fridge at home."

"Why's that?" Her voice was hoarse, despite the drink.

"Reminds me of my dad." He spent more time looking at the glowing orange liquid than sipping it. "We lost him when I was young."

She caressed his back. "I'm sorry." He leaned into her touch, and she continued. "But I've got to think that any father would be proud of a son in the Marines, then working for secret operators protecting people."

He set the bottle down. "Not yet. He's not proud or at rest. Not until the job's done."

"I don't think you can know that." This was a darkness she hadn't seen in him. A deeper tension, and it frustrated her that she didn't understand how to soothe it.

"I do know. I'm the only one." Somber, serious eyes turned to her. "Those fucking mobsters have no idea I'm part of Automatik. That'll shock them good." He took a breath. "And they have no idea why I'm perfect for this job…"

She felt him searching, trying to find a way to say something.

His gaze remained on her face. "This mob. They killed my father. When they were establishing themselves in San Diego."

"Oh my God." That was how deep this ran. Straight through Art's heart and far into the past. She pulled herself closer to him.

"And when they find out *that*…" He seethed through a clenched jaw, "It'll scare them straight to hell."

She placed her hand on his fist and felt it loosen a trace. "Does this work?" she ventured, tentative. "Can you do this job if it's personal?"

A sly smile spread across his face. "I do it *because* it's personal. For my dad." His fist opened and enveloped her hand. "For you."

"But you barely know me." Not that she was trying to convince him to abandon his fight for her. She had to test their connection. Was it just the sex? The danger? Was it a meal that would be forgotten after dessert?

"And you barely know me," he countered. "But you still understand I'm not going to quit until you're safe. I'm not going to lose you, too."

"I'd never doubt you." The man before her was a constant, with a motor that never stopped turning.

"And I'll never doubt that you'll always be in the fight." He picked up her hand, looked at it, kissed it. "You were kicking ass long before you met me."

He didn't judge her or try to put her in her place. From the light in his eyes as he stared at her, her determination had a positive effect on him.

She leaned forward and kissed him. His lips were

sweet from the sticky soda. "We kick ass together." If they could just stay in the hotel room, leaving only to eat at the restaurant on the corner, fueling themselves for days and nights of sex on the creaking bed.

"Hell yeah." The hollow darkness in his voice told her that he wished for the same time and space.

The sound of power tools blasted up from the street outside the hotel. Concrete was broken by a jackhammer, and saws cut what sounded like miles of wood. The peace and calm between her and Art was shattered.

She laughed at the real world chiseling into their moment. Art's face, though, drew down to a serious expression. He stood and started collecting his clothes with quick urgency. She didn't wait for him to urge her to do the same and covered her naked body.

Tension chilled her. The power tools continued, rattling the window glass.

She stepped close to Art and asked under the din, "What's up?"

He had dressed and assembled all his weapons onto him, hiding them under his jacket. "I didn't see any work crews out there when we found the hotel."

For a second they sat next to each other on the bed again, tying their shoes. Was it all gone? All the comfort and security? She clutched the passion and the calm she'd shared with him deep, close to her heart.

He stood and took up some of the produce bags. She picked up the rest and joined him at the door. After listening through the wood to the hallway, he removed the chair under the knob and opened the door.

The hall looked empty. Art led, and she crept behind him, trying to expand her awareness to every possible angle of the closed doors, torn carpeting and rattling light fixtures. The construction continued and seemed to grow louder.

She and Art moved cautiously toward the stairway at the end of the hall. The sound of her rustling produce bags was enveloped by the shrieking saws and hammers outside. She struggled to keep her thoughts together as the chaos pounded in her ears.

A shadow knifed across the hallway, just where it joined with the stair landing. She froze. It was only ten feet away.

Art dropped his bag of produce. Instead of running away from whatever was out there, he sprinted toward it.

Two men rushed around the corner. Their hard, mean faces gaped with surprise when they saw how close Art was. Both men had pistols in their rough hands, one silver and the other black.

What should she do? Fleeing up the hall, back where she'd come from, seemed like a death trap. That would leave her exposed to the bullets. But could she run *toward* the men the way Art had? Then what?

Art didn't break stride. He attacked the closest man, chopping at his wrist and making the gun spin to the ground. The next man, who wore a crisp gray sweatshirt, swung his black pistol to aim at Art's chest.

She shouted, "No!" but the man didn't pay her any attention.

Before he could pull the trigger, Art had leaped away from the first man and was entangled with the man in the sweatshirt. Art locked his arm up under his, keeping the barrel of the gun away from him. But it swung across the hallway toward her.

Art glanced back at where she was and shifted his weight to slam the man into the wall. The gun stayed in his hand, but he grimaced in pain. With his free fist, the man punched Art in the ribs over and over.

She dropped her bags and started to run toward him. But the first man blocked her path. His squinting eyes glanced from her to his silver gun resting on the floor.

Behind him, Art smashed the other killer into the wall again, cracking the plaster. Releasing his grip on the man's arm a bit, Art took a step back and swung a wicked elbow into the man's temple. Blood immediately poured down the side of his head.

The man in the sweatshirt tried to yank his arm free and fired his pistol. The bullet dug a long gash down the hallway wall.

The sound was muffled by the construction sounds, but Hayley's killer jumped, startled, when the shot went off behind him. He hurried for his pistol, and Hayley dove toward it.

The man was faster. She was still on the ground when he snatched up his pistol and started turning it toward her. But he was close. She kicked up as hard as she could, catching him in the crotch with her shin.

He doubled over, dry heaving and clutching his groin. Before he could stand up, two shots blasted through the hallway and tore through his chest.

When he fell, Hayley could see Art behind him. He was locked up with the man in the sweatshirt, but had turned so he and the man both held his gun. The barrel smoked. Rage creased the man's face. Art's expression remained that of stone.

The man fought harder, and Art moved easily, letting the force carry the man off balance. As soon as Art had the advantage, he twisted the gun from the man's hand, turned it around and fired point-blank into his heart.

Art let the man's body drop to the ground then hurried to her, the gun in his grip.

She scurried backward in the hall, finding her footing and struggling not to peer at the twisted bodies that had just been living men. All she saw was Art kicking the gun away from her attacker's hand before she turned to stare at the pale yellow wall.

"Are you okay?" His voice was close. His body was close.

"You…" Her jaw shook and she didn't know if she could make words. "We have to stop…being in situations…where you ask me that."

"I'm sorry. I'm so sorry."

She trembled as she tore her eyes from the wall and tried to look at him. But his back was to her, his focus down the hallway where the men had come from. Fear gripped her again. It wasn't over.

New shadows moved like black vultures at the stairway landing. How many more killers were coming? Art had his pistol aimed in their direction.

A man's voice called out over the construction noise. "Detroit! Detroit!"

Art sighed relief and lowered his gun. A blond man hurried into the hallway, carrying a gun of his own. Behind him was Mary from the farmer's market. They both scanned quickly over the dead assassins and came to her and Art.

The man clarified in a quick burst to Art, "We were too many steps behind. Couldn't catch up without breaking our cover."

"I get it, Harper. I get it." Art handed over the pistol, then rubbed at his ribs, wincing.

Mary stepped between Hayley and the sight of the bodies. "You good?"

Hayley shook her head.

"But you're not hurt?" Mary gave her shoulder a comforting squeeze.

"No." Though if she was, she didn't think she'd know it for a long time because of all the fear and adrenaline jamming her senses.

Art still stood next to her, giving her a body to lean on. "The master chef is a warrior. Engaged her target. Took him out at the balls."

Mary smiled. "I knew I liked this girl for a reason." She put out her fist, and Hayley bumped it with her trembling hand.

Harper was thick with muscles but balanced like an athlete. He gave Art a pat on the chest. "You cooked, we'll clean."

"Thanks." Art remained remarkably steady.

Mary nodded to Hayley. "Get gone."

Art didn't move until Hayley did. She took a tentative step, testing her legs. She managed to stay upright and move in a somewhat straight line. Art was right with her but stopped to pick up a few of the produce bags.

"Are you kidding?" How could anything normal like cooking and eating ever happen again?

"We've got to make it look like nothing happened." He hefted the bags. "We came to town, we shopped, we ate, spent a little time, then left."

Her legs remained unsteady and she had no choice but to walk with him as he progressed up the hall. When she tried to lean down to pick up a bag, he stopped her.

"Leave that one." His hand was gentle on her forearm.

Then she saw the spattering of blood on the plastic and the green leaves. Her stomach turned. She fought back retching.

Art had her moving again, walking down the hall and not looking back at the bodies or Mary and Harper. The sound of construction stopped. Her ears rang.

As they walked down the creaking stairs, Art explained quietly. "It was Garin. He hired them."

"Who were they?" The men were dark and tanned, not like the Russian guards at the house.

"Local bad guys." Art was careful at each landing of the stairs, checking up and down. "He must've booked them when he was in town, told them to look out for us."

They reached the ground floor. The front desk was empty. There was no one in the lobby or in the street she could see through the glass doors.

"But Garin can't know how it played out. It'll just make it worse." Art got them to the doors and checked up and down the street. "And it'll make him think a little too hard about me, about who's helping me out here."

He pushed the door open and scanned the area. She could smell the concrete dust from the construction but didn't see any sign of them. Even the soda vendor was gone.

It was two blocks to the car. The longest two blocks in the world.

"I don't know…" She didn't trust anything. No car that passed or cloud in the sky. She and Art walked closer to the square. The people paid little attention to them, but she felt menace in everyone's eyes. "I don't know how I can pretend…"

His steady presence at her side kept her moving. Without pushing, he maintained a hand at the small of her back, guiding her toward the car. His touch was the only thing that grounded her. If she lost him, she would spin off into the grinding teeth of the carnivorous world all around her.

"Deep breath." How did he sound so steady?

"There's no air." Her lungs felt half the size as usual.

"Panic is the enemy now." Though he appeared calm, his gaze moved about the area, taking in all the angles.

"I'm not a soldier." Admitting this pushed the fear deeper into her. Two men had just tried to kill her and Art. He was trained for it. She wasn't.

"But you dance with fire and steel every day." When his eyes turned to her face, a kindness for her surfaced.

"Not like…" Her throat might completely close up any second.

"Deep breath." This time he gave her an example, drawing long through his nose, then out through his mouth.

Her attempt wheezed short.

"I'll bet—" with quick caution he checked around a corner, then led her up a street where she finally saw the SUV, "—you had to deal with some real monsters in the kitchen while you were coming up."

Her brain conjured the chef from her past, but could only nod her answer.

"What was his name?" He angled them both to the passenger side of the car. The keys were noiseless in his hand.

Struggling to relax enough to make her mouth and jaw work, she said, "Noonan."

Art opened the back hatch, and they piled the bags of produce in the SUV. He scanned over her shoulder, up to the roofs of the buildings, his awareness charged as he opened the passenger door for her. "I already hate him," he growled with a smirk.

Falling into the story helped find her breath. "I line-cooked for him when I was in LA for a couple of years."

"I didn't know you hit that city." He stepped aside so she could get in the seat, but stayed with her at the open door.

"Not for long. I wasn't a good fit. Too many ass-holes like Noonan." The time in LA had been rough and lonely. Everyone had an agenda, cannibals who would do anything to get what they wanted. "He'd insult everything we did. Take the knife out of your hand and do it himself. Splash boiling water from the pots at you if he didn't think you were moving fast enough."

"Son of a bitch." The muscles in Art's jaw twitched. "But you made it through that. You're still cooking."

"I'm a better cook than him. On my last night, when I knew I was out, I took this stupid recipe he had for duck breast with cherries and flipped it up. Roasted apricots. Candied rosemary. This crazy penne pasta risotto with the duck cracklings." She laughed, breath filling her again. "Just left it on the prep station and walked the fuck out."

"Badass." Art's grin was filled with admiration. His arms spanned from the open door to the car frame, blocking her from the world. "You've got this."

And a small part of herself had to believe him. She'd lived through Noonan. She'd lived through that hallway in the hotel. Her pulse slowed. The tunnel vision that had crowded, claustrophobic, around her widened.

She told Art, "I'm still cooking."

How fast? How far? He'd wanted to floor the SUV out of town. Tear up the desert and take Hayley as far away as possible. But the operation wasn't over. They had to return and finish the Orel Group for good.

The men in the hotel had probably never heard of the organization. They'd just taken the cash, listened to the descriptions of Art and Hayley and thought they had an easy gig. Now they were dead. He'd placed the bullets himself. But Art had the urge to double-check. Anyone who came after Hayley like that shouldn't get a second chance.

Harper and Mary would do a good job of the cleanup. Even if Harper was a Navy man. Mary's time in the service remained sealed and encrypted. Art suspected she was Delta but never asked and understood he'd never get a straight answer from an operator with that kind of background.

Hayley sat in the passenger seat with her knees drawn up to her chest. She'd shaken off some of the trauma of the assault, but he knew she'd be feeling it for quite a while. And there was no chance she'd ever forget.

After a few turns on the streets, they were out of town and back into the desert. Past the trucks. Past the power lines. They would be alone until they reached the house.

"Is there anything you won't cook?" He feared she'd wind herself into a ball and never be able to stretch out into the fierce, determined Hayley he knew.

"Octopus." Her answer came immediately. "They're too smart. Too cool." She stared out the window, still distant.

"But a lamb?" It was a risk to needle her too much.

That brought out a smile and a shake of her head. Slowly, she lowered her legs to the foot well. "They taste too damn good."

"How would you cook it for me?" He watched her come back, eyes focusing, mind turning.

"Sear it hard, roast it good. Garlic. A few sage leaves. Simple. Primal." She was breathing again, loosening. But a deep red shadow lurked in her. "Do you remember the first person you killed?"

"Of course." He'd warned her earlier that the car might be bugged. No part of these Russians could be trusted. But this information wouldn't give them anything they could use against him or Hayley. "In Afghanistan. On patrol in the mountains. Checking out what we thought might be a backdoor route for moving munitions. We got hit with an ambush and fought back. Man in my unit had his thigh torn up by four rounds. I got the guy who got him." It sounded simple, but she didn't need all the details of panic and shouting and blood. Or the sickening feeling deep in his guts and mind after the noise had quieted and he'd seen the body.

The first of a few. Two added that day.

He hadn't realized how cold he'd felt until her hand rested on his thigh. A mile or three sped by. Distance had helped memory. Her touch healed deeper. He placed his hand on hers, completing the charged loop between them. The world had just twisted before her eyes, showing new pits of darkness. Words had done what they could. Art gave her everything else he could with his skin on hers.

The bruises from the brief fight started to throb. His ribs tightened up. He welcomed the pain. It meant he was still alive and she was, too.

The gunmen had failed. Their blood money was in someone else's hands by now, unearned. Garin wasn't done paying. When the time was right, when the bullets were screaming death, Art was going to have his final say with Garin.

"I'm right here." Hayley shifted her hand beneath his, and he realized that he was gripping her too tightly.

He loosened his fingers over hers. "I've got to keep you here."

"You have been." Her hand turned over so she could hold his. "You will. I…" There was more, but she didn't say it. She looked about the SUV, wary. "I trust you."

A new fever flushed through him. A cleansing fire. No one had ever told him that. With Automatik, his closest friends now, it was always implicit. None of the top-level operators would enter into a dangerous situation unless they trusted one another. But to say it, to give it like a gift the way she did, was unknown.

He held the heat deep, not wanting to ever give it up. "That makes you…" Damn the words that couldn't say it all. "Everything."

She held his hand tight, and he gripped her. Miles passed. The sun started to set behind them. The road was rough and would only get rougher ahead. Late light knifed over the rocks, drawing their shadows out. Manmade right angles broke the desert in the distance. The cinder block wall around the house.

Hayley's hand curled tighter into his when she spotted it.

"What's for dinner?" They both had a job to do, and he knew how hers kept her calm.

"Chicken. Roasted, with onions." Her fingers moved as if plotting. "A salad with those tomatoes and some salt and vinegar."

"Can't wait." He made his own calculations. "I'll be under your feet repairing the propane lines."

Worry flashed across her eyes. "Be safe down there."

"Always." His voice sounded lighter than he felt. Once they were inside those walls, the smallest spark could set off the whole place.

Taking the car off the dirt track that made up the highway, he angled them back to the compound. Sunlight rusted behind them as it tried to push through the dust the SUV kicked up. Garin would know they were alive by then. He'd have to play it as cool as Art, neither admitting they knew what had gone down.

Hayley released Art's hand and crawled over the partition and into the back section. He wanted her next to him again. It would take all his training, all his focus, to get them through this op.

He pulled up to the gate. A guard walked around the car, peering inside as he and Hayley assumed their roles. All business. Cook and killer.

The guard nodded and motioned to someone inside the wall. The gate chattered open, and Art took his time driving through. The front of the house was lit by the sun, but the wall's shadow already covered the yard. A new car lurked in the darkness, fresh dust covering its white paint.

Another boss had arrived. The countdown spun faster.

He didn't know if Hayley had caught the change, but she definitely wasn't relaxed as she stepped out of the door he'd opened. They both retrieved the grocery bags from the back and carried them toward the house.

Rolan was on the front steps. Garin was there. If he'd been surprised by their return, he suppressed it, replaced with barely veiled menace.

Art murmured under his breath to Hayley. "We've got to go on vacation sometime."

"Fuck yeah." Her game face masked any fear. The woman was positively determined, rocking him with more admiration.

After greeting Rolan, Art followed her into the house and placed the produce on the island. Garin had remained outside, glaring at them until they were out of sight.

As soon as Hayley went to put the food away, Rolan appeared, motioning for Art to follow into the living room. He had to leave her. They had their jobs. Stepping away, he gave her a small wave. She returned a nod. Her defenses were up. If there was trouble, she would fight.

The other guards cleared out of the living room as Rolan and Art walked through.

"A good time in town?" Rolan asked in casual Russian but couldn't suppress a bit of leering interest.

"Very good, thanks." Art hated thanking him for

anything, or asking permission, but that was just part of the gig. For now.

"Glad to hear it." Rolan glanced in the direction of the kitchen. "Don't break her heart; there's still cooking to do and I don't want the meals to suffer."

"What if she breaks my heart?" he joked back, but knew he was further off balance than he'd ever been. She could wreck him if she really wanted to.

"We can't have that either." Rolan wagged a finger. "You have work to do. Yemelin has arrived. Florida and Texas. He'll need to hear what you have to say about southern borders."

Art nodded and held back from explaining that not all people south of the United States were the same nationality and couldn't be taken as a whole. "I always do my job."

"I know." Rolan stood, formal, his hands folded neatly just below his belt. He hid something. Was he in on Garin's plan to off Art and Hayley? Did he know about Automatik? From the purse of his lips, he reveled in whatever he knew and wasn't going to give it up quickly.

Rolan turned, pulling his secret around him like a cape, and left the living room.

Four bosses out of five were in the house. One more, and Art would call in the strike. Prep work remained to be completed. But they were close. Any day, any second, the bullets would start flying in the house. There were already two bodies behind him. Two dead men who'd made the mistake of trying for him and Hayley. How many would he have to stop before he knew Hayley was safe?

FIFTEEN

COOKING COULDN'T SAVE her life. She knew when murderers like the men in the hallway showed up, guns out, no one would care how well she folded her eggs for a soufflé. In the house, she was surrounded by the potential for violence. It was inevitable. Art's mission would set it off.

But if cooking couldn't save her life, it might save her sanity. Ingredients. Heat. Time. She focused on the chicken, coating the pieces in oil and herbs before getting them into the oven. The direct killing instructions from Mary swept into her mind as she chopped the tomatoes. Hayley tried to push that danger aside and concentrate on the bright red segments and their natural gloss. But Mary's eyes returned to her. They were kind, knowing. There was sympathy in them, because Mary knew that Hayley had seen real violence and death for the first time.

If only Hayley could've stopped the day when she and Art had been in the hotel room. Frozen time, so her world was filled with the good of their connection. The intensity of the sex had been driven even higher by their understanding of each other. And the search to learn. Could that kind of life and discovery survive all the brutality?

She tried to orbit around that memory. Art's body

and his passion for her. Even with all that and the food on her cutting board, the other parts of the day kept crashing back into her.

Dead bodies. Twisted and heavy. Art had been so quick and precise. But if he hadn't been...

Garin stalked past her kitchen. His leering gaze held extra hate and an edge like a scalpel. He was trying to pick her apart, discover how she'd survived. His brutality appeared barely restrained. Art had explained that the man had hired those men at the hotel. Was the next step Garin doing the job himself?

More bodies.

Garin moved past the room, but she still felt his anger radiating like a fresh burn from a hot oven grate. One whisper from him, one shout, could bring out the guns and the blood.

She put her knife down and leaned on the island, trying to fight her mind. The image of Art's body, dead, completely motionless, persisted. She knew it wasn't true. He was alive, more so than almost anyone she'd ever met. That energy kept him aware and moving. The rhythm of his body as he walked. The bright awareness in his eyes as he scanned a room. But what if all that was gone? What if she lost him?

Maybe he heard her mind screaming the question. Art rolled into her kitchen, calm as if the day had been spent at the market and in bed and not the deadly hallway. He gave her a quick wink and rummaged through her produce bags until he found what he'd bought at the hardware store.

With that in hand, he moved to her side, so they both

stood over the cutting board with the half-chopped tomatoes.

"You holding up?" He kept his voice low, brushing
the back of his hand along her hip.

"I'm a wreck." The fear in her mind shook her. Imagining he was dead, seeing him alive. It was all tearing
her apart.

"Understandable." He nodded. Quick fingers snatched
up a slice of tomato and popped it in his mouth. He
chewed for a moment, savoring. "From the outside, you
look rock steady. Give yourself credit, Master Chef.
You're doing great."

"Doesn't feel like it." She leaned harder into him.
Their voices were too quiet for anyone else in the house
to hear. If anyone was watching, which they were, it
would appear like just a small, intimate conversation.
"I don't know how long I can do this."

"It's a ton to process." He reached for another piece
of tomato, but she knocked his hand aside. "But you're
strong as hell. And harder than any of these fools who
need guns to prove something." His gaze bounced along
the edge of the kitchen and deeper into the house.

Then his body moved closer. She felt the rise and fall
of the breath in his chest. He placed his hands on her
shoulders and turned her to him. He was very alive. She
tried to take that energy and confidence into herself.

He kissed her cheek and whispered into her ear, "I
trust you, too."

When he stepped away, she saw the emotion in his
eyes. It had taken a lot for him to say it. The same as
when she'd told him in the car. But he didn't look away

or shrink, ashamed. He held her gaze. Linking them. Locking them together.

Her heart beat faster, proving she was alive. Life was very different with Art. She wanted more and more of it.

She reached up and tugged on the collar of his shirt, pulling him down for a long kiss. *Let them watch. Let them know that Art and I can't be defeated.*

The kiss slowly ended. Their bodies parted, but the shared energy remained. The fear wasn't gone, but it felt less potent, muscled down until it didn't shout as loud.

Art blinked slowly, his eyes lingering on her face. She took him in. Strong body. Stronger will.

He collected his things and stepped from the kitchen, one last glance back. The depth remained in his eyes. Beyond words. Beyond the kiss or what their bodies had shared. Further than she'd known with anyone else.

The events of the day hadn't changed, but she was able to see them from a greater distance. Art was out of the kitchen, and she resumed working on dinner. Yet she didn't feel alone.

ONE MORE BOSS would tip the balance. Like stepping on a land mine. Just enough extra pressure to set off the explosion. Art was almost ready. Each corner of the house had been laid out and conveyed to Jackson. He'd explained the plan. The two SEALs, Jackson and Harper, would come over the wall to the north. They could take care of the guards on that side of the house and cover for James Sant, the former SAS man, and Kip Raker, retired Green Beret, as they pierced from the west, blocking the gate and any exit. Mary would set up to the south with the fifty caliber so she wouldn't be shooting into the sun, no matter the time of day. The strategy was to have the propane lines and tank blow, taking out the south wall and side of the house so she had a clear shot at anyone making trouble for the assault team.

To get this piece of the tactic in place, Art now worked in the basement, "fixing" the propane lines with the explosive patches Automatik had stashed for him at the hardware store in town.

The oily paper wrapped around the pipe, then a long steel fitting was clamped around it and screwed down. Hidden along the hinge was a tiny primer attached to a Wi-Fi receptor. One signal from his phone and the charges would go up, igniting the propane in the line, then burn back to the tank and blow the whole damn thing.

Five men in the compound and a woman behind a fifty caliber should be enough for the house. A helicopter would be nice for air support, but it would take a while to get it in position after the shooting started. It could only be counted on for cleanup.

Art had messaged Jackson as soon as he'd had a moment to himself in his room after being in town, alerting the field man of the upped time frame. After the charges were set, he would inform the team. Then it was a waiting game. There might be time to prep improvised explosives around the house, but he'd have to be extra careful as not to arouse suspicion.

The one key gap in the plan that bit into him was Hayley. The kitchen was over the propane line and near the tank. She had to be cleared out when the assault began. But where? Preferably behind him, but there were no guarantees where he might be when everything got going. He was the point man and had to have eyes on the primary targets so the mission was a success.

He had to know where the guards were so his team would meet the least resistance.

Garin would be easy to find. He was always close. Sneering. Itching to fight. Things had almost gotten bloody before Art had left for town. Now that he was back, without a scratch from the hit men Garin had sent, things would get deadly.

Maybe even in this basement.

The stairs down creaked with Garin's heavy feet. The Russian stepped out of the light of the stairway, remaining in the shadows just at the edge of the basement. Art finished securing the first charge to the propane line, feeling the waves of hate from the guard.

Garin's gun was on his ankle. If Art saw the man start to reach, he'd have his own pistol out and two rounds into the son of a bitch's chest.

"Greasy worker," Garin spat in Russian. "Three hundred years." He pointed to himself with his thumb. "My family, unbroken for three hundred years."

"Thanks to the greasy workers." If Garin wanted fists, Art would pull his knife. If Garin had a knife, Art would shoot him. "What did your people ever do for themselves?"

Garin laughed like wheezing out poison gas. "I will do it. Then the good Russian girl will know what it's like to have a pureblood."

Art took a single step forward, and Garin fell to deadly silence. It would be over in a second. Both men knew how to kill. And they both knew that whichever one of them emerged from the basement alive wouldn't live long after the bosses learned what happened. Rolan had already fired a warning shot. Dissent like this wasn't tolerated. The next bullet would hit flesh.

"Finish it," Art goaded Garin. "Finish it."

Garin pointed at him. "You will be finished. In my hands." He started up the stairs backward. The light revealed his wild eyes. "You'll die knowing she is next in my hands."

Art took another step. Garin backpedaled quickly, then turned and hurried away. His hired killers hadn't worked, and now he was plotting and planning. Garin was too paranoid to just think the men had taken his money and not tried to fulfill the job. Art knew Garin would suspect bigger trouble. Art hoped the fifth boss would show up before Garin escalated his aggression.

It was tempting to chase the guard up the stairs and see what he was plotting, but Art had to set the second charge on the propane line. He returned to the work and quickly secured all the parts.

He ascended the stairs, knowing the assault was cocked and ready. He would call it in, then set off the explosion. After that, it didn't matter what the hell Garin suspected. Art would be free to stop him from ever getting what he wanted.

Tension buzzed on the first floor. The guards held their guns tighter and balanced on a finer edge. They all peered above the wide stairs to the second floor, where Garin talked to Rolan and Dernov.

What the fuck was he doing?

The bosses weren't reaching for their guns, but they did seem to nod in agreement. Garin disappeared before Art could get to the second floor.

Rolan shot him a warning glance.

"Anything I should know?" Art asked, trying not to sound too concerned about what was going on.

Rolan spun his finger in the air. "We're collecting all the phones. Safety precaution."

Bullshit. Art knew there was only one phone Garin was interested in. But his general paranoia was enough to convince the bosses to tighten security.

"Makes sense," Art replied calmly, while inside he was churning. How the hell was he going to call in an assault to a team that may or may not be fully assembled around the compound?

Garin returned, all business, shaking an open canvas drawstring bag, like something he kept his slim shoes in. "You first, *denga*." The guard couldn't disguise an ugly smug smile.

Art pulled out his phone, powered it down and put it in the sack. "Now you."

Garin paused but caught the eyes of Rolan and Dernov on him. He pulled his phone from his slacks and placed it in the bag, shooting venom through his eyes at Art the whole time. The two bosses appeared satisfied and walked off to the stairs for the third floor.

At the top landing, Rolan called down to Art, "Help him collect."

Art chuckled quietly, and Garin seethed. They stood at least five feet apart as they moved about the house, gathering the phones from all the guards. Vasily stared at both of them with dead eyes when Garin explained what they were doing. For a minute it looked like he was willing to go down shooting before giving up his phone. Art kept silent, and Garin spewed garbage about it being just a formality and there was no reception out there anyway.

Vasily finally conceded, placing his phone at the top of the pile with careful precision. Art suspected the quiet guard had a memory card full of bizarre porn loaded into the device. The trip just got a whole lot longer for Vasily.

But for Art, the complications knotted tighter. Any attempts to signal Jackson or the team would have to be physical now. That meant risking getting caught. He'd have to go dark until the very moment Automatik could come knocking. But how would he pull that trigger? And would they be ready?

HER FRIENDS THOUGHT she was cooking for yuppies. Snacks for golf and dinners for wine tastings. Hayley had learned to work in that world long ago. She didn't even wince anymore when she saw ice in a glass of pinot grigio. And now she didn't look twice when a man with a submachine gun walked by her kitchen on his way to the dining room.

She was part of it now. No longer on the outside peeking in. And she was tuned enough to know that the stress had tightened in the past few hours. She'd seen Art and Garin collecting the phones but didn't know what had precipitated the new caution. Maybe the eminent arrival of the fifth boss. Who wasn't just another mouth to feed. He would escalate Art's mission, then she'd truly learn how much she fit into this world.

The chicken and onions came out of the oven and rested for a bit as she put the finishing touches on the tomato salad. Men started to collect in the dining room and would slow as they passed her kitchen so they could breathe in the aromas. Vasily's eyes remained emotionless, but he nodded his approval to her.

Even Garin appeared to appreciate the smells, but that didn't stop him from oozing his sticky gaze over her. Art was outside the kitchen almost immediately after him, ramping the friction even higher. Both of them were poised to attack at any second.

The arrival of Rolan and Dernov brought an unsteady truce, but she knew it was only for show. Under the surface of deference to the bosses, the men were ready to kill.

"You nailed it again." Art hovered by her island, looking at the chicken while she plated it.

"The onions were fresh from today's market. Beautiful." She dished salad onto plates and let Art stack them on a large tray. "They didn't even make me cry when I cut them."

Art checked the tray's balance. "If they did, I'd smash them."

"Oh, Art," she swooned, continuing to move chicken from baking trays to plates, "you're everything a girl could ever want."

He smiled, and his chest and shoulders moved with a silent laugh.

A burst of quick pops exploded outside.

Fireworks?

Art had his gun out, and she hadn't even seen him draw it. It was the assault. His team was firing at the house.

"Is this…?" She stared at him, wondering what to do as she fought the panic back.

He shook his head and pointed at the ground. "Get down."

She huddled at the base of the island and heard the men's thundering footsteps throughout the house. Shots crackled outside. Glass broke upstairs. Angry shouts could be heard between the bullets. Two cars revved high and ripped through the dirt somewhere on the other side of the wall.

"Over here." Art crouched down and helped her to the face of the island farthest from the gunfire. Then he sprang up and hit the switches, killing the lights in the kitchen.

Other guns joined in the deadly chorus outside, these higher-pitched. The exchange lasted for a few of her rapid heartbeats, then the bigger guns fell silent and the cars tore away.

Now it was the Russians' turn to shout. They argued something, many of the men bunched in the front foyer.

Art informed her, "They want to go after them, but it's a bad idea."

"Who them?" If it wasn't his team, then why would anyone else be attacking the house?

"Stay here. Stay down." He was immediately up on his feet and hurrying away.

A few lights remained on in the house, and she saw him sprinting up the stairs. She was exposed and vulnerable without him next to her, and crouched tighter to the base of the island. Was this how the fight started? Was this the start of the war she'd been thrown into?

THE FIRST SHOT made Art think his team had started the assault without him. Now that communication was cut off, things could escalate very quickly. The second bullet in the spray told him Automatik wasn't launching the attack. They wouldn't fire until they'd made it within the walls, when the targets were close and identified.

Whoever was out there was just trying to send a message. Luckily, Hayley had been insulated in the kitchen on the ground floor. Though that didn't make it particularly easy for him to leave her there to investigate what the hell was going on.

He made it to the third floor, killing the lights along the way, in time to see the cars bouncing west along the desert. Broken glass crunched under his boots when he stepped closer to the windows. This was their only damage. No one had been up on this floor during the attack. If any of the bosses had been tagged, his strategy, and the entire operation could've been wrecked. The whole meeting might've been called off.

Downstairs, the men made the right decision to not pursue the attackers. Outside the walls was the other men's territory. The Russians would be wiped out. Classic guerilla tactic. A brief assault to draw out the enemy, then pick them off at your leisure.

He didn't think the men in the cars even knew who they were shooting at. They must've been tied to the hit men at the hotel. Mary and Harper would've made those bodies disappear, but that didn't mean the guys weren't missed. And if two killers from an organization went missing, any gang would definitely suspect the mysterious new compound out in the middle of the desert.

But the gang didn't trade bodies for bodies. Word was relayed through the house that the guards at the gate and wall weren't hit. The locals would have to be satisfied with rattling the nerves of the house.

"Who?" Rolan came up the stairs, in a crouch, his pistol out.

Art holstered his own. The cars disappeared into the darkness of the desert. "Looks like a gang from town."

The boss moved closer to the window, then stepped back when his shoes hit the chips of glass. "What did you do out there?"

"Nothing they'd care about." Fucking Garin was bringing this all on, but Art couldn't prove anything and needed to keep things tight for now. "We were there for privacy." And the world would be a better place if everyone left him and Hayley alone.

"So what would provoke this?" Rolan put his gun away and traced the trajectory of the bullets from the holes in the windows to the ones in the ceiling.

"This is their territory." He wondered if Rolan or anyone in the Orel Group remembered when they'd killed his father off on his own street. "You know how it is."

"I do." The light from downstairs illuminated a cryptic look in his eyes. "It's a good thing, when the bullets started, that you didn't have to choose between her and me."

There was no choice at all. Hayley was worth saving.

He blew off Rolan's concern. "Nothing to worry about like that out here."

The boss took a long, pointed gaze at a trench dug by a bullet into the drywall above their heads.

Art shrugged. "Stay off the ceilings."

Rolan cracked a smile, laughed once as a concession.

But he held something back, unsaid and reserved until it would have maximum impact. "Now let's see if we can pick the bullets out of our dinner."

The secret unnerved Art. The boss had some kind of ammunition, but what would its impact be?

With his fine hand, Rolan motioned for Art to take the stairs down. He followed the direction, aware that the back of his head would be a perfect target if Rolan wanted to take him out. Every creak of shoe on step was noted, the rustle of clothes as the silver-haired man descended behind him. Any variance in the patterns, and Art's operation would take a quick turn.

But they made it to the bottom of the stairs, and to the kitchen, where the lights were just coming back on. Pale and shaken, Haley stood near her food, glancing at the massing guards warily.

Rolan glided into the dining room, and Art went to Hayley.

"Everything okay?" Her voice was tight.

"Yeah." He went to the tray full of prepped plates. "Dinner still hot?"

"You can't want to eat." She blinked from him to the food, disbelieving.

"Getting shot at always makes me hungry." He lifted the tray. "Can I take these?"

She checked them over quickly, testing temperature with her finger. "They're not piping hot, but if I put them back in, they'll dry out."

"Extenuating circumstances. These goons'll understand." Many of the men remained edgy, but most of them followed him and the food into the dining room.

The plates were dispersed onto the table, and Art returned to the kitchen with the empty tray.

Hayley was ready with additional plates.

They arranged them on the tray and he stood close and explained low, "AK-47 has a very distinctive sound. We don't use them."

She discreetly nodded her understanding. "How will I know?"

His appetite waned. The muscles between his shoulder blades knotted. "I have no idea yet."

He carried the food to the dining room, knowing that any sense of security the guards had developed had been shattered by the brief attack. Fingers tensed, closer to triggers. His latitude to operate had been dialed down to a narrow trench, and his communication had been cut off. It might be him versus the world in order to get Hayley out of this house.

How could they want food? Her nerves jumped with every sound, waiting for another round of gunfire. But there they were, two tables full of men. All of them armed. Art sat with the guards, who all waited as she addressed the bosses.

Four of them. Only one more seat remained empty. The latest one to arrive was very tan, younger than the others. He wore a blazer over a T-shirt, and his hair was brushed forward into high, tight bangs. This man smiled politely, though somewhat bored, while she described the dinner and Art translated.

"Roast chicken with onions fresh from the market today." Was that just today? The market. Mary. The hotel room. Art. The hotel hallway. The dead killers. "The tomatoes are from there, as well."

"Very nice," Rolan complimented, and Art translated. The other bosses, except Dernov, nodded. He just scowled as usual.

She started to leave but stopped. "I'm sorry if it's gone a little cold. As you know, there were some…distractions."

A few of the men snuffled laughs. Others looked like they wanted to pull their guns.

"If any of you would like, I'll reheat your dish." But she hoped that no one would take her up on that and she'd have a few minutes to herself in the kitchen. She hadn't found a way to get her screaming blood pressure down.

The men all dug in and seemed happy enough with the temperature of their food. She and Art shared a quick glance, reassurance that their link continued, then she stepped quietly from the dining room.

Cleaning up calmed her hands. Taking greasy pans and bringing them back to the shining stainless steel gave her a sense of control. Uncomplicated. Distant from the guns and death.

After dinner, Art returned with a tray full of dirty dishes. He eyed the stack of clean pots and pans. "You didn't leave anything for me."

"You get the plates." She took a step back from the sink, giving him room.

"And then dessert?" He attacked the dishes without hesitation.

"If you do a good job." She wanted to touch him and

feel his motion as he went about his task. But she didn't think that she'd ever let go.

"You know I do." He turned and winked, brash.

She rolled her eyes and went to the pantry in search of something for dessert. "I've discovered that as soon as you think you've got something under control, you lose it."

The water ran. He turned to her. "I won't make that mistake."

"Good."

Tacit promises for their future hung on a knife's edge. She wanted to believe it could all be true. She knew bad things were coming.

He returned to the dishes, and she put together a simple dessert of chopped apples with honey and pistachios. Once the cleanup was complete, they turned off most of the lights in the kitchen and leaned on the counter to eat.

The main contingent of guards had cleared off the first floor, leaving a corner of peace for their silence and dessert.

But she couldn't slip into any calm. The tension hummed in Art. She felt it as their bodies were close, eating, then collecting the last two bowls to clean. When things were good, they were tuned for pleasure. She understood how he moved, and he'd shown that he could find whatever she needed on her body. Now, though, he remained tense. A slight flex in his muscles. Not locked up, but cocked and ready.

The night had quieted, velvet thick. Voices and footsteps drifted down from the second and third floors.

Art tilted his head, listening, and scanned the immediate area around the kitchen.

"I want you to have this." He reached to his back pocket and retrieved a short knife in a sheath.

"I'm surrounded by knives." Could she use any of them to hurt someone?

The stout black blade slipped silently from the sheath. The handle formed a T behind it, and Art gripped it into his fist so the blade extended from near his knuckles.

"It's called a push dagger." The weapon and the man were deadly. "You hold it like this, and it'll never slip."

He sheathed it and handed it to her. The knife felt like a heavy, poisonous scorpion that he'd somehow soothed to sleep.

"Keep it with you," he said. "Under your chef's coat. Under your pillow."

She didn't have to ask if he was serious. She knew his world now.

"That way—" his voice was deep and held back emotion, "—I can be with you even when I'm not with you."

He started tenderly unbuttoning her coat. Her breath slowed, and heat blazed up from deep in her. Running his hands along the lapels of the coat, he peeled it open. She arched forward, seeking a touch, a kiss, anything that proved there was life beyond the violence. Art was alive. Holding her coat, he pulled her to him. One kiss told her how much he wanted, how much more there was for them to discover. Then he had to step away, resuming his ready diligence.

"If only," she whispered.

"If only," he answered, then helped her clip the knife sheath to her belt.

SIXTEEN

HAYLEY DRESSED FOR bed after her shower while still in the steamy, locked bathroom. Half a hallway down was her door. One lock to another. It had to be quick. Wearing sweatpants made her feel too vulnerable, even if she had the new knife tucked in the roll of her dirty clothes.

Dry air prickled on her skin as she stepped into the hallway. The heat from the shower mixed with exhaustion, urging her toward her bed. Any other time she'd savor the heavy pull of sleep and relaxation. In the house, she couldn't let down her guard.

And there was one of the biggest reasons, leaning on the wall next to her bedroom door. Garin had his large arms folded across his chest and a disappointed frown on his face.

As she came closer, any traces of calm from the shower were lost in the tightening of her nerves. She reached into her bundle of clothes and coiled her fist around the handle of the knife Art had given her.

Garin straightened himself with her approach, stepping away from the wall and lowering his hands to his sides. She tried to keep track of all his moving pieces. If he attacked, where would it come from?

He started with words. She could pick out the meaning in only a few of the hissed-out statements, but she understood the angry and disappointed tone.

"…high…low…bad…" His eyes were in constant motion, looking at her, up the hallway, the ceiling and floor. He kept his voice down, obviously concerned about being detected.

She didn't think he'd care about Art knowing. It seemed like the kind of conflict he'd invite. But the bosses could come down on him very hard.

His words hit a desperate pitch and he took a step toward her, hands out and palms up. She moved back, ready to draw the knife. The leering monster had the audacity to look hurt as she pulled away.

He implored and explained in long Russian sentences she didn't understand.

She replied calmly. *"Nyet."* It hadn't worked with him in the past, but it was all she had. *"Nyet."* And she tried to remain steady and keep things from escalating by even adding "please."

"Nyet, pozhaluysta."

But it only made him press his case harder. And his anger started to show through, brighter than the dim lights at the ends of the hallway. His chest swelled and his hands curled.

They moved in unison, him forward and her back. She shook her head, leaving no room for discussion.

He wasn't convinced and pleaded more rapidly, almost letting his voice get loud enough to escape the hallway. One hand made a fist.

He took another step and she drew the knife. The large man gaped, shocked. His gaze snapped between the knife and her face, unable to put the two together. She knew he carried a knife, had seen it open when he fought Art. But where did he carry it, and how quickly would he draw it? She clenched her jaw to keep her teeth from chattering. He had cornered her, and she was ready to fight like hell if she had to. The balance in the hallway shifted and buckled. If Garin pressed, things would get bloody.

It was then that she saw the shadowy figure over Garin's shoulder at the far end of the hallway. Art was coiled, half crouched and ready to attack. His eyes shone like a predator.

Any closer and he'd be in the light, easy to detect. But she'd seen these fights start in the blink of an eye. He wouldn't reach Garin in time to prevent her from having to defend herself.

She prepared, trying to take on the ease she'd seen in Art when he battled. His movements had been fluid, adapting to what was happening around him. But he was trained for it.

Seconds stretched like steel cables. Garin hesitated, as if running through scenarios while his body waited for orders. She kept the knife high, in view. Just like throwing a punch, she thought. She was ready to slash out, again and again, and prayed that no pain would come her way.

Maybe Garin sensed her determination. Bullying a woman was easy when she couldn't fight back. Hitting him with the spoon in the kitchen had only fueled his rage. This time she had an edge.

The large man muttered again, sentences dripping with bitterness and disappointment. He shook his fist slowly and turned his scowl from her as if he couldn't stand to see her face.

The air felt less combustible when he stepped around

her, not bothering to even glance back and continuing to mutter. She knew better than to let her guard down. If he didn't come rushing back then, he would tomorrow, or the next night.

She hurried to her room, and Art was by her side by the time she was throwing the door open. He closed and locked it behind them.

Tremors shook her legs and she paced to release the energy.

"The knife." Art held up his own fist as an example.

It took effort to line up her shaking hand with the sheath, then she pushed the blade in and hid its deadly edge. She tossed her roll of clothes onto the bed and continued to walk in the narrow space between the wall and the door.

"You handled it," Art whispered, even and soft.

"It helped seeing you there." Every step through this ordeal, Art had been close.

His carnivorous grin flashed. "It's good to have friends in dark places."

She flexed her hand. It wanted to grip a tight fist, even though the knife was put away. "I'm in there now, in the darkness." Her pace slowed, legs growing steady.

"Not completely." He stayed by the small table in the corner, allowing her room to walk. "We're going to keep you out."

"By giving me a knife?" She stopped, facing him. Yes, he'd been there all along. Because he was the reason she was among the killers.

"I..." He rubbed his shaved head, frustrated. "I can't just leave you defenseless. But there's more. There's so much worse..."

She knew he'd seen it.

He remained on his side of the room. "I would've finished Garin if he'd come a step closer. I can do that. I've done it. You don't have to."

"I might." Garin had been a heartbeat away from her, his eyes wild.

"Not while I'm alive."

He'd made that promise before. The death she'd seen, at his hands, revealed what it meant. How far he'd go. How dark. Into the shadows that she could never see into.

And then she might lose him forever.

Art left her room quietly, the door clicked in a whisper behind him. She locked it and watched the shadows of his steps under the door as he disappeared.

THE GUN WAS in his hand. He'd unloaded it, checked the action, loaded it and now waited. Art perched at the edge of his bed, feeling like he was about to leap into the void. Usually, on this mission, this was where he'd be relaying the day's intel to Jackson. But contact was dead. Only Garin and Dernov had the combination to the safe. Art had a pretty good idea that Mary, with her shady training, could spring the lock, but that wasn't even close to a possibility.

It might be satisfying to get the combination out of Garin. Especially after the way he'd cornered Hayley in the hallway. The psycho had been babbling about how her family would benefit from a pureblood like him, and Art's bad lineage would just pollute her. Maybe his hired killers were only supposed to off Art at the hotel. He didn't want to think about what plans they had for her. Snapping Garin's neck while he was focused on

Hayley outside her door would've been easy, but his disappearance would've made a lot of waves.

As soon as the fifth boss arrived, all safeties would be clicked off. The house would be a free-fire zone, and if Garin got in the way of the mission, so be it.

But there was no way to know when that would happen. He still hadn't worked out a signal. Simple gunfire wouldn't bring in Automatik. The situation was so volatile that the crack of bullets would be as normal as the crack of eggs. The bursts of AK fire from the local heavies didn't trigger the assault. Art needed something big.

The largest bang he could make was the propane tank. Without the phone as an electronic trigger, he'd have to do it the blue-collar way: a well-placed bullet on the charge around the pipe. Which positioned him somewhere in the basement, not the safest place during the blast. And it meant he wouldn't have eyes on Hayley, unless she was down there in danger of getting blown up with him.

She'd have to be somewhere other than the kitchen. At least half of it would go up with the tank. That was her safest zone, though. Taking her to another part of the compound put her in greater danger.

His mind spun and his grip tightened on the pistol. All the moving pieces of this speeding clock had sharp edges. It didn't seem like there was any way to time them so blood wasn't spilled.

BURTON DIDN'T PLAY tennis, but in her dream he stood holding a racket and wearing all-white gear on a green-painted court. He complained that she was late and fucked up their chances of taking the cup. His face was red and distorted as he shouted, spitting. The bright sunlight made her head spin. She tried to shade her eyes but couldn't move her hands.

A gunshot blasted, loud, and a bullet snapped Burton's racket in half. He didn't stop shouting. Art stalked onto the court, shirtless, his scars and tattoos vivid. The push dagger glinted in his fist.

She shouted, *"Nyet!"*

Art punched Burton in the stomach, completely burying the knife. Blood covered his arm.

He dragged his fist from the now-pale Burton and turned to her.

Hayley woke up kicking the covers off her legs, ready to run.

The high window was dark, hours before dawn. She tried to slow her pulse, taking long breaths and sitting up. Each time she blinked, she saw the bright green court and red blood.

A splash of cold water on her face would help bring back the real world, but unlocking the door felt like a very bad idea. The real world wasn't much better than the terrible dream.

Art was better than that, and even though this version had been generated by her subconscious, she felt guilty at the way she'd depicted him. She did trust him and knew he wasn't just a killer. The constant danger ground her down, confusing everything.

She ran her fingers through her hair several times, trying to soothe herself. After a few strokes, she lay back in the bed and tried to find her way past the dream and back to sleep.

Early light woke her. Sleep without rest. She dressed, clipping the knife to her belt just behind her right hip before putting on her chef's coat.

Unlocking the door, she let it fall open quietly. Most of the house except the night shift of guards remained asleep.

Not Art. He sat on the bottom of the service stairs, where they'd had their first kiss. There were dark rings under his emotionless eyes.

"I had a rough night, too." He managed a wry smile.

"I'll make extra coffee." First she hit the bathroom for her morning routine and finally splashed cold water on her face.

Art was standing when she emerged, and the two of them walked into the kitchen. The first coffee was just for them. She couldn't tell him the dream. He was reserved, as well. The discomfort edged into her. They'd found a connection and now it was strained thin as a champagne glass.

"I want…" He searched. "I want to take you out to dinner. In San Diego."

The meaning was clear. Once this was over. If they survived.

She stepped closer to him. "I want that, too."

"Or would that be too much like work for you, being in a restaurant?" he asked with concern.

"Depends on where I go. There are a few places that work good for me." And it would be a pleasure to share them with him.

"I'll let you pick." Some of the natural rhythmic sways returned to his movement.

She nodded. "You drive. But I sit in the front."

He clinked his mug of coffee with hers. Weariness

etched on his face, little lines dragging down the corners of his mouth and his eyes. Somehow he pushed through, maintaining his energy and awareness.

"The goons will be coming in soon." He refilled his mug, moving his focus from the back door to the open edge of the kitchen.

Breakfast had been prepped the night before. She was ready. "This is the easy part." Drawing on deep reserves of energy, and the caffeine, she tried to will herself awake.

He looked her up and down. Bits of heat gathered across her skin, as if he was touching her with just the tips of his fingers. "You packin'?" he asked intimately.

The heat waned. But enough remained to make her wish they were a thousand miles away from this house, alone in another hotel room. Maybe high in a city, with the curtains open so they could watch the people from a distance.

She brushed her palm along her back where the knife was.

"Don't pat it," he instructed gently. "Lets them know where you stashed it." He swirled the coffee in his mug. "Give me a turn."

She hesitated. Fully clothed, and still she felt exposed. She hadn't opened herself up to that kind of scrutiny from a man. But it was Art, and the trust remained. She lifted her arms slightly and took a slow turn.

When she returned to her view of Art, he was nodding appreciatively. "Good." He was all business. "I can't see it." Then a different light crept into his eyes. He murmured, "You do that for me again sometime? Maybe naked, or just in bra and panties."

The thrill of exposing herself to him like that shot through her. "Only if you'll soap me up and shampoo me in a long shower."

A few days under pressure with Art had felt like years of peeling away his layers and revealing her own. He seemed like a man who could belong in her life. But was that just because of the danger? What about after? Would their bond continue?

"Woman." He tilted his head back slowly, reeling. "You're the best."

They both snapped to attention when the first wave of guards started shuffling to the kitchen. The men gathered their breakfasts, and Hayley kept the coffee-pots and food supplies full. Art helped silently. The guards talked to each other, but none of them engaged him. The attack last night highlighted the friction. Art was on the outside. She was neutral to them. The cook.

The edge in the room suddenly hummed sharp. Men reached for their guns, resting their hands on the grips. Art remained poised, his attention toward the front of the house. A car arrived. The gate squeaked and tires crunched the dirt. Guards left their breakfasts half-eaten and strode out.

After a moment, the men appeared to take a collective breath. Martha walked down the service hallway toward the kitchen and slowed when she saw all the attention on her. She stashed her purse in a cupboard in the kitchen and set about cleaning and organizing the counters.

Hayley and Martha and Art exchanged a brief *"Buenos días,"* then fell back to silence.

The bosses arrived for their breakfasts, Rolan leading the way. Dernov was rumpled and angry-looking, as usual. The young, tan boss was the kind of guy who was used to going to bed at this early hour and was bleary-eyed.

Martha worked her way out of the crowded space, taking cleaning supplies into the other parts of the house. At least she could be where no one else was, partially separated from the ongoing stress in the house.

Murmured talk toward the front of the house skipped back to the kitchen, perking up the bosses and drawing them away. The guards went with them.

She shared a quick look with Art, asking what was going on.

"Hang tight," he told her through a tight mouth, then trailed after the group.

Tight was the perfect word. What was coming next? She'd learned to mistrust innocent construction sounds. Every corner could hide someone who wanted to kill her. Anything could trigger an explosion.

She resisted the urge to tap the knife on her belt. It was there. She'd clipped it on earlier, and nothing had changed that. And if she needed, there were other knives nearby. Once, they'd been only for cooking, but she saw their other potential and would use them to stay alive if she had to.

The voices grew louder at the front of the house. She walked to the edge of the kitchen but couldn't see. The tone was genial enough, but she knew better than to rely on that.

Art stalked back toward the kitchen, his face unreadable. Other guards started to filter around in the space behind him, occupied with tasks.

"The final boss," he said as soon as he was close enough to murmur.

"Five?" She tried to keep her voice down.

He answered with a clipped nod.

Here came the explosion. She expected every window in the house to crash in with black-clad commando while a roaring helicopter hovered overhead.

Nothing.

"What now?" The whole building was supposed to snap as soon as the last boss showed up.

"You have another guest at the table." Art's grim face didn't reveal everything he was thinking. "We do our jobs."

It didn't make sense. He'd explained most of the mission, and she thought she understood. Why the delay? Was there a problem? Was it all called off? She couldn't ask everything she wanted to know while vulnerable in the house.

All she could hold on to was Art's cryptic, "I'm doing my job," spoken as he walked out of the kitchen and into the activity.

BAD TIMING. All the guards were awake. The night shift remained stationed around the house and front gate, waiting for their relief to finish their breakfasts. Everyone turned out for the fifth boss's arrival.

Art was once again drafted into bellboy duty. He hefted the bags while Rolan and the other top leaders greeted Krylov, the biggest man in the northeast. Krylov's driver/bodyguard looked like he spent twenty-seven hours a day in the gym, lifting every weight at once. A fully zipped tracksuit struggled to surround his thick neck.

The guard didn't even peek at Art, but shook hands

and gave back-thumping hugs to other guys while catching up on whatever bullshit was flying. It was good for Art to fly under the radar.

Until he could pull the trigger.

After the night shift was asleep. After Martha was out of the compound. He couldn't track two noncombatants and assure their safety. It would be hours until he could set off the assault, hoping the other members of Automatik would show up to the shooting party.

Art remained invisible throughout the trek to the third floor to deposit Krylov's bags. The boss's shoes were perfectly polished, just like his manicure. His hair was slicked back, dyed black. His dark mustache stretched out as wrinkles formed in the corners of his eyes. He was free with his smile for the men around him, as long as they brought the admiration.

Krylov's man, who Art heard someone call Stepan, asked about Art as he left Krylov's room after placing the bags at the foot of the bed. Other guards filled him in. Of course Garin added, *"Denga,"* while slicing at Art with his eyes.

Stepan nodded his understanding, squinting down his broken nose at Art.

There was no sense in going at the gorilla. Even if he took him out, proved his strength, it would never rank him with the others. He was as close as he needed to be.

The procession headed back downstairs. Art spotted Martha moving into the voids left behind by the men, staying clear of the activity. She'd be almost impossible to track.

If only there was a way to get Hayley out with her. But there was too much scrutiny now. The phones had been collected and security tightened since the brief assault from the locals. There was no room for variation in the routine.

In the kitchen, where Krylov and Stepan dug into as much food as their paws could gather, the talk started up again. Hayley was explained as if she was a display behind glass. Art knew she didn't understand all the Russian but would get the meaning. She kept her face politely neutral, not giving up her power as chef.

Rolan even went out of his way to compliment her food. Art did translate that for her, and she gave the boss a small appreciative bow.

Both Krylov and Stepan hammered Art with harder looks when he chimed in.

"He speaks Russian?" Krylov asked in his native language.

Art replied in Russian, "And Spanish and English when I need to."

Rolan explained Art's assets to the new boss, while Garin stood in the back of the group, clenching his jaw. Krylov tipped his head back and forth, considering if he should be impressed. Stepan wasn't and spent most of his time flexing his traps.

As soon as Krylov continued his tour with the other bosses, the talk among the guards rose up. Art and Hayley's relationship was poorly and sometimes lewdly summarized while Stepan's expression dropped to disappointment. Garin's anger rose, the veins on his forehead showing. Vasily remained stoic, though shifting his squinted eyes from person to person.

Art was even further on the outside, and now Hayley was with him. They were both expendable after this week was done. Hopefully not sooner.

The guards filtered out to follow the bosses or to take their positions throughout the house. He wasn't alone with Hayley and wouldn't be until the operation was over, but had to communicate how things were shaking down.

He leaned an elbow on the island and tried to sound as casual as possible. "You'll need to make five extra desserts for after Martha leaves."

"Artem." Rolan's voice called to him from the front of the house. The boss continued in Russian, "You're needed to speak."

Art straightened but stayed with Hayley.

"Desserts…?" She caught up quickly, processing with a quiver in her lips and nervous eyes glancing past him to the rest of the house. "I can make enough for more people. I'll be ready."

"Good." He hoped Automatik was also ready. "I love your desserts."

Rolan walked toward the kitchen, becoming insistent. "Artem, you must explain to them what you told me about last night's attack."

"It's good." Art gave her a wink, staying loose. "Just a little business."

She half smiled, but the worry tugged her mouth back down. "I can't wait for dessert."

"Me, too." He left the kitchen, heading toward Rolan and the other bosses. Training and planning would only get an operator so far. Once the first bullet left the chamber, life became death.

SEVENTEEN

SHE RELIED ON what had gotten her here to help get her through it. After cleaning up the breakfast service, Hayley turned to the ritual of the pelmeni. The process of making the dough, the filling and the broth took every surface of the kitchen and nearly every pot and pan. The space was hers. No matter which guard or boss came by to watch or smell the cooking aromas, none of them ventured closer than the far side of the island.

Even Art maintained a respectful distance. His presence was always felt, and no matter which stage of the cooking she was in, she would always look up when he walked by to check in on her. They shared flashing glances. Anything longer would become too agonizing. She wanted time with him in a safe place. But that wasn't possible until the day was over. And how horrific was that going to be?

He'd given her the message earlier. Nothing would happen until Martha was out of the house. Then the rest of his team would show up. He'd said five extra desserts. Were five soldiers enough?

His concern for Martha's well-being spoke well to the planning of his operation. He'd also seemed to do everything he could to protect Hayley. A full-out assault of the house was something completely different, though. She'd seen how the guards had reacted when the locals had fired a few shots into the top floor. It didn't take much for all the guns to come out.

"Los Angeles?" The young, tan boss stepped closer to the stove than anyone and stared into the pot of simmering broth. His English was good. She would have to be careful.

"San Diego." She shaped pelmeni, wrapping dough around the filling and setting them out on baking sheets to rest.

The man clicked his tongue. "I could get you a restaurant in Miami."

The prospect of her own restaurant was always appealing. At what cost? How much further would she be willing to get into business with these men? "I think Rolan would rather have these pelmeni close."

Art's plan had to work. She had to be free from all these poisonous snakes.

"We're lucky to have you here." The boss nosed around her prep bowls. "But if you ever get tired of cooking old-fashioned for the dinosaurs, I'll get you a place. Up-to-date. Full liquor license. Near the clubs."

He knew how to lure a chef. Temptation was his art, then the business would take over and this man would own her. The same way she'd been "offered" the job of cooking for a house full of criminals. No choice at all.

"Thanks." The pelmeni demanded she maintain her pace and she didn't glance up. "I'll see what shakes down."

"Good girl." Confident and patronizing.

She was probably older than him. And she had a paring knife close at hand from cutting out the dough if he tried to touch her.

Even with her focus on the food, she felt Art's presence approach the kitchen. She glanced up at him, taking in the tilt of his shoulders while he strutted toward her. His eyes questioned, looking between her and the tan boss. A quick nod from her told him everything was alright. But he still hung out at the perimeter of the kitchen.

All the while he maintained a cool presence, as if today was like any other day and the only thing he had to worry about was making sure his stubble was perfectly dusting his strong jawline. On the inside, he must be revving high. His motor never appeared to stop. She'd felt what it was like to be on the receiving end of all that attention. She'd also seen what he could do when threatened. This calm Art was just a mask. He was ready to break out at any second.

The tan boss didn't even register the man who was set to dismantle the whole operation. The boss left the kitchen, sidling around the island with his focus two rooms away when he passed Art.

She said to Art, "Lunch in ten minutes." The first batch of pelmeni hit the broth. She was running to the end of the ritual, and the nerves started to coil tighter around her joints again.

"I'll pass the word." He started to leave, then stopped. "Smells great." The depth in his eyes soothed her. "I've known people who've forgotten all their training when things get tight." His admiration heated her. "If you've fallen down, you've always gotten back up."

She tried to absorb what he'd said, deep, as if it could strengthen her bones and fill out her muscles. Confidence was elusive.

Art walked off as if it was just another lunch, talking to whichever guards he ran into, she presumed about the meal's timing. They then sauntered away to spread the information. It wasn't long before most of the house paraded past the kitchen, eagerly glancing at the bowls of steaming pelmeni, complete with side salads and condiments.

The fifth boss, who seemed most revered by all, including the other heads, patted Rolan on the back, as if to indicate the man had done good by hiring her. Rolan beamed and preened his silver hair a bit, taking on some of the glow of the top man.

By the time she served the food in the dining room, Rolan was in the midst of an animated story. He pointed at her and Art, made gestures toward the dumplings as well as somewhat awkward karate chops similar to what Art had used on the men with knives outside the club. He spun her tale while the guards and bosses listened intently. There was surprised admiration in their eyes for her. Less for Art, though there were a couple of grudging nods his way. Garin seethed. Vasily paid little attention to the story, staring instead out the window at the bright day. The newest bodyguard, who was a giant, sided with Garin. If either of them glanced at Art, it was just to send dirty looks and promises of pain.

Art was outnumbered. How many people did he have on the outside? Only five? She'd met Mary and Harper, and they looked capable, but them and three others coming at the house wouldn't be nearly enough to neutralize all these armed threats.

Rolan's story hit a crescendo and he ate a pelmeni as punctuation. Lunch was officially underway, and the men fell silent as they devoured the food. Organized crime wasn't her ideal customer base, but she couldn't suppress her pride at creating food that was so well appreciated.

She took her leave of the dining area, bits of Russian conversations springing up behind her. Art's voice joined in. Maybe they were asking for more details on the fight. Or sizing him up, trying to determine his moves.

Martha was already in the kitchen, helping clean up the piles of bowls and pots used for the pelmeni. Hayley had saved food and made a couple of plates for her and Martha, who smiled appreciatively.

The two of them ate automatically, standing near the work that waited for them. Hayley tried to keep her focus on the dumplings. The taste and texture. She'd made hundreds of pelmeni in the past. Maybe thousands. What could she do different? Firmer dough? Additional spices in the filling, or the broth? She let these thoughts take her, rather than wondering if this was the last meal she'd ever have.

Silverware clinked on empty plates, and men made satisfied sounds in the other room. Conversations popped and swerved. Chairs scraped the floor as people stood. After a minute, stacks of dirty dishes flowed into the kitchen.

Hayley and Martha finished their own meal and got to work. Art came in with the last batch of plates.

"I'd help, but the bosses are taking a meeting in the conference room and I'm in on it." His casual rhythm was gone, replaced by something dark and edgy. "If it's too hot, get out of the kitchen."

And he was off, leaving her to figure out what all that meant. The man was going to be in a room with all the targets of his operation. Possibly the very same men who'd ordered the hit on his father all those years ago. And he somehow maintained his cool. Waiting. But he was apart from her. Behind how many locked doors? His caution shook the floor under her feet and thinned the air. The kitchen had been her only safe space. Leaving it would expose her. And that was why he warned her. There were no safe spaces anymore.

FIVE BOSSES IN one room. He was armed. A pistol and two knives. Enough bullets to take them all out. But that wasn't his mission. There were authorities around the world who wanted these men. Exposure in a courtroom and the justice of a jail cell would do more damage to the Orel Group than leaving behind a pile of bodies. Split apart, most of these men would turn on each other. Seams would tear, and the power of the organization would leak out.

But Art was tempted.

Tactically, he knew it wouldn't work. He'd maybe take out one or two bosses before the others had their guns out and filled the air with lead. He had to hold tight.

As tight as his fist. Like he was closing his fingers around Rolan's throat. The boss was still riding high after telling the story of how he'd met Hayley and her fabulous pelmeni. The food she cooked was moving him up in the esteem of the powerful bosses. Krylov, the New York man, licked his lips noisily when the dumplings were mentioned again in the windowless conference room.

There were even a few compliments passed out to Art for how he'd handled the two attackers outside the club. He thanked them and could hear what they didn't say. "Good job, *for a half-breed.*"

"*For a Mexican.*"

His father wouldn't have been proud of him saving Rolan's life that night. But the man's ghost had to know that it was part of a bigger plan. By the end of this day, he could rest in peace.

Until then, Art kept playing along. He sat on the side of the table opposite the five bosses, telling them what he knew about the flow of drugs over the border into Arizona and California. Dernov and Yemelin complained about the Latin American gangs, how they controlled too much and couldn't be trusted. Art knew the same could be said about the Orel Group but kept that to himself.

Most of the bosses perked up when he suggested infiltrating the gangs. Krylov brushed it off, saying they were too loyal. But Art countered, saying that if they found a top man while he was in prison and isolated from his support network, they might be able to turn him.

The information went over well, and Rolan beamed brighter.

Keep smiling, Art thought. *Even when your face is in the dirt and my boot is on the back of your neck.* Even when Rolan was being handed over to the authorities in an unmarked helicopter.

This was the time to call in the strike. All the bosses in one room. But Art had no access to his phone. The signal would be crude. It had to wait until after Martha was gone, as well.

Meanwhile, he was in the perfect position to execute the op.

And he was separated from Hayley, who was alone with the rest of the guards in the house. There was nothing to stand between her and Garin except the knife Art had given her. It had worked the other night, but Garin wasn't going to give up that easily. Art knew the man would sacrifice a gallon of his blood to get what he wanted.

The only sliver that kept Art close to sane in this room was knowing, or hoping, that Garin wouldn't make his move in the light of day. Hayley was smart enough to not let herself get isolated with him. There'd be too many witnesses for him to make a play. Unless he'd become completely unhinged. Which was getting to be more and more of a possibility.

Art raged inside as he talked to the bosses about what kind of lawyers to pay off to find out about incarcerated gang members. He was through helping them, the same men who'd taken away his father. It cost him too much. This whole operation might cost him Hayley. He had to pull the trigger soon.

SHE WATCHED THE CLOCK. She watched the sun's downward arc after lunch. She watched the attitude of the men. None of the timekeepers told Hayley when the world would change around her. Martha's departure was the only clue, but she wasn't sure exactly when that would happen. And how long after would the assault start?

The one person with the answer was somewhere upstairs, locked in a room with the enemy. He was forced to play a part for them. She had to, as well. While acid seethed in her gut and worry lashed out like barbed wire whips, she prepped dinner.

Potato after potato was peeled, then sliced to discs for a gratin that would fill several baking dishes. She cubed beef for a stew and felt how the blade popped through the first layer of the muscle. The red striations parted, revealing the deeper cuts. Her knife shook and she hurried through that part of the process, sweeping the meat into a bowl and washing her hands a few times.

Garin stalked into the kitchen while she was washing her knife. Even when the blade was clean and dry, she kept it in her grip. He maintained a distance but pointed at the prepped food, speaking in streaming Russian sentences she didn't understand.

His vehemence betrayed a deeper hurt. The man had been trying to get her this whole time. Her rejection lanced his pride, making him very dangerous. His focus for the moment was on dinner.

The word *rassolnyk* kept coming up again and again. All she knew from her memory of her father and aunt talking about food was that it was a kind of soup, but she'd never learned how to make it.

Garin wanted it. He wanted her and would probably destroy her as soon as he had the chance. They stood on opposite sides of the island. His eyes kept flicking to the knife in her hand. He knew about the other one, the gift from Art. Garin might not know where she was keeping it, but she couldn't count on surprising him again.

For now they danced around the pretense of him wanting a specific soup for dinner.

She pointed with the knife to the bowl of beef, then the large pot waiting on the stove. *"Ragu iz govydiny."* Beef stew. She repeated it as many times as Garin insisted on the soup.

The looping conversation became so bizarre that a collection of guards were pulled closer to the kitchen to see what was going on. Of course none of them came to help, though Gogol watched her with sympathy.

The bosses had leashes strong enough to pull Garin off his goal, and they were all sequestered somewhere else. And Art, the only man who stood up to the blond guard, was locked in with them.

Even stone-faced Vasily rolled his eyes as Garin continued to press for the soup. The latest bodyguard, who was a mountain in a tracksuit, snickered at Garin's insistence but made no effort to curb him.

The odd conversation angled into an argument when Garin started to touch her prep bowls and baking dishes.

She rapped the butt of her chef's knife on the top of the island and insisted, "My kitchen. My kitchen."

The language didn't matter. He understood.

The escalation hit the other guards, as well. Vasily spoke up softly, staying just at the border of the kitchen and the dining area.

Garin turned on him, fury in his eyes, but held himself together and didn't challenge the other man. They exchanged sentences while the new, giant guard looked on, disappointed that the whole scene was being defused.

Most of Garin's fuel had burned off. But he couldn't leave without a parting shot. He circled his hand over the whole kitchen and enunciated very clearly for Hayley, *"Rassolnyk."*

With a last glance at the knife that remained in her hand, he turned and left the kitchen, sweeping a wake of bad energy throughout. She worried that the soot of his anger would settle on what she was cooking, spoiling it all before it hit the stove.

The curtain dropped on the scene, and the other guards went from being spectators back to their jobs of scowling mean and carrying guns. She tried to return to her cooking but was too shaken and had to stand at the counter, taking deep breaths to bring her racing pulse down. The house was on the brink. Somehow she'd managed to hold it together during her confrontation with Garin. But when things really snapped, it would be chaos.

And that son of a bitch would not give up. He'd set them up at the hotel, failed and continued to exploit every opportunity to harass her when Art wasn't around.

When she was calm enough to cook again, she set back into the process. It didn't last long enough. After a few extra touches to what she'd already done, the food was off, taking care of itself. Beef stewed and the gratins roasted.

She watched the clock again, not knowing what it meant.

Art had the answers. But he'd been gone so long. Had they found out who he was? The house was dead quiet. Maybe this was the way they did things. Silently. With the casual and polite calm Rolan used to button his coat.

If they knew about Art, they would come for her next.

The back door of the kitchen was unlocked. She could run. But on the other side of the dirt yard was the wall. Too high to climb. The guards would see her by then. She stared out the windows on the door, trying to plot any path to safety. There were none.

Art had told her to get out of the kitchen if it wasn't safe anymore.

It was time to leave.

She put her hand on the back doorknob, and a voice whispered over her shoulder.

"Not that way." Art placed his hand over hers. "You're right to get out, though."

She swallowed the rising dread from the too-quiet house and turned to him. "Are you okay?"

He nodded slowly. "I will be." Potent energy resonated in him. He was focused, the way she'd seen him when he fought. "Martha's leaving soon. You should walk her to her ride. Stay on the front steps." His hand brushed over the small of her back, then found where the knife was clipped under her coat. "Be ready."

Like a dance, they turned. He led until they both faced the front of the house. Martha, tired from her day's work, came into the kitchen and retrieved her purse from the cupboard.

Art told her, *"Gracias por todo."*

"De nada." Martha smiled, friendly. Her attitude grew guarded as she faced the rest of the house.

Hayley pointed at her own chest, then the path to the front door. *"Camino..."*

Martha nodded her understanding, and the two women left the kitchen together. Hayley took one peek back and saw Art angling out in the direction of the service hallway.

She made a silent promise and wish and prayer to anyone listening that it wouldn't be the last time she ever saw him.

A guard who'd made the run to town, either picking up or dropping Martha off, was already in the car with the motor running. He smoked a cigarette, hanging his arm out the open window and down the door.

Hayley exchanged *"adiós"* with Martha while they were still on the front steps of the house. That was where Hayley stayed. The guards at the gate pulled it open while Martha got into her car. There were other guards along the front of the house behind Hayley.

As soon as the car pulled through the gate, it closed with a solid clang. Hayley tracked the car into the desert. The sun was low enough now to be in her eyes, and she shaded them, watching the squirrel tail of dust twitch toward the horizon.

Hayley had positioned herself where Art had told her. It was about to happen. Armed men patrolled in front of and behind her. She waited, heart pounding, exposed on the front steps. Her trembling hand unbuttoned her chef's coat. She couldn't breathe any easier, but she would be able to reach the knife as soon as Art ended the world.

THROUGH THE SMALL window in the service bathroom, Art watched Martha's car leave. Last he'd checked, the bosses remained in the second-floor conference room. All the objectives were in one place. Hayley was outside the house.

It was time.

His last act as an undercover agent was flushing the empty toilet, false justification for why he'd been in the room. From this point forward, he was an operator.

He left the bathroom and went down the hall to the utility stairs. No one paid him any attention as he descended, pulling his pistol. Hopefully his team would pay attention to his upcoming signal and show up. If not, then his objective would narrow down to one task. Get Hayley out alive.

From the bottom of the stairs, Art aimed his pistol across the basement at the charges attached to the propane lines. No more lies or pretending. He was a member of Automatik. The attack started now.

Art fired the shot.

AN EXPLOSION KNOCKED the wind out of Hayley's chest. The windows on either side of the front door blew out, scattering tiny shards of glass across the stairs at her feet.

Guards ran, guns at the ready, mouths open with shouts she couldn't hear. Her ears rang with the blast, and she stumbled to maintain her footing. It felt as if the front steps of the house were pitching and buckling, but she didn't know if it was the wood and concrete moving or her equilibrium being knocked off axis.

An angry plume of yellow fire and black smoke rose from the back of the house.

Art had shaken everything.

But how could he do that from safety? Had he sacrificed himself to make the blast?

Terrified by the thought, she hurried toward one of

the tall windows on the side of the door but was bumped out of the way by one of the rushing guards. He pushed her to the ground and leaped for the front door.

A crackling sound burst behind her, loud enough to push through the wool that seemed to fill her ears.

Several bullets tore into the guard's back, and he toppled into the open doorway. Hayley spun, scraping her hands on the hard steps and glass bits, to see where the shots had come from.

Two men, dressed in all-black tactical gear, were working their way up through the parking area in the front yard. There were already three dead guards in their wake, by the gate.

The two soldiers moved with crisp efficiency from one car to the next. Louder shots blasted from the second floor above Hayley's head. The men took cover and fired back. Chips of plaster and concrete and glass rained down on her. She remembered that Art had told her to stay outside, but it felt like only a matter of time before one of the bullets from the steady stream that burned past her would find its way into her flesh. The one path she could run was toward the house.

The flames from the barrels allowed her to keep track of where the shooters were. She scrambled up the stairs to the front landing of the house. It was a challenge to get her legs to work, but when confronted by the dead guard at the door, she stood and bolted into the foyer of the house.

Chaos. Yes, Art's team had arrived, but the Russian guards weren't going to lay down their weapons without a fight. The men she'd been feeding for the better part of a week were now sprinting from corner to corner, guns drawn.

Shots popped throughout the house, kicking up plaster and punching deadly holes in the walls. The intensity of the panic cranked higher when the lights of the house all snapped off. Only the late sun, cutting into the windows from the edge, illuminated the rooms. The shadows were deep enough to not be trusted.

At the end of the main hallway on the first floor, she saw more daylight than she expected. The explosion had torn a hole that smoked from a ragged edge. The damage extended beyond what she could see. Was Art in that destruction?

He'd told her to get out of the kitchen. To find somewhere safe.

But there was no safety. One of the guards skidded to a stop in the middle of the foyer, staring at her, wide-eyed and howling in Russian. He raised his gun, aiming it at her chest.

EIGHTEEN

THE BULLET STRUCK the charge on the pipe, shattering it and sparking the first small explosion. Flames swirled around the rupture. Knowing the destruction would escalate quickly, Art turned to sprint up the stairs.

Burning propane hissed out behind him, then popped with the bursting lines. Wood and drywall shattered. He knew the kitchen was being torn out from under its floor. He was halfway up the service stairs when the fire reached out to the propane tank and blew the whole thing.

The hot wave rushed along his back and shoulders, jetting up the narrow stairway. He stumbled to keep his footing and found that the walls weren't square anymore as he banged along them. When he'd been planning this stage of the operation, the thought had crossed his mind to have Hayley with him. He'd know she was safe if she was at his side. But he was glad he'd gotten her to the security at the front of the house, even if she wasn't immediately behind him or directly within view. There'd have been no way for the two of them to cram their way up the steps fast enough with the flames raging.

It felt like it took a day to get to the top of the stairs. Fire growled behind him, and the building crashed and collapsed. Finally in the service hallway, he saw the destruction.

The kitchen was gone. Water pipes angled, broken from where the back wall had stood. The floor had been bitten away as far as the island, leaving the counter-tops in shattered piles that crumbled into the basement.

Blowing the tank had done its first job. The cinder block wall on the south edge of the compound had been breached, a fifteen-foot section lying in rubble. Beyond it was the desert, and hopefully "Bolt Action" Mary, if his team was in place.

Art had to act as if the team was coming. Hayley was out front. He knew she'd be safe there for a moment and could find cover at the edges of the house. His first objective was in the back.

Guards moved in a panic all around him. The majority of them kept their heads and found cover, guns drawn and peeking out to try to assess what was happening. Four or five were at a loss and stood exposed, shouting questions to each other. The most loyal acted on instinct, streaming up to the second floor where the bosses were. Art and his team would meet them there. That was where the heavy fighting would be.

A submachine gun chattered from the front of the house. Art recognized the methodical pattern. Automatik had arrived. The guards knew they were there as well and opened fire in opposition.

The battle had begun.

Art ran to the edge of the destroyed kitchen, then up past the dining area to the abandoned living rooms. All the windows had been blown out by the blast. He sped through the jumbled furniture to the open frames. The can lights in the ceiling blazed, contrasting the darker sky over this side of the horizon.

He fired four shots out of the house, two bullets into each generator. The motors sputtered, sparked and popped, then died.

Immediately the lights in the house flicked off.

Gunfire crackled from the nearby outside corner of the house. Someone fired blind at the sound of Art's shots. With his objective complete, he didn't need to stay and engage. His only thought then was to find Hayley.

Sprinting back through the house, he saw that most of the guards were now either upstairs or had taken up defensive positions around the perimeter. They shouted to each other, trying to keep tabs on where the attack was coming from, but it was a deafening chaos. There was no one leader to coordinate, and there had never been a set plan for something like this.

From down the long central space of the house, Art saw Hayley stumble into the foyer. Inside was not a good place to be. It sounded like the firefight at the front of the house had reached a temporary back-and-forth stalemate and must've driven her in through the door.

Before Art could call out, a guard blocked his view of her. It was the same man who'd mad-dogged him when he'd first arrived and was trying to get into the house with Hayley's food cooler.

Now the man shouted at Hayley and raised his gun to point at her.

Art ran toward them, his pistol drawn. If he fired now, the man might pull his own trigger as he died. Hayley would be hit. But if Art reached him, he could knock the gun away and finish the man while Hayley was in the clear.

She acted first, yelling broken Russian to the man. Sentences sounded like a mix between a menu and a string of insults. The man appeared confused but finally peered in the direction where she pointed, insistent.

As soon as he glanced away, Hayley dove to the ground in the opposite direction. The gun was no longer pointed at her. Art raised his own weapon and fired twice, killing the man.

The guard's gun went off as he fell, shattering a wooden banister behind where Hayley had just been standing.

Art sped to her. She pushed backward until her back hit a wall. Her eyes were so wide, taking in the shocking, destructive world. When she looked at him, a different level of awareness rushed in, sharpening her.

He reached down, and she reached up. Their hands connected, and he helped her stand.

"Any injuries?" he asked, gripping her close with one hand, his pistol in the other. He wanted to check her over and linger on her face, relieved to know she was with him, but had to keep scanning the house for threats.

"No. None." Breathless, she hurriedly questioned, "You? Are you okay? That explosion…"

"I'm good." He dodged forward to grab the fallen guard's gun, then took cover again with Hayley behind a corner next to the large stairway. "And my team is here."

She reported, pointing at the door, "Two out front."

"Pinned from the second floor." Shots continued from that level. "Jackson and Harper can't flank up there from their position." Though shots did come in from the north, where the SEALs were. But the upper house defense was too dug in and would slow Raker and Sant from the west. He handed her the guard's pistol, with the quick instruction, "Use it."

She held it correctly, though without a lot of confidence. "Are we getting out of here?"

"To get out, we have to go through." He tugged on her hand, and the two of them edged quickly into the service hallway. "Front's a dead end. Can't get out the doors or go up the main stairs."

He'd hoped the utility stairs on this end of the house would be a clean way up, but there were too many men moving up above in the guards' rooms' hallway.

"Holy shit." She stumbled, gaping at the wreckage where the kitchen had once stood.

"I was looking forward to that stew." He tested the floor for stability and moved them around the hole in the house.

Hayley cursed. "My knives."

He understood what it was like to lose a trusted tool. "We'll get you new ones to train."

Fragments of a man breaking cover on the outside edge of the house caught in Art's peripheral vision. He pulled himself and Hayley down and away as shots popped and bullets streaked in steep angles from the ground up. Holes burst in the ceiling.

Art returned fire; a few bullets to keep the man pinned. But it took him away from the newest threat. Stepan, the massive bodyguard, rushed toward Art and Hayley, his huge hands open and ready to crush anything in his path.

As Art swung his pistol around toward Stepan, a bullet parted the air, entered the giant man's chest and exited out the other side of his rib cage. He stumbled forward and crashed to the ground, skidding to a stop several feet away.

Hayley gaped. "How…who…?" She glanced around without breaking cover.

"Mary's got our back." The shot had come from the south, where the cinder block wall had been toppled.

Another large bullet from her rifle smacked into the base of the house, near where the guard had been shooting up at Art and Hayley. The man had to keep down in order to stay alive, leaving Art with the opening he needed.

He sprang to his feet and hurried himself and Hayley into the broad living room. The path to the back stairs was blocked. He and Hayley threw chairs and a table out of the way to get access.

They started to mount the stairs, but Hayley hesitated.

"Wait." She swung her gaze from the dark stairway to the blown-open windows in the living room behind them. "Why the fuck are we going deeper into this?"

"Because if we go outside that way—" he gestured toward what appeared to be freedom in the back, "—the guards at the perimeter will get us. Mary can't keep them all pinned down." He took the first step up. "We take our time, stick to cover, the rest of the team joins us and contains the bosses."

Which might take a while. From the sounds of the firefight on the other side of the house, both teams had yet to make it within the walls of the house.

But the attention of the guards was forward, allowing Art and Hayley a quiet ascent to the second floor. They crept up the steps. Any sound they made was masked by the periodic gunshots. The guards were setting up their defenses and making a stand. It was unclear if the bosses were threatened enough to join the fight or if they were just huddled together in the conference room, waiting for their men to take care of the problem.

Art was three steps away from the top, where he could see only a piece of a room, sliced bright and dark by the low sun. Hayley remained close behind him. The second safest place for her would be five hundred miles away from the battle. But that just wasn't a possibility. He maintained his mission directive, knowing he'd protect her through every twist and turn.

The silhouettes of two rushing guards cut off the light at the landing. They reared up, shocked and ready to fight, when they spotted Art and Hayley.

EVERYONE WAS SHOOTING around her. But could she pull the trigger? Two guards barreled down toward her and Art. They would kill her if they had to.

Even if she was psychologically ready to shoot at them, there was no way to aim without putting Art in danger. He stood between her and the guards, putting himself in harm's way.

He acted fast, firing twice, once into each man. One of them arced backward, falling away from the stairs. The other guard staggered. He looked like he was about to collapse, but something held him up.

All the energy drained out of the man, yet he stood. Somehow he lurched forward and flung himself down the stairs at Art. The impact drove Art's back into her, and she stumbled on the stairs. She dropped her gun, afraid that if she gripped it too tight it would go off.

Art twisted, pushing the limp man past him and beyond her down the stairs.

Then she saw how the wounded guard had maintained his attack. Vasily had thrown him, and now rushed down at her and Art.

Art tried to bring his pistol into the fight, but Vasily was already too close. He pinned Art's wrist to the wall. The Russian's face was as calm as stone while he punched Art twice in the gut.

He tried to strike him again, but Art drove a knee up hard, catching Vasily in the stomach and pushing him back to the opposite wall. The bodyguard didn't even wince. He continued to control Art's gun hand and reached behind his back to pull a short, hooked knife.

Art saw it coming and twisted so the blade scraped along the wall. By the time Vasily swung back for another attack, Art had drawn a long, thin blade of his own and countered the strike.

The two men struggled and turned on the narrow stairs, knocking into the walls and cracking the wooden banister. Hayley was pinned between them and the body of the fallen guard behind her.

Her gun was long lost, and the back stairway was too dark to search. She could get only glimpses of Art's intense face and the flashes of the blades in the murky shadows. It felt like any second, more guards would pour in from the top or come scurrying up from the living room below.

They had to get out of the stairway.

Art obviously knew it. He bared his teeth, smashing Vasily on the wall again and again, even as the hooked blade dug into his left shoulder.

Hayley had her own blade. She tightened her fist around the push dagger and dragged it from its sheath. Vasily was too intent on Art to see her attack coming. She had to stop him from hurting Art. She punched and slashed at the guard's hand.

His eyes popped wide with shock. The wounds on his hand opened up, making him drop his knife. Vasily raged at Hayley as if betrayed. He started to make a lunge for her but stopped short. A jagged groan escaped his throat, and he slouched.

Art muscled Vasily to one side of the stairs, then let the man fall down where the other guard lay. As Vasily descended, Art's knife pulled free from his chest.

"Thank you," Art whispered, leaning close and helping her sheathe her knife.

"You're hurt." Seeing him take the wound had been too much. She was part of this war now. She'd drawn blood. The violence was hers.

"It ain't a thing." He put his knife away and pulled off his jacket. It draped over the fallen men in the stairwell. After searching over the stairs for a moment, he turned back to her, placing the dropped pistol in her hand.

Trapped. In the house. On the stairs. She had no choice and took the gun. The same way she'd been forced into violence. Anger burned in her. Other people tried to control her life. She couldn't let them anymore.

At first her rage had been aimed at Art. When she'd thought he was just a criminal, it was easy. Then after the truth of his mission was revealed, the complications fractured the fury. He was cornered, as well.

He'd done everything he could to protect her. Now he was fighting to get them free.

Once again starting up the stairs, Art murmured without taking his focus from the top, "You're the master chef. You showed me a thousand new ways to taste. You're beautiful and unstoppable and nothing that these people do, nothing you do to survive, takes that away."

His words led her up through the shadows of the stairs to the landing where sunlight streaked in hard planes. Art held up a hand to slow her, then checked over the area quickly. Shots popped through the house, but not in the immediate area.

Art stepped forward, waving her with him, and the two of them hurried away from the stairwell and to cover at the corner, where the room opened up between two long hallways. From the height of the second floor, she could see more of the destruction below. Smoke continued to pour from the burning edges of the wrecked house. The blast from the propane tank had left a crater in the dirt and a halo of devastation that stretched beyond the toppled cinder block wall.

Taking aim down the long hallway, which had been where the guard's rooms were, Art fired a volley, then quickly reloaded. Bullets answered him, and he ducked out of the way. A pool table absorbed the attack. Chips from the shattered balls and splintered wood flew through the room.

The fighting intensified at the front of the house, where Art had been shooting. He ducked into that hallway long enough to let loose another barrage. When he returned, avoiding the returned deadly answer, he tilted his head to the hall on the other side of the room.

"That's where the bosses are." His pistol clicked,

metallic, as he checked it with expert hands. "We converge on this point."

Footsteps thundered up the hallway where Art had been shooting. Wild gunfire came with them, clearing a path. She shrank closer to the wall, knowing she would never get small enough to avoid the bullets.

Somehow Art watched the situation with his usual calm confidence, picking it apart and staying balanced. "Let them panic. We stay cool." He bumped his hip on hers. "You cool?"

"Ice-cold." And hot. She went from numb to burning to back again, trying to process the war around her.

Three men burst out of the guards' room hallway. Art shot the first, and the guard stumbled and spun to the ground. The other two scattered—one leaped to the cover of the stairwell, while the other kept running and dove under the pool table, slamming his head and shoulder hard on one of the thick legs.

Art traded shots with the guard at the top of the stairs. The man didn't have a good angle on them and was temporarily pinned.

The man under the pool table gathered himself, rubbing at the back of his head while still holding his pistol. It was Gogol, one of the few guards who'd had a genuine smile for her, especially after they'd made the *syrniki* together.

His swimming eyes focused and he gaped when he saw Hayley and Art taking cover together. She raised her gun and pointed it at him before he could collect himself any further.

"*Nyet*, Gogol! *Nyet!*" It was all she could think of.

Art barked in a steadier stream of Russian while maintaining his concentration on the man in the stairwell.

Torn, Gogol glanced at the hallway behind him, where Art said the bosses were. The gun was in his hand, but it was on the ground, where he'd been trying to steady himself. His mouth moved as if in conversation with himself.

The pistol shook in her grip. She continued to tell Gogol, *"Nyet,"* praying he wouldn't make her pull the trigger. Art didn't stop working on him, too, sounding forceful but not threatening.

To counter them, the man in the stairwell spat sentences. She didn't understand his words, but he was angrily shouting orders at Gogol.

Reeling, Gogol squeezed his eyes shut. Could she shoot? The metal in her hand was the heaviest thing she'd ever held.

Gogol shook his head and shouted over everyone else's voices.

Her finger tightened on the trigger.

When he looked up again, it was into her eyes. He was drained. Releasing his grip on the gun, he pushed it so it slid across the floor toward Art and Hayley. Gogol placed his hands behind his head and sank into the ground, no fight left in him.

But the man in the stairwell wasn't ready to give up. Gogol's sudden silence must've spurred him, because he became reckless, firing wildly as he sprinted back onto the landing.

She and Art ducked out of the way. If he continued to fire like that, she would be hit. There had to be better cover somewhere. Before she could run, Art fired a single shot. The guard fell, his attack over.

The battle at the front had stopped, and in the silence she heard footsteps hurry up the guards' rooms' hallway. Hayley tugged on Art's arm, conscious now of the blood that streamed down his biceps.

She whispered urgently, "We have to move."

"Not yet." He held up his hand and waited. "Friendlies."

The two men who rushed from the hallway were the ones who'd attacked from the gate. They immediately spread out when they reached the room, covering the angles behind the walls, including Art and Hayley.

The man closest to them wore a helmet and goggles, but his smiling mouth was exposed, surrounded by a tight, dark beard. "You were right, mate." He had a roughened British accent. "That is a terrible hallway."

The other man circled around, making sure the room was clear. His complexion was much lighter than his partner, and he was clean-shaven. He put his fist out for Art and received a quick bump. "Thanks for the assist." A bit of country twanged in his words. "We still on the rails?"

"Affirmative." Information came from Art in quick, efficient packets. "One POW." He pointed at Gogol, who remained under the pool table with his head down. "Targets remain in one or both of the rooms in that hallway."

"Injuries?" the British man asked, quickly scanning over Art and Hayley.

"Nominal." Art turned to her. "And...?"

If she was hurt, she couldn't feel it. "I'm fine."

"More than fine." Art gave her a wink, helping the blood run in her body and chasing some of the cold.

All three men suddenly raised their weapons, ready. She hugged closer to the wall and tried to keep her hands steady on her pistol. There was no shooting below, or on this floor. A new threat approached, but she wasn't as tuned as Art and the others. Where was it? What was coming?

Then she heard the quick footsteps. The two men in tactical gear relaxed a bit, and the British man whispered to Art, "SEAL Team Zero."

Art bit back a chuckle as two men sped out of the hallway. Their equipment was strapped to heavy vests across their broad torsos. Even with his helmet, she recognized Harper from the hotel. The other soldier with him was an African-American man with a black bandana tied above his alert eyes.

Harper shook his head. "Who fucking designed this house? More blind spots than a goddamn minivan."

She noticed that while the soldiers spoke, none of them stayed in the same place very long. All four of the men in the tactical gear circulated around the room, checking out windows and down hallways, their guns loosely gripped but ready.

Art put his hand out. "Can I get a radio so I can avoid surprises?"

The African-American man pulled a small walkie-talkie out of a pouch on his vest and handed it to Art, who snapped it to his belt and ran a cord from it into his ear.

"Trigger's on com." Art barely uttered the words, and the other men nodded.

Harper stepped closer to Hayley. He bristled with weapons but still asked gently, "You still kicking ass?"

"I guess." There was a lull in the battle, but she knew better than to relax. She might never catch her breath.

"She is," Art answered definitively.

"Then you were right, Diaz." The African-American man gave Art a friendly pound on his uninjured shoulder. "She isn't a liability."

All her kitchen knives had been destroyed, but she found some steel. "And you should taste my meat loaf."

The men chuckled, and the soldier backed off a bit.

Art explained, "Jackson was our man in the dirt this whole time. He's finding his way back to civilization." Art pulled ammunition from Jackson's vest and reloaded his own pistol. "Glad you got my message."

Jackson smiled, as relaxed as if it was a sunset beach meet-up and not a gunfight. "Nothing like a fifty-foot fireball to start the party."

"How many heavies remaining?" The man with the southern twang was back to business.

"Unknown," Art answered. He made quick hand gestures to the others, and they fanned out through the room and started approaching the hallway with the doors leading to where he said the bosses had been.

Her exploration of the house had only taken her to where the guards' rooms were. This part of the floor was unknown. It felt airless, a hallway leading to a dead end. No windows. The sun shot all the way through the house and streaked the walls with amber and orange.

Art stalked behind the other members of Automatik, and she followed. Together, the team moved silently and coordinated. All the angles were covered. The hallway ahead was quiet. At least five armed men waited there. She couldn't imagine that any one of them would want to be taken without drawing blood.

The soldiers moved around the pool table and Gogol. Scattered furniture piled like bones. The room narrowed into the hallway. She stared at the shadows and light on the doors, searching for movement with such intensity that the shapes persisted when she looked away.

Art shook his head and scowled, something bothering him. He reached forward and tapped Jackson on the shoulder. Once he had the man's attention, he indicated the edges of the room with hand gestures. The other soldiers watched and understood, and quickly spread out, away from the hallway and along the perimeter.

Three quick shots roared, louder than she'd heard so far. The room shook with the concussion. Huge chunks of plaster and wood sprayed out from one of the walls next to the hallway.

None of the soldiers were hit, but if they'd been walking through the room as they had been before Art had redirected them, at least one would've been wounded. Or killed.

Three more blasts rattled off. The bosses weren't using the doors—they shot their way out.

Led by Garin. He smashed through the perforated wall carrying a huge shotgun that fired and fired again. His eyes were red with rage, and he shouted what sounded like Russian curses and oaths. Strapped to his chest was a loaded black tactical vest.

His shots drove the Automatik soldiers to cover. Behind him came two screaming guards, firing pistols. Then the bosses streamed out of the actual door of the conference room, guns barking and filling the room with bullets.

Art hurried backward, taking her with him. They avoided the initial outburst of the escape. The wall of gunfire chased them. Returning fire as he retreated, Art bought them a sliver of space. The other soldiers were pinned behind narrow pillars and broken furniture and couldn't knock down the attack.

Garin brought hell with him. Fire and hot metal. Death.

She still had her pistol but couldn't figure out where she could shoot to stop the onslaught. And if she stopped long enough to aim, she'd be torn apart.

Art and Hayley passed the pool table, and Gogol sprinted out from beneath it, disappearing down the guards' room hallway. A stray bullet caught him in the leg, and he crashed into a wall, then the ground. Her stomach flipped as she heard his agonized scream.

Art continued to move them from cover to cover, shooting when he could, but barely keeping ahead of the mayhem. How long could they run?

One of the Automatik soldiers pierced a shout into the fight. "Grenade!"

The deadly metal explosive clanked on the ground in front of Art and Hayley.

NINETEEN

THE UNKNOWN FUSE could set the grenade off in a split second. Art dove at the weapon, shoving it away with his outstretched hand. The alloy sphere, designed to fragment and tear flesh apart, skittered across the wood floor then exploded under the pool table.

He turned and found Hayley taking cover farther up the room, toward the guards' rooms' hallway. Safe from the grenade. The shooting continued, though he couldn't hear it after the blast. But he could feel the wake of the bullets as they streaked in all directions. He fired a couple of wild shots into the mix, gaining space so he could rush the few feet between him and Hayley.

Another grenade arced through the air and thudded to the ground near them. Art shouted to Hayley as he shot in a different direction, clearing a path for her escape. She ran toward the back stairwell.

One of the two guards with Garin swung a gun around toward her. Art spent too many bullets eliminating the threat, but he wasn't going to conserve anything until he knew she was safe.

She made it into the top of the stairwell.

Two seconds had passed since the second grenade had fallen. Art leaped into the guards' rooms' hallway just as the explosion hit. He pulled his feet around the corner and watched the destructive wave take the wood and drywall apart.

He jammed himself to standing, then was rocked by a third blast, somewhere between him and Hayley. It had to stop. She was in the middle of a firefight.

After reloading his pistol, he took himself to the edge of the hallway to assess the fight in front of him.

Hayley was gone. The top of the back stairwell was a collapsed jumble of plaster and exposed wood studs. Cold fear boiled off to rage.

He stepped into the fight, bullets flying all around him. A boss, Krylov, turned in a circle, firing a submachine gun erratically to hold anyone back. The jumping barrel came around toward Art, and he fired a shot into Krylov's knee. The man buckled in pain. Art put another bullet through his shoulder. The gun fell from the boss's hand. Harper tackled him and bound his wrists with zip ties.

Two other bosses were already subdued and on the ground. The youngest, Yemelin, kept Sant and Raker pinned with a flurry of pistol shots.

The big noise of the fight was gone, though. Something was very wrong.

Garin was missing. Rolan wasn't among the bosses.

Alarm knifed deeper into Art.

He leveled his aim and shot Yemelin in the forearm. The boss's hand sprang open, and the gun fell to the floor. Sant broke his cover and took Yemelin to the ground, restraining him and shoving him toward the other captured bosses.

"Only four." Raker scanned, checking for where the other threats might be.

A truck engine screamed below the second floor. Art rushed to a window in time to see Garin jumping onto the running board of the water truck as Rolan drove it around the house.

Holding on to the passenger door, Garin fired a spray of bullets up at Art and the others. They ducked, avoiding being injured but allowing the truck to gain distance on them. Different shots popped from the first floor. They sounded a bit unsure, the pace slow, but managed to strike the truck in loud thumps.

Garin's attack passed, and Art peered down the broken windows.

Hayley stood, smoking pistol in her hand. Her face was stern, resolved.

Art breathed for the first time in his life. He wanted to vault himself out of the window to her, but when she saw him, she pointed toward the escaping truck with her gun.

"I'm okay," she shouted through rushed breaths. "Get them."

For her, he would. For his father. For anyone else they might hurt.

The rest of his team was occupied with the bosses in the room. He sprinted across the space to the opposite windows. The glass was all blown out, but the wood framing remained. It wasn't enough to stop him.

He picked up speed and barreled into the window. Wood snapped and shattered. Jagged edges scraped at his arms and shoulders. Through the barrier, he landed on a short roof that curved above the edge of the first floor. The surface buckled under his weight, but he managed to run a few feet on it before leaping off.

The truck was just passing the wrecked corner of the house when Art jumped. Water sprayed from the holes Hayley had punched into the back of the giant tank. He hit the top and bounced on the hard metal. One of his hands held his pistol, making it hard to grip the curved surface. He scrambled to stay on as the truck bounced over the rubble from the fallen cinder block wall, grabbing one of the metal fittings that protruded out of the top of the tank.

Art sprawled, finding the center point of the tank just as the truck hit the desert and tore across the hard-packed earth. Jackhammer impacts bounced him, chest down on the metal. He crawled forward until he could hook a grip on the front edge of the tank, where the desert air burned across his face.

Voices from Art's team came over the radio in his ear.

"The fuck?"

"Mission's not over."

"Not until Art finishes it."

Holding the lip of the tank with one arm, Art fired into the passenger section, where he'd seen Garin climb in. The jumping truck threw his aim off, and the bullets punched through sections of the roof or skipped over the hood or were lost into the desert.

More radio chatter: "Dragonfly, time to dust off this roundup."

They were calling for the helicopter. The house had been secured.

Jackson's voice carried extra urgency. "Chef is unaccounted for. The chef is unaccounted for."

Fuck. Hayley needed him. He had to end this fight and get back to her.

As calm as a redwood tree, Mary's voice crackled over the radio. "Art, you have an armed heavy prepped for egress out the passenger side."

Garin swung the door open and fired a burst from a submachine gun. The bumping terrain threw his shots off, the same as had happened to Art.

Art tried to shoot back, but each time he pulled the trigger, the truck lurched and the bullet went wild.

The terrain grew severe, and the truck bucked like a bull. Garin swung out on the door, slamming back and forth. Art went airborne, then slapped back to the top of the tank, knocking the wind out of him.

The truck hit another hard rut, and Art had to decide between keeping his gun or holding on. The pistol skipped away into the growing shadows on the desert floor. By the time Art had collected himself, Garin had moved out of the cab and was now crawling onto the top of it, submachine gun in hand.

Before Garin could fire, Art lunged forward and grabbed the barrel. He twisted the gun from Garin's sweaty grip. But he couldn't maintain a hold, and the weapon was lost to the speeding landscape around them.

Garin snarled and leaped onto the top of the truck with Art, who had to scuttle backward on his knees. He banged against the pipes and fittings on the top and barely rolled out of the way as Garin stomped down toward him.

The guard shouted into the wind and swung out a vicious kick that caught Art in the ribs. The pain made his side seize up, but he managed to wrap his arm around Garin's lower leg and hold on.

Art drove his fist again and again into Garin's lower belly, then spiked his elbow into the side of the Russian's knee.

Howling with pain and rage, Garin kicked with his unpinned leg in an attempt to lurch himself out of Art's control. And the truck continued to bounce, barreling through the desert.

Art couldn't let Rolan escape. If he made it to town, he might disappear, then be able to rebuild the organization. And he'd have Art's and Hayley's identities.

Blows landed on Art's shoulders, the side of his head, but he wouldn't let go. He turned his body so Garin's leg twisted under him. Garin then pounded on his back with the edge of his fist.

Both men started to slide down one side of the tank. The hard dirt sped beneath them. Art used his free hand to draw the knife on his belt and slashed out to slow Garin's attack.

The blade bit into Garin's arm, and he recoiled. The truck bounced hard, knocking Art against the tank and forcing him to lose his hold on Garin. As soon as the guard pulled away, he snapped open his own knife.

Finally. One of them would die. Art promised that it would be Garin. The man had antagonized Hayley since the beginning. Now he was keeping Art from her one last time.

Crouched low for balance, both men swept forward with bladed attacks. The knives scraped each other, but no flesh was cut. Garin tried again quickly. Art turned out of the way but stumbled and couldn't counter.

The clock that had wound so tight in him now spun completely out of control. Wild rage fought against his trained calm in the face of danger. His mission was here, on this speeding truck. And all he wanted was to find Hayley, to get her to safety.

With their positions reversed, Art now faced the back of the truck. Another car charged through the desert, gaining on them. It was his SUV.

Hayley drove.

Garin glanced at where Art stared. When the guard swung back around, his face was tight with fury.

Art shouted to him in Russian, "You're not going to leave this desert alive."

The guard readied for another attack, steadying himself on one of the fittings at the top of the truck.

Art yelled into his walkie-talkie, "Mary, give me a full stop on the water truck."

She answered smoothly, "Stand by for a fifty-caliber parking brake."

He sheathed his knife and motioned for Hayley to get parallel to the truck on his left. She struggled with the wheel but managed to bring the car closer.

Close enough for him to jump.

She gaped with shock when he flung himself off the side of the water tank and slammed onto the hood of the SUV. As soon as he had a grip on the edge of the sheet metal, he looked up to the truck.

Garin was just coiling to jump when the truck's engine burst into a sputtering ball of flame and smoke. Rolan made the mistake of slamming on the brakes. The chassis screamed and torqued as the truck ground forward, then curled sideways. It hit a rut and groaned, toppling over in a roll that sent Garin flying into the shadows. The water inside the tank jerked the truck, sloshing and booming.

Hayley brought the SUV to a relatively controlled stop, and Art rolled off the hood and onto the ground. He'd staggered up to a hand and knee when she reached him.

"Are you hurt?" Just having her hands on him lifted some of the pain.

But not all of it. He strained out a laugh.

"Much?" she added.

He stood, still buzzing with adrenaline. "You can't shoot, but you sure as hell can drive."

She curled an arm around his waist and tried to guide him toward the passenger side of the SUV. Her voice shook with emotion. "Did you think I was really going to leave you out here alone?"

His eyes glossed and he clenched his jaw while his mouth searched for words. He whispered back, "Never leave me."

"I won't." Her hands curled tighter around him. "I—"

A shuffling attack came from the desert dark. Garin, streaked with blood and dust, flailed toward Art and Hayley with his knife drawn. Art thrust himself between Hayley and Garin, but she was way too close to the conflict. The first swipe from the thick blade almost cut Art across the chest.

Garin hissed blood through bared teeth. He was fighting to the death.

Art would give it to him.

The next slash came down, and Art sidestepped it. Before Garin could pull back, Art grabbed his wrist and elbow. Twisting with all his strength, Art turned Garin's knife, still in his hand, toward the Russian's chest.

Garin tried to wrestle free from the grip, but it was too late. Art threw his weight into the bellowing man, driving the knife in under his ribs. Both of them fell to the dirt.

As Garin breathed his last, Art whispered to him, *"Adiós."*

The dying man tried to shake his head in denial of the word and his fate at Art's hand. Stillness overtook the body, and he lay heavy on the desert ground.

Art stood, Hayley immediately with him. She didn't look at Garin. Her face was grim, tired, but not defeated.

But he resisted letting her take him to the car. "The mission's not over."

The wound in his shoulder started to burn. His ribs were bruised. Every joint ached. He pulled himself together and walked to the crashed truck. Hayley remained with him, cautious.

The SUV's headlights striped blue through the swirling dust, shining on the growing pool of water and mud.

The three-quarter roll had crushed the truck's roof and bent down a corner of the driver's door. Art wrenched the door open and dragged the semiconscious Rolan out. Blood stained the man's silver hair, and his eyes swam, unfocused on Art and Hayley.

Art paid no care to any injuries Rolan might've had as he searched the boss for weapons, then dragged him to his feet by his lapels. "The Orel Group is dead." He fumed in slow, clear Russian. "Tony Diaz ended you."

"Who?" Rolan winced, his brows bunching as he tried to form thoughts.

"Tony Diaz." Just saying the name brought the emotions up through Art. His breath came in ragged rasps.

"My father, who you had killed. And now he's at rest, because you're done."

"Tony…" Rolan processed while his head lolled from side to side. "I don't remember…"

"But you knew something." Art shook him, needing to know if there were any leaks about Automatik. "You knew something about me." A secret that Rolan had kept, like a poison knife under his coat.

Rolan laughed, cut short by wheezing pain.

Art pushed him against the leaking water tank. "What do you know?"

Rolan looked over his shoulder and frowned, disappointed. "You could've been…strong…with us. Power… But a woman… You were a fool…to fall in love with her."

Hayley stood behind Art. The last light of day outlined her in amber. She was scraped and dirty and exhausted and undefeated and beautiful.

Art released his hold on Rolan. "Dead wrong."

Without his support, Rolan couldn't stand and flailed. He slid down the side of the tank and onto the ground. Art grabbed his lapel and dragged him through the dirt and mud toward the SUV.

Hayley opened the back passenger door, and Art shoved Rolan in. The former boss only had the strength to lie in the foot well, his dirty clothes twisted all around him. Art closed the door and leaned on the car with Hayley.

He put his arm around her shoulder, and she hooked her fingers into the waist of his jeans. Feeling her next to him was life. His injuries didn't matter. The pain remained but couldn't overcome the realness of her. Hayley was alive. She was safe.

To the north, a helicopter hovered over the compound.

She stared at it, eyes a bit remote. "Is that our ride?"

"Yeah." And he couldn't wait to get out of this corner of the desert.

She asked without bringing her eyes to him, "Are you going away?"

"No." He held her tighter, taking in her thoughtful face. "I'm me again."

Her shadowed gaze moved to him. "Because the mission is over?"

He shook his head and leaned forward. The moment was so contained and private, the distance between them small. Their connection was delicate and strong enough to survive the bullets and the fire.

"Because you," he said, and he kissed her.

She returned the kiss and the emotion. They shared each other. For the first time in a very long time, he was safe.

FLYING IN A helicopter with open doors might've scared her a week ago. Maybe even a day ago. But as the vehicle climbed high enough to get another peek at the sun, which had dipped below the horizon, Hayley had no gulp of fear.

She sat with Art on small benches that folded out of the walls in the middle of the vehicle. The cut on his shoulder had been tended to by the British soldier after they'd loaded all the Russian mobsters onto the helicopter. But Art remained dirty, bloody in places. He was a warrior, exhausted from giving everything in the fight and defeating anything that had stood in his way.

The Russians were all bound, with dark sacks over their heads. Some of them had bandaged wounds. Gogol's leg was in a long splint. Even Martha's driver had been nabbed by unseen members of Art's team after he'd dropped the woman off. Art had explained that there was another set of helicopters waiting to take the bosses and surviving guards to the necessary authorities. Rolan was headed to the Netherlands.

The boss who'd "hired" her for the job had been silent since Art had thrown him in the car. Instead of going to the compound, Art had spoken on his walkie-talkie and had given Hayley directions to an empty patch of desert, where she'd witnessed a perfectly camouflaged Mary emerge from the dirt. The sniper carried her rifle to the waiting SUV and on the ride back.

The rest of Art's team was also on the helicopter. They leaned on the walls or each other, as if on a bus on the way back from a camping trip. She couldn't be that nonchalant about the circumstances, but she was a step closer to Art's world.

Explosions had gone off around her. Watching Art dive for that hand grenade had seized her with fear. But he hadn't hesitated. He'd kept his word and done everything he could to keep her safe. Which was why she'd had to go after him in the SUV when she'd seen him on the back of the water truck. She'd never promised him protection, hadn't thought it was in her power, but all that had been erased when he'd started to disappear into the darkness of the desert.

The helicopter banked, and she slid her hand into his. He held her tight and turned to gaze into her eyes. The motor was too loud to speak, and they didn't have the headsets that the others did.

He asked if she was okay with a tilt of his head.

She nodded, yes.

EPILOGUE

HAYLEY DIDN'T FEEL guilty that their restaurant had been opened using a percentage of the cash found at the compound after the raid. The Orel Group was dead, its bosses in dark prisons and everyone else scattered. Because Automatik was unofficial according to any government on the planet, they had the ability to parcel out enough money to pay back her mom, donate to several charities around town and to kit the simple kitchen out with a better stove and flat top griddle.

The good reviews were beginning to come in on social media, despite the rocky start Art had working the front of the house. But he'd picked it up quickly, and the people started digging his slightly surly attitude.

His demeanor was always more agreeable when they were together in the small house they'd rented. The tension from the compound was behind them. They made love with the bedroom door open, whenever they wanted.

There were nights when she woke, confused and wondering if the place was secure. He would soothe her with an easy voice, then check all the locks before returning to bed. She would read him, too. When the darkness would gather behind his eyes. Sometimes talking out the memories helped. Other times she would just sit with him, keep a hand on him so he knew he wasn't alone.

Neither of them was alone.

This night there was still company at the restaurant, despite the doors being closed and locked. She shut down the fires in the kitchen and carried two serving trays out to the wood-paneled dining room. As soon as Art saw her coming, he sprang up and took one of the trays from her.

Together, they set the food down at one of the two large tables in the middle of the restaurant, where Harper, Jackson and Mary sat. The sniper glanced from the pile of steaming rice pilaf to Hayley, emotion in her eyes.

"Lebanese?" Deep surprise crossed Mary's face.

"I don't break a food promise." Hayley arranged the platters, revealing chicken kabobs, small phyllo pies filled with ground beef, and several side salads.

Jackson clinked his beer with Mary's, which rested on the table. "Good thing you shoot straight. Otherwise we wouldn't be eating all this."

She smiled with swagger and picked up her beer for a long drink.

Art handed Harper some large spoons. "Serve it up."

Hayley watched them dig in, piling the food onto their plates. "You know our menu, a little Russian, a little Mexican, but I kept a corner of the kitchen separate for this tonight."

And it had been a decent take for a Wednesday. The place had a shot.

The Automatik soldiers, her and Art's friends, all thanked her.

Art started to sit, then remembered something. "I've got to get the light."

He strode toward the front of the restaurant, and Hayley went with him. A flick of a switch by the entrance darkened the sign over the door that read *Da/Sí.*

She put her hands on his hips and stretched up so she could kiss the back of his neck. An appreciative growl rumbled through him. He double-checked that the front door was locked, then turned to her.

"Expecting trouble?" She peered out the glass door to the quiet dark street beyond.

"Maybe outside, maybe inside." He smirked, glancing at his friends at the table.

"You want trouble?" Her fist lightly tapped his chest.

"If it's you…" He took her hand in his and kissed her knuckles. "Then, hell yeah."

"Good." She snarled, loving how he bared his teeth with her. "Then let's make trouble."

"Yes, Master Chef."

* * * * *

ACKNOWLEDGMENTS

Many thanks to Angela James for guiding me toward romantic suspense. Her encouragement and the support of the Carina staff are big reasons writing romance novels is so rewarding. Also much appreciation goes to my new editor Rhonda Helms, who made this process like an awesome conversation over a few beers.

ABOUT THE AUTHOR

Nico Rosso discovered the romance genre through his wife, romance author Zoe Archer (AKA Eva Leigh). He's published a wide range of romance stories including demon rock stars, sci-fi space opera, steampunk Westerns, and now romantic suspense with the series Black Ops: Automatik. When he isn't at his desk, he can be found in the workshop, building furniture and other projects for his new home with Zoe in central California.

REQUEST YOUR FREE BOOKS!
2 FREE NOVELS PLUS 2 FREE GIFTS!

(H) HARLEQUIN®

ROMANTIC suspense

Sparked by danger, fueled by passion

YES! Please send me 2 FREE Harlequin® Romantic Suspense novels and my 2 FREE gifts (gifts are worth about $10). After receiving them, if I don't wish to receive any more books, I can return the shipping statement marked "cancel." If I don't cancel, I will receive 4 brand-new novels every month and be billed just $4.74 per book in the U.S. or $5.49 per book in Canada. That's a savings of at least 12% off the cover price! It's quite a bargain! Shipping and handling is just 50¢ per book in the U.S. and 75¢ per book in Canada.* I understand that accepting the 2 free books and gifts places me under no obligation to buy anything. I can always return a shipment and cancel at any time. Even if I never buy another book, the two free books and gifts are mine to keep forever.

240/340 HDN GH3P

Name _____ (PLEASE PRINT)

Address _____ Apt. #

City _____ State/Prov. _____ Zip/Postal Code

Signature (if under 18, a parent or guardian must sign)

Mail to the **Reader Service:**
IN U.S.A.: P.O. Box 1867, Buffalo, NY 14240-1867
IN CANADA: P.O. Box 609, Fort Erie, Ontario L2A 5X3

Want to try two free books from another line?
Call 1-800-873-8635 or visit www.ReaderService.com.

* Terms and prices subject to change without notice. Prices do not include applicable taxes. Sales tax applicable in N.Y. Canadian residents will be charged applicable taxes. Offer not valid in Quebec. This offer is limited to one order per household. Not valid for current subscribers to Harlequin Romantic Suspense books. All orders subject to credit approval. Credit or debit balances in a customer's account(s) may be offset by any other outstanding balance owed by or to the customer. Please allow 4 to 6 weeks for delivery. Offer available while quantities last.

Your Privacy—The Reader Service is committed to protecting your privacy. Our Privacy Policy is available online at www.ReaderService.com or upon request from the Reader Service.

We make a portion of our mailing list available to reputable third parties that offer products we believe may interest you. If you prefer that we not exchange your name with third parties, or if you wish to clarify or modify your communication preferences, please visit us at www.ReaderService.com/consumerschoice or write to us at Reader Service Preference Service, P.O. Box 9062, Buffalo, NY 14240-9062. Include your complete name and address.

HRS15

REQUEST YOUR FREE BOOKS!
2 FREE NOVELS PLUS 2 FREE GIFTS!

H HARLEQUIN®

INTRIGUE

BREATHTAKING ROMANTIC SUSPENSE

YES! Please send me 2 FREE Harlequin® Intrigue novels and my 2 FREE gifts (gifts are worth about $10). After receiving them, if I don't wish to receive any more books, I can return the shipping statement marked "cancel." If I don't cancel, I will receive 6 brand-new novels every month and be billed just $4.74 per book in the U.S. or $5.49 per book in Canada. That's a savings of at least 12% off the cover price! It's quite a bargain! Shipping and handling is just 50¢ per book in the U.S. and 75¢ per book in Canada.* I understand that accepting the 2 free books and gifts places me under no obligation to buy anything. I can always return a shipment and cancel at any time. Even if I never buy another book, the two free books and gifts are mine to keep forever.

182/382 HDN GH3D

Name   (PLEASE PRINT)

Address   Apt. #

City   State/Prov.   Zip/Postal Code

Signature (if under 18, a parent or guardian must sign)

Mail to the **Reader Service:**
IN U.S.A.: P.O. Box 1867, Buffalo, NY 14240-1867
IN CANADA: P.O. Box 609, Fort Erie, Ontario L2A 5X3
**Are you a subscriber to Harlequin® Intrigue books
and want to receive the larger-print edition?
Call 1-800-873-8635 or visit www.ReaderService.com.**

* Terms and prices subject to change without notice. Prices do not include applicable taxes. Sales tax applicable in N.Y. Canadian residents will be charged applicable taxes. Offer not valid in Quebec. This offer is limited to one order per household. Not valid for current subscribers to Harlequin Intrigue books. All orders subject to credit approval. Credit or debit balances in a customer's account(s) may be offset by any other outstanding balance owed by or to the customer. Please allow 4 to 6 weeks for delivery. Offer available while quantities last.

Your Privacy—The Reader Service is committed to protecting your privacy. Our Privacy Policy is available online at www.ReaderService.com or upon request from the Reader Service.

We make a portion of our mailing list available to reputable third parties that offer products we believe may interest you. If you prefer that we not exchange your name with third parties, or if you wish to clarify or modify your communication preferences, please visit us at www.ReaderService.com/consumerschoice or write to us at Reader Service Preference Service, P.O. Box 9062, Buffalo, NY 14240-9062. Include your complete name and address.

HI15

REQUEST YOUR FREE BOOKS!

2 FREE NOVELS
FROM THE SUSPENSE COLLECTION
PLUS 2 FREE GIFTS!

YES! Please send me 2 FREE novels from the Suspense Collection and my 2 FREE gifts (gifts are worth about $10). After receiving them, if I don't wish to receive any more books, I can return the shipping statement marked "cancel." If I don't cancel, I will receive 4 brand-new novels every month and be billed just $6.49 per book in the U.S. or $6.99 per book in Canada. That's a savings of at least 19% off the cover price. It's quite a bargain! Shipping and handling is just 50¢ per book in the U.S. and 75¢ per book in Canada.* I understand that accepting the 2 free books and gifts places me under no obligation to buy anything. I can always return a shipment and cancel at any time. Even if I never buy another book, the two free books and gifts are mine to keep forever.

191/391 MDN GH4Z

Name   (PLEASE PRINT)

Address   Apt. #

City   State/Prov.   Zip/Postal Code

Signature (if under 18, a parent or guardian must sign)

Mail to the **Reader Service:**
IN U.S.A.: P.O. Box 1867, Buffalo, NY 14240-1867
IN CANADA: P.O. Box 609, Fort Erie, Ontario L2A 5X3

Want to try two free books from another line?
Call 1-800-873-8635 or visit www.ReaderService.com.

* Terms and prices subject to change without notice. Prices do not include applicable taxes. Sales tax applicable in N.Y. Canadian residents will be charged applicable taxes. Offer not valid in Quebec. This offer is limited to one order per household. Not valid for current subscribers to the Suspense Collection or the Romance/Suspense Collection. All orders subject to credit approval. Credit or debit balances in a customer's account(s) may be offset by any other outstanding balance owed by or to the customer. Please allow 4 to 6 weeks for delivery. Offer available while quantities last.

Your Privacy—The Reader Service is committed to protecting your privacy. Our Privacy Policy is available online at www.ReaderService.com or upon request from the Reader Service.

We make a portion of our mailing list available to reputable third parties that offer products we believe may interest you. If you prefer that we not exchange your name with third parties, or if you wish to clarify or modify your communication preferences, please visit us at www.ReaderService.com/consumerschoice or write to us at Reader Service Preference Service, P.O. Box 9062, Buffalo, NY 14240-9062. Include your complete name and address.

REQUEST YOUR
FREE BOOKS!

2 FREE NOVELS
FROM THE ROMANCE COLLECTION
PLUS 2 FREE GIFTS!

YES! Please send me 2 FREE novels from the Romance Collection and my 2 FREE gifts (gifts are worth about $10). After receiving them, if I don't wish to receive any more books, I can return the shipping statement marked "cancel." If I don't cancel, I will receive 4 brand-new novels every month and be billed just $6.49 per book in the U.S. or $6.99 per book in Canada. That's a savings of at least 19% off the cover price. It's quite a bargain! Shipping and handling is just 50¢ per book in the U.S. and 75¢ per book in Canada.* I understand that accepting the 2 free books and gifts places me under no obligation to buy anything. I can always return a shipment and cancel at any time. Even if I never buy another book, the two free books and gifts are mine to keep forever.

194/394 MDN GH4D

Name	(PLEASE PRINT)	
Address		Apt. #
City	State/Prov.	Zip/Postal Code

Signature (if under 18, a parent or guardian must sign)

Mail to the **Reader Service:**
IN U.S.A.: P.O. Box 1867, Buffalo, NY 14240-1867
IN CANADA: P.O. Box 609, Fort Erie, Ontario L2A 5X3

Want to try two free books from another line?
Call 1-800-873-8635 or visit www.ReaderService.com.

* Terms and prices subject to change without notice. Prices do not include applicable taxes. Sales tax applicable in N.Y. Canadian residents will be charged applicable taxes. Offer not valid in Quebec. This offer is limited to one order per household. Not valid for current subscribers to the Romance Collection or the Romance/Suspense Collection. All orders subject to credit approval. Credit or debit balances in a customer's account(s) may be offset by any other outstanding balance owed by or to the customer. Please allow 4 to 6 weeks for delivery. Offer available while quantities last.

READERSERVICE.COM

Manage your account online!

- Review your order history
- Manage your payments
- Update your address

> ### We've designed the Reader Service website just for you.

Enjoy all the features!

- Discover new series available to you, and read excerpts from any series.
- Respond to mailings and special monthly offers.
- Connect with favorite authors at the blog.
- Browse the Bonus Bucks catalog and online-only exculsives.
- Share your feedback.

Visit us at:

ReaderService.com